Peace
of Pie

# Peace of Pie

SAVOR EVERY TASTE OF LOVE.

# LEE BARBER

RADIANCE

## RADIANCE

An imprint of Roan & Weatherford Publishing Associates, LLC
Bentonville, Arkansas
www.roanweatherford.com

**Library of Congress Cataloging-in-Publication Data**
Names: Barber, Lee, author.
Title: Peace of Pie/Lee Barber |
Description: First Edition | Bentonville: Radiance, 2024.
Identifiers: ISBN: 978-1-63373-935-2 (hardcover) |
ISBN: 978-1-63373-936-9 (paperback) | ISBN: 978-1-63373-937-6 (eBook)
Subjects: BISAC: FICTION/Romance/Later in Life | FICTION/Women |
FICTION/Romance/Contemporary

Radiance trade paperback edition November, 2024

Cover Design by Casey W. Cowan
Interior Design by Michele Jones
Editing by Staci Troilo & Lisa Lindsey

*Honoring Partial to Pie. Every neighborhood should have such a wonderful pie shop.*

# ACKNOWLEDGMENTS

I am beyond grateful for all of my family, friends, colleagues and co-counselors who believe in me. The love and confidence is mutual.

# BRYONY GREEN, ON VACAY

*A* shadow fell over Bryony's face. She opened her eyes.

"Hey." Nathan stood over her.

"Hey," Bryony said back, her gaze traveling up the tanning-bed-shaded legs to the bottom of his blue cotton shorts.

*Why are men's legs still shapely and sinewy after their bellies have a middle-aged bulge?*

"Sorry about this morning," Nathan said. "Forgive me?" Sunlight framed his salt and pepper curls with a halo glow.

"It was a silly argument." Midway through brunch, he'd blamed her again for his weight gain. Tired of hearing it, Bryony had pushed back, softly. Nobody had forced her desserts down his throat. He knew how to excuse himself from the table.

"I signed up for another snorkeling class," he said.

"What time?" she asked.

"It starts in half an hour."

Bryony sat up and brushed sand from the edge of her towel. "I wish you'd said something sooner." She grabbed her floppy flowered hat, sunblock, phone, and paperback.

He squatted and put his hand on her arm. "I meant for me. I didn't sign up for both of us."

"Why not?"

"You swim like a fish, Bryony." Straight white teeth flashed. His cheeks and chin were smooth. "Give me a chance to catch up?"

When had he shaved? As soon as they de-boarded, he'd announced plans to grow a beard. Maybe he'd finally heard her one quiet lament about how short whiskers abraded her face.

"I guess so," Bryony said. "But I love to snorkel."

Yesterday had been a dream for her. While the busty blonde instructor worked with Nathan to ease his anxiety about breathing under water, Bryony explored nearby. The underwater world provided a surprising new way to experience Earth's unending variety of gardens. Floating through a sea of blue, while taking in so many shades of fuchsia, green, turquoise, and chartreuse, surrounded at one point by a school of bright orange fish—heaven.

"Stay on the beach." Nathan stood. "We'll hook up for dinner later." He walked backward, saying, "Thanks for the vacay, Bry. This is fun!" And turned to jog toward the hotel.

Bryony watched until he disappeared between the potted palms lining the patio area behind their high-rise accommodations.

"Vacay?" she asked herself aloud, since no one else could hear or would bother to listen if they could. Clearly Nathan had not read the brochure. A "vacay" returned one to the same-old-same-old. Their two-week Florida "Romantic Gestures" package was supposed to infuse passion into a floundering six-year relationship.

Dropping the lotion, book, and phone into her hat, Bryony plopped the bundle onto the corner of the towel, muttering, "Brother!"

A gull landed on the sand a few feet away and opened its beak to call out.

Fish scent rolled in with the next wave and her stomach waved back with a hint of nausea.

She picked up both sides of the hat brim and pinched them together to make an impromptu bag, which she grasped with her right hand. With her left hand, she picked up the edge of her towel and shook out sand.

A group of teenage boys emerged from behind her. Bare-chested and rambunctious, they ran to the water whooping and laughing, attacking with words, pushing and shoving each other into the sand, then into the water. She stopped to watch them dive, disappear, and break the surface to splash and slander again. In spite of the name-calling, they appeared to be having fun. Bryony would never understand the kind of fun that included maligning one's peers.

"Oh, to be young again," she muttered to herself, folding the towel.

"Cheer up," a gravelly voice said from nearby.

Bryony raised her head, the towel now draped evenly over her arm.

A jolly-faced bald man smiled. "Growing older allows you to deliver on dreams you only discover because you lived long enough to dream them."

A woman, her short silver hair curled tight to her head, clutched the man's arm. "Don't mind him, dear," she said. "He talks to everybody. Never met a stranger in his life." She looked up at the man beside her and grinned.

They walked on, their slow pace indicating the kind of care demonstrated by those who know the risk of falling. Bryony watched them for a few minutes, the sweet woman hugging the friendly man's arm.

"Realize my dreams," she scoffed. What dreams? She turned and trudged to the hotel.

AFTER A NAP and a shower, Bryony blew her hair dry and styled it into a loose knot on top of her head. Soft curling tendrils fell over her ears and neck. Wearing nothing but a light green terrycloth robe, she sank into the hotel's blue wingback upholstered chair to read the novel she had started on the plane.

Nathan returned from his lesson as she turned a page. He pecked her cheek, showered, dressed for the evening, and left the room for an "errand." The door clicked shut behind him, and Bryony snuggled deeper into the chair. She looked back down at the book, a hint of a smile easing tension inside and out.

An *errand*, he'd said. A small gift for her, perhaps? Valentine's Day was less than two weeks away, the day before they would fly back to Ohio. Maybe he was finally on board with the intent of the trip. Maybe he, too, would take the opportunity to infuse spice into their lives.

Reading straight through to the end of the book, she closed the back cover and stretched her arms upward, satisfied with this ritual accomplishment, the uninterrupted reading of popular fiction indicating downtime. Nathan had yet to return. Bryony wondered where he was, but noticed she was happy he had taken his time.

She should have scheduled a break months ago. She would remember when planning for next year—include vacations.

Thirty minutes before their dinner date, Bryony slid into her new dress and emerged from the hotel room to peer in both directions. The hall was empty. She stepped back into the room and closed the door. Odd for Nathan to be gone so long, but anticipatory excitement made the wait tolerable. Would he return with chocolates? Flowers? Something soft and frilly and feminine?

She smoothed silky fabric over her hips, validated herself for choosing a bold tropical print, sat on the edge of the bed, and picked up the TV remote. The evening news focused on tragedy, mayhem, and political chaos. She clicked the remote to a station that catered to romance. Why not?

An hour later, the door opened.

"Hey, Bry!" Nathan walked in, his tie loosened, his pants legs rolled up, empty-handed. "Ready to go?"

Unable to keep the irritation out of her voice, Bryony said, "You're late." She clicked off the television, and asked, "Where have you been?"

"Lighten up!" Nathan walked into the bathroom and turned to stand in front of the mirror.

Bryony followed, her stomach roiling. She noticed sand on his rear end and on the back of his shirt.

"I took a stroll on the beach," he answered.

His relaxed ways used to intrigue Bryony. Now they irked her. Clearly the relationship depended on her ability to bend, but how much, and in what direction? Clueless about whether to continue communicating her upset or resort to her usual forgive-and-forget method of resolution, she stood silent, watching him comb his curls into place, until the cell phone on the nightstand buzzed.

Bryony stepped over to look at the caller ID, picked up the phone, and slid her finger across the screen, worried. "What's up, Mitch?" she asked. Her brother had said he would only call if there was a problem.

"You'd better come home. I can't take off work right now, and Mom's not looking good."

"What do you mean?" Their mother had been fine when Bryony left Fieldstone. Aides were scheduled to come in three times a day to care for any personal needs, provide balanced meals, and a bath before bed. Bryony's father could handle the rest, which would amount to making sure his wife did not walk out the front door and become lost before she exited her own yard.

"She's in the hospital," Mitch said. "I don't know, Bry. She has a high fever, and some new medication seemed to make her worse. She looks bad. The assistant principal is out with the flu, and a couple of teachers called in sick today."

"How bad is it?" Bryony asked.

"I think they're all doing okay, just the usual aches, pains, fever." Mitch answered. "You know, the flu."

"Not them. Mom," Bryony said. Her brother could be oblivious at times. "How bad is she? What did the doctor say?"

"I don't know," Mitch answered, his voice rising. "I don't do this stuff, Bry. It's your job. Be the daughter. Come home and take care of her and Dad. I have enough on my plate."

"I'll be there as soon as I can." She was already moving to the closet.

"Hurry." Mitch ended the call.

His abrupt goodbye and the helpless tone of that one word startled her. Mitch rarely *showed* fear, even when he lectured *about* his fears.

*I'm afraid you're making a mistake there, Bryony.*

*I'm afraid that's not the right choice.*

*I'm afraid you're not acting in your best interest.*

Always he voiced his concerns with confidence bordering on arrogance. Tonight, he sounded like a scared little boy. Anxiety took root in Bryony's midsection.

Nathan walked out of the bathroom and propped his foot on the bed to unroll his pant leg, spilling sand on the carpet. "What are you doing?" he asked.

"We have to go. Mom's in the hospital. Will you please call the airline and book flights out as soon as possible? I'll pack." Bryony pulled both suitcases out of the closet and flung them on the bed.

"Slow down." Nathan put his hand on her arm. "Come here."

He pulled her into his arms. "Breathe. It'll all be okay. She's a tough bird."

While he stroked the back of her head, Bryony rested her cheek on his chest and took a deep breath. Gentle, calm, nurturing Nathan was back. She pulled away to look up at his face. "Thank you," she said. "Thanks for not being upset about having to leave early."

He smiled down at her, his eyes warm and caring. Unlike her father and brother, Nathan really was kind and considerate. He pulled her in for one final caress before stepping back to grasp her shoulders and gaze into her eyes. The air between them stilled.

"You're gonna be fine, babe," he said. "You're always fine. Whatever happens, you're the one who sees all the pieces and the order in which they need to be placed. You'll go there, and before you know it, everything will be back on track."

Her breathing relaxed. Nathan was right. One foot in front of the other. She could do this. Having Nathan made it all so much easier. "I'm sorry," she said. "I wanted this vacation to be special, something we would always remember. I arranged for dinner on the beach our last night here."

Stroking her hair again, he inhaled deeply, and then exhaled saying, "Ah, Bryony. You are so competent, so capable and accomplished." Their eyes locked for a full thirty seconds. The vacation had been worth this one sweet, loving moment she would never forget.

Suddenly, Nathan dropped his arms to his sides and stepped back, the pace of his words quickening. "You don't need me to come with you. The package you purchased was nonrefundable after a certain point, right? And I'm sure we're long past the expiration date. No sense in both of us missing out on the rest of the vacation. I'll be back in Fieldstone before you know it."

# CALLUM FORSTER JR.'S V-DAY PARTY ROCKS

*V*alentine's Day at last! It was second only to New Year's Day on Cal Forster's list of favorite holidays. He had planned the mid-February bash commencing in—he checked his watch—T-minus twenty-two minutes. He had been at it alone since noon, and now his condo's community room dripped with pink and white crepe paper hung above red tablecloths, plates, and napkins.

"At last, the long-heralded time has come," a familiar voice said from behind him. "The Plain Dealer should cover this event —the Top Rated Valentine's Celebration in all of Cleveland."

Cal turned and hugged the man leaning on a cane. "Pops! How did you sneak in? You're first this year. I should have had presents for those arriving first, third, fifth, seventh, and eleventh."

"Your mother made up the prime number door prizes for your third birthday," his father said. "She loved math."

"C'mon on, Pops. Let's sit for a minute." Cal guided his ninety-six-year-old father to the couch and sat with him. "Who drove you?"

"Your sister did. She's parking the car." His father leaned back into the cushion. "I could have driven myself, you know, but Heidi insisted. I've been driving for eighty years and never had a wreck."

"Except for that time you ran the car through your mother's garden," Cal said. "You crashed into the barn, killed a chicken, and almost did in the dog, who limped for the rest of his long, differently-abled life. If he'd had a sharp attorney, he could have sued your pants off."

His father smacked Cal's leg. "Don't get smart. I was twelve years old. Didn't know how to drive yet." He looked around the room and harrumphed a few times. "You outdid yourself, Cal. You would have made someone a fine wife."

"According to Mom, I was born for bachelorhood." Cal surveyed the room. A large decorated valentine box, ready for the distribution of handmade cards, sat at an angle on the table, off-center. Symmetry killed the mood.

Juice boxes, soda, and beer stocked ice-filled tubs. Disposable silver serving trays displayed heavy appetizers. The full dessert table promised skyrocketed blood sugars. A game table stood ready for action. He crossed his fingers there would be no broken bones or ruined carpet this year.

"Are you ever going to settle down and get married?" his father asked. "Generally marriage comes before retirement, but there's no law saying it's too late, you know."

"Haven't found the right person yet." Cal's mother had predicted no other woman would be able to keep up with him. She once tried a leash when he was four years old, but stopped when he wrapped it one too many times around a parking meter.

"I thought you and Leslie would be hitched by now," his father said. "But I'm glad you're not. I wouldn't have said this while you were still seeing her, but she wasn't right for you. Not enough up here." He poked his skull with a gnarly finger.

"She had a PhD in history," Cal said. "We simply didn't work out."

"PhDs do not make up for a lack of common sense." Cal's father shifted on the cushion. "Did the breakup with Leslie motivate you to retire and travel?"

"Sure," Cal said, comfortable with his lack of transparency. His father would see the real motivation as *mollycoddling*. The breakup might have played some small part in Cal's decision, but mainly he would retire at the end of the school year to be his father's travel surrogate.

"Whatever floats your boat, Cal." His father sighed. "I have to say, I'm looking forward to your trip. It's about time you got to see the world."

Cal smiled. He had no strong desire to see the world beyond the amazing places and people he encountered every day. But when he was younger, his father had expressed a yearning to travel. The one time he had been out of the country was during the war. Cal's mother died young, and his father single-parented Cal and his sister through their teen years. By the time Cal Sr. retired in his mid seventies, the urge to travel gave way to a string of health issues. Over the past twenty years, he slowly wound down to be the tired, aged man who sat in his favorite worn out chair most of the day.

Though his father seemed good today, some days his moods were darker than Cal had ever witnessed. The decision to retire and travel was based solely on wanting to give his father something to look forward to—calls, photos, letters, emails. They were learning together how to Zoom. Cal would do anything to make his father's last days, however many there were, the best they could be. Teaching again could come later, after his father was gone.

The outside door opened. "Good afternoon, Mister Forster and Mister Forster," Cal's best friend, Rudy, sang out. "Are we ready for a love-fest here?" A young woman clung to his arm. Her smile dazzled, and she looked to be about eighteen.

"Looks like you are," Cal's father said under his breath.

Cal's sister, Heidi, entered before the door closed behind Rudy and his date. Heidi moved toward the couch as Cal stood. They embraced briefly before she sat down beside their father. Cal moved to the door to greet Rudy and the young woman as they shed their coats.

While Rudy went to hang their coats in the closet, Cal stepped over to escort the young woman the rest of the way into the room.

"Hi," Cal's father said, his tone provocative, flirtatious.

Inwardly, Cal groaned. Knowing his father mimicked Rudy for Cal's benefit, he made introductions before his father could continue. "Welcome. I'm Cal and this is my father, Callum Sr., and my sister, Heidi."

"Nice to meet you Callum Sr., Heidi." The young woman shook their hands as she greeted them, then, giggling, turned to Cal. "Don't you recognize me, Mister Forster? I'm Rochelle. Rochelle Robertson? I had you for English when I was a senior. It's been a long time, six years. I lost a lot of weight, and my hair is long now." She blushed.

"Rochelle Robertson?" Cal said. "Of course I remember you. You wrote a lovely essay on the loss of your cat. I cried when I graded it."

Rochelle smiled and teared up. "He was one of the family."

Cal smiled, too. He had never expected to see her again, one of those above-average students who sailed through his life and dropped off the horizon for lands unknown, at least to him. "What are you up to these days, Rochelle?"

"I finished my BSN, and I work at the Cleveland Clinic. Right now I'm a floor nurse, but someday I want to be a nurse practitioner. You always said, 'Achieve your current goal, and it opens the door to the next one.'"

Sometimes they listened.

Rudy rejoined them. "What did I miss?"

Cal eyed Rochelle, looked at Rudy, and returned his gaze to the young woman. He had to ask. "What are you doing with this guy, Rochelle? He's old enough to be your grandfather."

"I am not!" Rudy said.

Rochelle giggled again. "Rudy is my mom's old boyfriend. He agreed to give Mom a lower price on new carpet for her living room if I came with him today. He's like a second dad." She punched Rudy's arm and smiled at him.

"Thank God," Heidi muttered.

"You weren't supposed to tell!" Rudy play-punched Rochelle back. "But it's true, and you wouldn't have known"—he looked at Cal—"if she weren't such a blabbermouth. I wanted to have a stunning date for my friend's party."

"You think I'm stunning?" Rochelle blushed again. "Thanks, Rudy."

"What a relief!" Cal's father said. "I thought we might have to call Children's Services." He hoisted himself off the couch and walked toward the restroom. "I gotta talk to a man about a horse."

The community room door burst open. Heidi's oldest daughter stumbled into the room, flanked by two of Cal's great-nieces. The children ran and threw their arms around Cal's legs, the three of them almost toppling over, but Cal managed to catch himself, regain his footing, and bend his knees enough to remain stable and in an upright position.

His two nieces' children possessed proper names, but to their mothers' dismay, Cal called the children Sweaty, Sweetie, Grimy, Blimey, Tooter, Scooter, and Hell-oh!

Scooter and Hell-oh! held on for dear life as Cal tried to shake them off, one leg at a time. "Help!" he cried out. "I've been attacked by ferocious alligators!"

The two preschoolers giggled and held on tighter.

And so the party commenced with the arrival of Heidi's second daughter, both sons-in-law, the rest of the great nieces and nephews, thirty-one additional guests, more plates of food, and a lap dog—courtesy of one of Cal's colleagues—that yipped the entire time.

Everyone engaged in the four organized games. There were prizes for all. Laughter drowned out the barking for the most part. Tears were limited to one incident, when Hell-Oh! ran into Sweetie, but after five minutes of ice packs, both were off their parents' laps and back in the fray.

Toward the end of the party, during the first lull in the non-stop action, Heidi put her arm around Cal. "You outdid yourself this year."

Cal hugged her back with one arm. "Wouldn't be much of a party without your family. Thanks for having great kids and greater grandkids."

"They do love their Uncle Cal," she said.

"I love them, too." Up to this point, in addition to being the teacher students sought for solace and support, Cal's entire life had revolved around bringing as much joy to his family as he could manage. He was a lucky man indeed.

Blimey interrupted to show his grandmother the book he received for winning the Hearts competition. "Great job!" Heidi said.

The young boy laid his head against Heidi's side for a moment and said, "Love you, Grandma." Then, he hugged Cal and said, "Thank you, Uncle Cal," before running back to the game table.

"They're going to miss you when you go," Heidi said. "You don't have to leave, you know. Nobody blames you for the breakup with Leslie."

"Tell your husband to warn me next time I start dating any of his relatives."

Hello-Oh's twin brother trotted their way.

"Uncle Cal, where's the bathroom?" Per his usual presentation, Grimy's face provided evidence of every treat sampled at the party, with a crumb of cookie here, a schmear of chocolate there.

Cal pointed toward the bathroom and asked, "Can you handle it on your own?"

"Yes, sir." The young boy trotted off, his chubby arms pumping.

"I tried to warn you about Leslie," Heidi said. "Mark always said she was his 'crazy cousin.' I'm surprised you put up with her for ten years."

"We had fun until she insisted on marriage and a move to South America." When Cal declined, Leslie went bonkers. She needed a therapist, not a marriage.

"We love her, but we all knew it would end someday. She's not your type, Cal. Too heady, too flighty. You need someone with a solid blend of spark and stability, someone like you."

"Aw, shucks, Heidi." Cal rubbed his knuckles across his sister's arm. "Sounds like you like me." Truth was, Heidi was right. He knew he'd been a fool to waste ten years with Leslie.

His sister laughed. "Guess I do a little."

"Where's Mark today?" Heidi and her husband had been high school sweethearts. Cal liked his brother-in-law, mostly because Heidi was happy with him.

"He's helping his sister install a new dryer, something about prongs and cords. He'll meet us later at the arena."

Meeting at the arena was the reason the party ended at the two-hour mark. Tickets for a Puppets on Ice show had been purchased months ago. Cal had declined the invitation to join Heidi and her brood. After they left, the other guests soon followed out the door.

Cal Sr. sat on the edge of the sofa, while Cal Jr. buzzed around the room, dismantling with deft movement what had taken hours of painstaking attention to set up. Only one misstep marred the perfection of his performance with an unscheduled round of fifty-two card pick-up. His father's gut-busting guffaw made the extra work worth the effort.

When the last batch of leftover food boxes were stored in the trunk of his Prius, Cal returned to the community room.

"Sit down for a minute," his father said. "Take a load off."

Cal dropped to the couch cushion and sighed. "What a great party!"

"Yes, it was," his father said.

They sat in silence for several minutes, the calm of the room's bland colors—tan, darker tan, lighter tan, brown—seeping into Cal's muscles. He shut his eyes and noticed dream images starting to merge with a surge of feelings related to deconstructing his life as a teacher.

"Well, son." His father's voice startled him awake. "Any definite plans about where you'll be going first when you leave?"

"Not yet." Cal sat up and stretched into an awake state. "You know"—he paused—"you could come with me."

"Ha!" His father coughed, recovered, and continued. "You don't want this old geezer slowing you down. Have an adventure. Maybe you'll meet the love of your life."

At fifty-eight, Cal did not count on that. There were perks to bachelorhood, the biggest being not having settled for someone who didn't quite fit, because he had never met a woman who did.

After inspecting the community room one last time, transporting his father home, and storing carefully packaged leftovers in the refrigerator there, Cal drove back to his condo.

Bailey—a light brown shaggy stray who had shown up a few years ago—ran circles around Cal's feet until he leashed the dog and took him outside to pee.

"What do you think, Bailey?" Cal said. "Are you going to be happy staying with Rudy while I travel the globe?"

Bailey sneezed and shook his head with gusto.

"Yeah," Cal said. "I'm a little worried about you staying with him, too."

# BRYONY'S BROKEN HEART

$\mathcal{C}$rimson hearts still hung in the window of BeanHereNow, Fieldstone's only coffee shop. When Bryony returned to work, she would remove the cupids she'd strung around her cubicle before leaving for Florida.

Valentine's Day used to be her favorite holiday. Now it would always be the anniversary of her mother's funeral.

Lillian, Bryony's oldest friend, breezed by with a plated bagel for a seated customer. "I'll be back in a minute, honey." She brushed by again on the return trip. "You doing okay?"

"I'm okay." Bryony watched her dearest friend swoosh back behind the counter of the coffee shop she owned and operated every day but Sunday.

In the days before Bryony's mother passed, Lillian had been an angel, supplying coffee and food to those keeping a round-the-clock vigil, showing up to sit bedside when needed, making phone calls and running errands while her husband and grown children stepped up to keep the coffee shop running. Without Lillian, the last ten days would have been much harder, maybe impossible.

Hugging a plain, black coffee mug between her palms,

Bryony's eyes settled on the single rose blooming in the bud vase on the table for two. The petals, ruby red, reminded her of the velvety Valentine's dress sewn by her mother when Bryony was eight.

A similar rose sat in the middle of each table in the coffee shop, though no two vases matched. An assortment of sizes and shapes, they shared the common motif of flowers painted on opaque glass. Bryony spent months scouring thrift stores to complete the collection. Lillian had not replaced them in the ten years since opening BeanHereNow. Sweet of her to hang onto them, and wonderful she had not replaced her best friend either.

Lillian returned to tug the mug from Bryony's grasp. "Let me warm it up for you." She headed back behind the counter and returned with a full pot of steaming coffee and a fresh mug. "The other one was chipped." She tipped the pot and filled the mug to one half inch from the rim.

"You just wanted to bring out my favorite." Bryony curled her fingers around the coral-colored smooth ceramic, covered in small white hearts, and inhaled the rich aroma.

"Hang in there, honey," Lillian said. "Give yourself time." She left to waltz around the other tables, make small talk with the customers, and top off their coffee.

When launched, few expected BeanHereNow to survive. Fieldstone, like most rural small towns in Ohio, was not an upscale coffee shop kind of place. There were a few local eateries, homegrown and hometown owned, but most townspeople either frequented a chain restaurant out by the highway and shopped at Walmart, or stayed home and watched television. Nobody could have predicted the coffee shop would become a magnet for folks who needed community in their lives. The regulars established rituals around being there, almost like having second homes.

The seating area occupied the entire front of a downtown

historic building. Twelve tables sported wrought iron legs with recycled wood surfaces. Each table included a set of high-backed wooden chairs, none of which matched by style, but did match by paint color for each table. With every color of the rainbow represented, Bryony often wondered if patrons picked seats depending on their mood.

Today she sat at the table with blue chairs. Fitting.

The door opened, and Bryony looked up to see Abby Dunaway enter. She wore a brown wool coat and a hat woven with bright colors, too many to count. The young woman smiled and made a beeline to Bryony's table, where she stopped, looked down at a stack of envelopes in her hand, peeled off the top one, and held it out while saying, "Happy belated Valentine's Day! Sorry it's late. I've been busy helping my Grandma."

Bryony forced the corners of her mouth upward as she accepted the envelope and placed it beside the rose.

Abby's expression softened. "I heard about your mom. I'm so sorry."

"Thanks, Abby." Bryony tapped the envelope with her finger. "Now I can't complain about not getting a valentine this year."

Abby smiled and moved on to the other tables, distributing cheerfulness and cards, before seating herself close to the two other "fixtures," Lillian's name for the three people who arrived around nine every day and stayed until almost noon.

Bryony only knew the fixtures through their presence at the coffee shop. In addition to knowing their names, she had learned that Abby Dunaway had grown up locally. She graduated from high school ten years earlier and worked in the evenings at a nursing home. Abby always carried a bag of yarn. Hats, scarves, afghans, and doll clothes flew off her crochet hook.

Mr. Parker, retired postal worker, went through his mail, paid bills, read a newspaper cover to cover, worked the

crossword puzzle, and ended the latter part of his morning stay
with a paperback novel pulled from his back pants pocket.

Bryony knew nothing about Etta Corning except her name,
which was written in black on her nylon computer sleeve. With
spiked black hair, tattoos, a nose ring, and intense focus, Etta sat
in front of her laptop every day, tapping away at who knew
what.

The fixtures bought one cup of coffee each, which seemed to
entitle them to take up an entire table until the noon crowd
arrived. Initially, Lillian shared her worries about others joining
them, taking up space during the busiest times—the morning
rush, noon to one, and three to four-thirty.

*Maybe having a few people sit around during the slow times makes
the shop seem more inviting,* Bryony remembered saying. She
wondered if they were lonely. After a bit of coaching, Lillian
agreed the fixtures could sit as long as they wanted, provided
they did not interfere with customers who used the tables for
eating or drinking and left in a timely manner, *as God intended.*

And they did not interfere.

The fixtures did not bother anybody, and nobody bothered
them. As far as Bryony knew, Lillian never had to say a word to
them, yet they knew when to leave. The first arrivals for the
lunch rush cued their departure. Evidence such as this renewed
Bryony's faith in the natural ability of people to cooperate.

Lowering herself to the seat opposite, Lillian pushed the
envelope from Abby toward Bryony and said, "Open it." Lillian
had one of her own. She slid her long, brown index finger under
the flap and pulled out a handmade card with a crocheted heart
sewn on the front. "You've hooked me, Valentine," she read
aloud from the inside of the card. "Hope your day is wrapped in
love." She held the card open for Bryony to see. "Look, there's a
picture of a woman wrapped in an afghan with hearts on
it, crocheting."

Bryony palmed her unopened card to the edge of the table, where she could easily grasp it with two fingers, and shoved it into the pocket of her skirt.

"Abby, honey," Lillian called out to the young woman seated about fifteen feet away. "This is so sweet! Thank you!" She waved the card in the air.

"You're welcome!" Abby called back.

Lillian turned her attention back to Bryony. "I'm so sorry I left right after the funeral."

"You can stop apologizing," Bryony said. "Being at the ER with your grandson made sense. I'm glad he only needed a few stitches."

"How was the luncheon?" Lillian settled forward in her seat, grasping Bryony's hand.

"Mitch drove Dad over to the church community room. People hung around until about two. The caterers packed up and left around two-thirty. Dad was awful. Mitch harped at me to move home."

"What?" Lillian reared back her head. "What is wrong with that brother of yours? You have a home. You have a full-time job. Why doesn't Mitch move back"—she finger-quoted "home?"

"Don't worry, Lil." Bryony managed a weak smile. "I have no intention of moving in with my father. We'd both be miserable."

"Nice of your coworkers to show up for the funeral." Lillian fiddled with the rose in the vase, turning the bloom toward Bryony. "Paul cornered me again about helping with the class reunion. He's eager to put together a committee. Next one will be our fortieth."

"You should do it. People who have never attended would probably come if you were in charge." Bryony went every five years because Lillian insisted. Trips down memory lane held no appeal for Bryony. The particular path paved by a high school reunion usually resembled a—to quote a song title from her teenage years—highway to hell.

"I wasn't popular," Lillian said.

"You were nicer than the popular girls." Bryony remembered them all as Charity and Susie's She-Devil Squad. "And your popularity has grown in the past decade. Don't underestimate the power of your presence. According to a trusted source"— she gestured to the framed Fieldstone Post article hanging on the wall—"you 'singlehandedly brought new life to a dying downtown.'"

"I wish he hadn't written that. I had so much help! Look at this place. You designed the whole thing."

Beams and boards fourteen feet above were painted black to match the vent tubing. The floors were sanded and polyurethaned. The writer for the newspaper called it "Industrial Chic." Bryony hadn't known such a thing existed. Lillian and she designed the interior based on pictures ripped from magazines, neither of them bothering to read the articles.

Bryony picked the colors—pale green for the walls and black for the cabinets—and provided the plants, now grown into dark green vines spiraling down from pots, their stems entwined, a few reaching the floor. She would come in next week to feed and trim them.

Lillian patted Bryony's hand and smiled. "Any other fallout from yesterday?"

"Dad didn't want to pay the caterer." Bryony brought the mug to her lips, sipped, and swallowed. "He pitched a huge fit until Mitch threatened to take over the checkbook."

"Why didn't he want to pay?" Lillian asked.

"He said I should have done the baking."

"Because he knows your baked goods are better." Lillian wrinkled her nose. "Those pastries were dry."

"Because he thinks I should take care of all things domestic,"

Bryony said. "I am the only woman in the family now, according to him."

"What about Carol?" Lillian asked.

"Carol hasn't been in Mom and Dad's house five times in the four decades she and Mitch have been married." Her brother's wife possessed the personality of a sugar-free cookie— disappointing from the first bite, but still hard to put down. She did, however, make a fine mate for Mitch.

"Right." Lillian nodded her head. "I remember. Something about her allergies. She sneezes every time she goes there."

"She's probably allergic to my father," Bryony said. "He has an ill effect on everyone."

With her mother gone, Bryony wondered what kind of relationship she would have with her father. In the past, her mother had buffered their interactions. When her mother became ill and her mind slipped, Bryony's caregiving tasks created a barrier to the insults her father hurled in every way possible. If he was not saying something demeaning, he was scowling at her, or rolling his eyes, or walking away clucking disapproval. Funny how he never treated Mitch like that.

"Where's Nathan?" Lillian asked.

"I don't know. He should have flown home by now, but he hasn't called."

"You're kidding!" Lillian said.

"I think he's become enamored with snorkeling." Nathan's absence stung, but seemed a minor inconvenience when compared to the misery of watching her mother die. And his lack of communication was not all that unexpected. From boys to men, Bryony had a long history of being left behind without a word. "Don't worry about me. I'm fine on my own. Say hi to Rick and the kids. Please thank them for all they did to help." She stood and slid her arms into her coat. "I've missed seeing them."

"They miss you, too. Come over for Sunday dinner again. You used to come every week." Lillian stood to wrap her arms around Bryony. "You are the sister I never had. You're always welcome in my family, Bry. You know that, right?"

"I do." Tears pooled in Bryony's eyes. Though like an aunt to Lillian's boys as they grew up, she had assumed they no longer needed her after they married. She lived with regret for not remaining a constant part of their lives.

She ended the hug first and told Lillian she would be in touch.

As soon as the coffee shop door shut behind her, a brisk wind hit Bryony's cheeks, and the memory of her mother's wooden face flooded her mind again. She had stared at it for two hours during the visitation, and before the casket closed for the service. Never again being able to look into her mother's kind eyes—Bryony's calm, safe place—seemed unbearable.

As she settled into the driver's seat of her ten-year-old Chevy, deep sobs surfaced.

Per her father's prediction, she'd become an old maid, and she would be one until she died. Unlike her mother, who Bry mourned deeply, no one—other than perhaps Lillian—would grieve her. She was a fixture in the lives of her family, co-workers, and clients, showing up and leaving when expected, minimally known, and easily replaced.

When the tears subsided, Bryony pushed the brake and started the car. On the way home, she would stop by to check on her father.

The last ten days had been hard on all of them, every possible moment spent first in the hospital, then the hospice unit, and finally the funeral home. She imagined empty cabinets in her parents' kitchen, some dirty dishes, a few loads of laundry. She would do what she could, but she had no intention of trying to fill the shoes her mother had gradually vacated. Her father seemed to have done all right on his own up to now.

After she parked in front of the house where she grew up, Bryony sat for a moment taking stock. The whole place grumbled with neglect. Gutters needed work, and bushes trimming. She chastised herself for not noticing sooner.

Trudging up the steps, she looked across the wide cement porch to a swing hanging from two fat chains secured to the bead-board ceiling. As far back as she could remember, her mother had rocked forward and backward in that swing every spring, summer, and fall evening, until one day she stopped, her mind no longer able to lead her to pleasure. Now the swing sat idle, skeletal slats, no breath of movement, a ghostly reminder.

Bryony tapped on the wooden door, inserted her key to unlock the knob, and stepped into low light and a blaring television. Her father, sporting one-day whiskers, lay on the couch in his robe.

Stale air assailed her nose. Bryony opened the front door wider.

"What are you doing?" her father growled, pulling his robe tighter. "It's freezing out there."

She fanned a few times before shutting the door. "When's the last time you had any fresh air?"

Her father turned back to the game show, where the announcer cracked jokes at people dressed in costumes.

Bryony stepped into the room and sat on the edge of the coffee table.

Her father threw a dirty look her way. "Can't see through you, Bry. Will you kindly move?" His voice dripped acid.

What was happening to her father? Never nice to her in the past, his behavior had been gruff and unfriendly, but now he spewed hate. Fear gripped her stomach.

"Daddy, what's wrong?" She felt lost.

"What do you mean, 'What's wrong?'" He threw off the afghan covering his legs, again pulled the robe tight around his middle, and stood.

Pale white skin covered the bones of his spindly legs. How much weight had he lost? Wrapped up in her mother's final days, Bryony had missed her father's sharp decline. She froze inside as guilt settled over grief like a frosty shroud.

"Are you eating, Daddy?"

He pinched his face until his eyes were slits. "What's it to you?" he mumbled, and turned to lumber toward the downstairs bathroom.

Dust covered the coffee table. An empty glass, the bottom dry, sat beside a box of fresh tissues. A paper bag with used tissues sat on the floor. At least he arranged for a proper way to handle his trash. She picked up the bag and carried it to the kitchen, where the visual shock forced a verbal burst of, "Oh my gosh!"

Soiled dishes covered every surface. A foot-high stack of newspapers climbed up from the stove's burners. Dazed, she opened the refrigerator. Deep green mold covered the end of an orange cheese bar. A bowl of something gray and bubbly grew white fuzz.

Her father appeared at her side.

"Oh, Daddy," she said. "How do you live like this?"

"What do you care?" he asked. "If you'd move back in and do what you're supposed to do, I wouldn't have to live like this."

Her brain worked to reassemble coherent thought.

He pulled out a chair and sat down hard. "What else do you have to do? You don't have a family."

"You are my family," Bryony said, her inner scramble for equanimity ongoing.

Her father looked at the floor, his voice lower. "You're selfish, like your mother."

Another insult to her perception of reality. Her mother had never been selfish. Her mother had been kind and generous. Her father must be losing his mind.

Bryony took a breath, pulled out a second chair, and sat

across from him. "There's a new place out by the highway. You would have your own room, and they provide meals and housekeeping."

"Places like that cost too much money."

"You can afford it with your pension and selling the house. We can help." Calm now, Bryony's mind reviewed numbers in preparation to lay out a solid plan for her father's future security and comfort.

"We who?" Her father looked up, sour-faced.

"Mitch and I can help."

"I don't want to talk about it." Her father pushed out of the chair and headed for the living room.

"What am I going to do?" she mumbled under her breath before calling after him, "What will you eat for dinner?"

"I'll order a pizza," he called back.

Bryony looked again at the stacks of dishes, pans with baked-on food, and fast food wrappers. Should she stay and clean up? No. She could not let herself be funneled into the vortex of tasks created by her father's state of mind. He was in trouble, and there would be no easy fix. The dishes were the least of their worries, though she did move the newspapers from the top of the stove to the back porch. The possibility of a house fire made her shudder.

Pulling out her cell phone, Bryony ordered her father's favorite pizza and a salad for delivery, and paid with her credit card.

Before she left, she kissed him on the top of his head.

"You're blocking my view!" he roared.

As soon as she was out of the house, before she was off the front porch, she dialed Mitch's number. His voicemail answered.

"Mitch," she spoke into the phone. "Dad's not safe at home. Please call me. We have to do something."

She was opening her car door when her phone dinged to signal an incoming text.

*Kind of busy here. You figure it out and let me know what you decide.* Mitch added a thumbs up emoji.

Where was the emoji for feeling crushed under the weight of grief and over responsibility?

# CAL'S HEARTY REUNION WITH AN OLD FRIEND

*T*ripping as he stepped out of the Rock & Roll Hall of Fame, Cal almost ran into someone arriving. He saw first the camel coat ending below her knees. His hand brushed her arm before he could catch himself. Cashmere, definitely. He started to apologize before he raised his head, but stumbled again, this time over his words, when he saw the woman's face.

Clear blue eyes opened wide with concern, not annoyance. "Are you okay?" she asked.

Cal managed to complete his apology before noticing the tall man by her side. The camel-coated beauty's companion was tall, Brad-Pitt-handsome, with broad shoulders and a gray wool overcoat.

Another woman stood just behind the man. She was tall, slender, with a runway model pose, sultry eyes, and a slight smirk.

Rudy came through the door behind him, laughing. "Way to go, Cal Forster. You're number one in grand entrances and exits."

By this time, Cal was upright and stable, though a bit embarrassed. "I'm really sorry," he said.

"Cal?" the man asked. "Cal Forster? By golly, it is you."

The man looked vaguely familiar, but Cal couldn't place him. Maybe the parent of a student from way back when?

"Chuck," the man said. "Chuck Henderson!"

Cal looked up into the familiar, albeit aged, face of his old friend. "Chuck?"

"Cal!" Chuck pumped his hand, and then hugged him around the shoulders. "This is Cal Forster, honey. I told you about him. Remember?"

The beauty on Chuck's arm smiled. "You're kidding." She offered her hand. "Chuck has pictures of you two as boys. Imagine running into each other after all these years."

Cal shook her hand as he looked at Chuck. "Unbelievable," he said. "Weren't we about fourteen when you moved?"

"Summer before our freshman year," Chuck answered.

Gesturing first to the woman by his side, he said, "Cal, this is my wife, Charity." His wife gave a little wave as the other woman stepped forward. "And this is Susie. She's an old friend of Charity's. We try to visit whenever we're up this way."

"Delighted to meet you," Susie said, extending her gloved hand. "Any friend of Chuck's is a friend of mine."

Rudy stayed long enough to be introduced, but made a hasty departure, calling over his shoulder while jogging to his car, "Sorry folks! Duty calls. Hey, Cal, since Susie's local, make sure you give her one of my business cards!"

"He's in the carpet business," Cal said, his attention back on the three people in front of him. "You want his card, Susie?"

"I'm good," Susie answered, wrinkling her nose, an amused smile on her lips.

"I thought so." Cal returned the smile, curious about her, more than mildly attracted.

"You here for the exhibit?" Chuck asked.

"Yeah, I wanted to see it again," Cal answered.

"We used to listen to them on eight track." Chuck laughed.

"We were cool."

Chuck smiled, bobbed his head, and then shook it in a show of disbelief. "Cal Forster. What a surprise." He swiveled his head to each of the two women flanking him and asked, "You two okay with having lunch now and coming back later?"

"Sure," Charity answered.

Turning back to Cal, Chuck asked, "You have time for lunch?"

"I know a great place," Cal answered.

Susie begged off, saying she'd catch up with Chuck and Charity at their hotel later. "Sorry to miss the opportunity to explore my new friendship with you, Cal Forster," she said before walking away. "I'm sure we'll meet again."

❧

AS THEY WALKED to the nearby restaurant in a biting March wind, Cal experienced a surreal sensation of time folding in on itself. Could childhood friendship survive over four decades of separation? Cal had no idea, but comfort and camaraderie with Chuck seemed embedded in his bones.

By the time they reached their destination and were seated at a table, they discovered they both had chosen teaching careers and earned advanced degrees. Chuck now taught business classes and managed a high school work study program. Cal had spent a few years doing the same, but switched to teaching English after finishing his doctorate.

They both favored not tying funding for school districts to property taxes. They both saw the value of programs for students who preferred to gather work experience as part of their high school program.

Their lives diverged, however, when it came to family and future plans. Chuck and Charity had two children, both grown, and there were grandchildren. Cal talked about his sister's kids and their families, but he knew being an uncle contrasted sharply with being a father. Chuck said he had no retirement plans thus far. He enjoyed working too much. Cal said he'd just turned in his retirement paperwork and laid out his plans to be his father's travel surrogate.

At one point, Cal apologized to Charity for not including her more.

"You two go ahead," she said, waving them on. "I'm having a great time listening."

Chuck talked about the town where he and Charity lived. "Fieldstone's population is about fifteen thousand," he said. "We have all the amenities enjoyed by many of Ohio's smaller cities and towns, including a declining infrastructure and an out-of-control heroin epidemic."

Smacking her husband's arm playfully, Charity said, "It's not that bad. We have a fine coffee shop now—I can't believe you haven't been in there yet—and we have a great library."

"Every county in Ohio has a great library system," Cal said.

"Touché." Chuck high-fived Cal.

They talked for well over an hour, their food going cold, half-eaten sandwiches whisked away to be replaced by multiple cups of steaming coffee, until Charity looked at her watch. "This has been lovely, but I think we need to get going if we're going to have time for the exhibit before it closes." She stood. "Meeting you, Cal, has been the highlight of my trip to Cleveland. Please say yes to the invitation I'll send for our July Fourth party. I won't take no for an answer."

"Of course I'll come," he said.

ON THE WAY to his father's house, Cal noticed a discernible lift in his mood. Turning in his retirement letter had left him sad, unsettled, lost. Teaching had been his greatest success. Besides feeding his need for accomplishment, the constant interaction with staff and students steadied him. Anticipation of a trip to southern Ohio and attending the Henderson's holiday party in early July gave him an anchor for the near future.

He planned to be on the road by August, but then what? And what would he do with his summer until then? The rest of his life was a syllabus waiting to be written.

Why not start right away? He would make a reading list, starting with *Travels with Charley* by John Steinbeck, and moving on to more modern travel memoirs. Come to think of it, maybe he should tour the states first. He could take Bailey with him.

Anxiety ebbed. He would stay connected. He could read and write and Zoom with or call his father every day.

By the time he parked his car in his father's driveway, Cal again knew he was on the right track.

Entering the back porch of his father's house, he wondered how many times he and Chuck had banged through this very door on their way to Cal's room to pour over comic books or compare the day's discoveries from digging in the backyard. He chuckled and shook his head in wonder. Life was a funny thing.

"Is that my favorite child?" his father called out from the living room.

"No, I'm the other one," Cal called back. "Need anything from the kitchen?"

"Bring a six-pack," his father answered. "Let's get drunk."

Cal breezed through the kitchen and dining room, down the hall, and around the corner. His father reclined in his chair in front of the picture window.

"Where's my beer?" his father asked.

"Hello to you, too," Cal said. "I think your beer got left behind in the 70s."

"I think it's time for the thirteenth step," his father said. "The one that goes, 'You're old and almost dead. Who cares if you drink yourself silly? Go for it.'"

"I care," Cal said.

Before his father stopped drinking, Cal Sr. would get too blasted to climb the stairs for bed. Cal's mother had laid out an ultimatum. His father could have alcohol or his family. Even Cal, less than ten years old at the time, knew she was serious.

He frowned at his father. "I thought you were kidding."

"I was kidding, Cal," his father said. "If I drank a beer, I'd probably pee myself. Oh hell, I do that already." His father slapped his thighs and made a show of sitting up straighter. "What's new with you, son?"

"I had a nice surprise today," Cal said. He recounted the whole story, from his misstep coming out of the Hall of Fame, to the invitation to attend the Henderson party in July.

"I remember him," his father said. "He was a good kid. Nothing like Rudy."

"Rudy's a good guy," Cal said.

"Yeah, sure he is," his father replied. "Underneath the bravado and behavior bordering on amoral, he's a stellar chap."

"You're still sore at him for nearly landing me in jail when I was fifteen," Cal said.

"I'm still sore at him for training you to choose eternal bachelorhood. Under his tutelage, you began to favor personal freedom over family. Any number of women you dated before Leslie would have made fine wives, but Rudy drove them off with his constant invitations to extend your adolescence. Rudy robbed me of grandchildren."

"You can't blame Rudy." The truth was Rudy acted as Cal's anchor, someone who seemed to understand him, accept him, serve as his one constant outside the world of Cal's family. "Besides, Heidi made up for a lack of progeny on my part."

"Nothing like having a grandson from a son to pass on the name."

"Hell-Oh might change her last name to Forster," Cal said. "She's a rebel."

His father laughed. "She'll teach us all a thing or two someday. Your mother would have loved that little girl." His voice trailed off.

"Mom would have loved all of them," Cal said.

His father nodded, his voice low, steeped in nostalgia when he said, "She had plenty of love to go around." He looked Cal in the eye. "You're like your mother. I'm not sure if you were born like her, or if she pushed you in a certain direction. You never stop learning, just like her. She always wanted to go back to school, teach someday."

If his mother had steered Cal's work life in the direction he chose, having his retirement driven by his father made even more sense.

LATER, DRIVING TO his condo, Cal again considered his decision to be his father's travel surrogate. Retiring now was the right choice, and maybe if there were a wife and kids, he wouldn't have the freedom.

When he opened his front door, Bailey greeted him with a swaying back end and a leash in his mouth.

"Hey, Bailey, I thought of a title for my memoir. *Travels with my Dad, Virtually*. Nice, huh?"

Bailey dropped the leash and licked Cal's hand.

"I knew you'd like it, buddy."

# NO CHARITY FOR BRYONY

*a* few spots close to her father's building remained open, but Bryony parked in the lane farthest from RestHaven Retirement Community. Her legs relished bearing weight after a longer than usual morning at the computer. They almost felt like part of her body again by the time she stepped onto the front porch.

"Hello," a woman in a white rocking chair said. "Pleasant weather we're having. April is upon us. Spring has sprung." In contrast to her positive statements, her manner was droll.

"I love all the pansies," Bryony replied.

The woman closed her eyes, laid her head back, and rocked. "The groundskeeper should be nominated for a Nobel."

Was she mocking the gardener's effort or truly appreciative? Bryony hoped the latter. A lowly petunia could brighten the day. Pansies were a step up.

Since moving her father into RestHaven last Sunday, Bryony had come to see diversity in the other residents. What had she expected? An entire population of sweet old ladies who wore flowered cotton dresses, and tidy aged gentlemen who held doors and uttered charming greetings? In contrast to whatever she thought she might find there, the residents ranged from congenial to crass. She'd received a proposition already, delivered with colorful language and some spicy details from a man who raced around in an electric chair. *He's harmless*, the nurse on duty had said. *Likes to shock people.* The third time Bryony saw him, she gave him a flower and told him to be nice to her or she wouldn't talk to him anymore. That seemed do the trick. He'd been pleasant and appropriate since.

At least she didn't have to worry about her father flirting with visitors or staff. Her greatest concern continued to be his ending up as the community curmudgeon, but staff had reported only docile behavior so far. Apparently, he reserved his surly side for Bryony's visits.

No one sat at the reception desk. Bryony signed the guest book and headed down the wallpapered hall. Halfway to his room, she found him in a furnished alcove in front of a bay window.

He was not alone.

A woman sat next to him on a loveseat. The woman wore blue polyester pants and a white sweatshirt with appliquéd songbirds amid winding stems and leaves. A mop of white curls covered her head, and pastel plaid sneakers covered her feet. She appeared to be absorbed in examining the face of Bryony's father. Her hand rested on his knee.

"Oh, you're kidding me," the woman said. "I had a car like that."

Bryony caught her father's eye, and he stood faster than she'd seen him move in years.

"Hey," he mumbled.

The woman swiveled her head toward Bryony, her upturned mouth wreathed in semicircles etched by the years. Round, red, metal glasses sat on her nose. Her blue eyes danced with delight, and her teeth shone like polished stones. Dentures, no doubt.

"This must be your daughter!" She extended her hand. "Hello. I'm Alma."

Noting swollen joints, Bryony leaned down to grasp Alma's hand gently. "Yes, I'm Bryony. Nice to meet you."

Her father continued to stand in awkward silence.

Alma stood and said, "Well, let me get on my way." She looked from Bryony to her father and touched his arm. "We'll catch up later, sweetie," she said before walking away at a fast clip.

Bryony's father sat down.

As soon as Alma was out of earshot, Bryony raised one eyebrow. "Sweetie?" she asked.

"I hate that kind of talk." Her father scowled. "Where were you last night? I thought you were coming to bring my mail."

"I told you I had to work late last night and would deliver your mail today." Bryony pulled a rubber-banded stack of sealed, postmarked envelopes out of her oversized leather purse and placed it in his lap.

"Your purse is big enough for someone to live in," her father said, and they were off.

He complained for the next forty minutes about being forced out of his home and made to live in a place with a bunch of "old" people who "annoyed" and "irritated" him.

Bryony interjected reminders of how her father, brother, and she had come to the decision together. The truth was less clear.

Her father refused from the start, adamant he would not move. In the end, Bryony enlisted Mitch's help to force their father's hand by overstating the dangers of mold found in the basement. Coached by Bryony, Mitch was able to convince their father he should vacate the house immediately and stay out for at least a month after the workers left, to be on the safe side.

A month turned into six weeks and in the end, their father capitulated, saying, "Go ahead and sell the damned thing."

Bryony sensed he knew he'd been snookered, but was too tired to keep fighting.

"And another thing," her father said. "The food here stinks. I wouldn't feed it to a dog. And speaking of dogs, did you know they have one here? First time I see poop on the floor, I'm calling the authorities. Animals belong outside."

As he railed and railed, Bryony remembered to "just listen." The administrator had coached Mitch and her about the importance of not arguing. Bryony's long history of not arguing finally served a purpose, but this new alternative to not arguing, this active listening without walking away or going blank inside as a defense, was new. She liked it. She liked where it led.

Over the past week, Bryony had begun to see her father in a new light.

Isolation seemed to be the source of his surliness. She'd never noticed his singularity, how he did not have friends, until now. That noticing, and the hours spent visiting, resulted in a growing tenderness toward her father, and the tenderness deflected his barbs. He might never be nice to her, but she was determined to be kind to him for the rest of his life.

"I could understand…," her father said, arriving at the low-blow of his diatribe. "I'd understand if you had a husband to take care of, but you have no one to think of but yourself. Your mother didn't raise you right. You're selfish, like her."

There it was again, the reference to her mother's selfishness. Someday Bryony would ask him to elaborate, but not now. The administrator had said her father might need six months to a year to process the trauma of moving from the home he'd lived in for over sixty years. Moreover, he was still grieving the loss of his wife.

Bryony would give him as much time as he needed.

"Did they hook up your cable?" she asked.

"It took a week," he grumbled.

"But now it works?"

"It's fine."

"And all the channels you need are available?"

"Yes."

"And who is Alma?"

Her father smiled.

Who *was* Alma?

"She's George Orman's little sister," he said. "They lived down the street when we were kids. I haven't seen her since high school. She married young and moved to Columbus."

"She seems nice."

"She's okay." He smiled again.

Bryony chose not to probe.

From the parking lot, she called Mitch to give him an update.

After she finished, he first asked her to donate something for the Band Boosters bake sale, then he too went on a tear about her refusal to offer care. "It's not too late," he said. "You've got a crew in there ready to start renovations on the house in order to sell. RestHaven is month-to-month. You could take a few months to update Dad's house, and then, instead of selling, you and Dad could move back in together!"

"I thought we were clear on this," Bryony said.

"Think about it, Bry. You could sell your house and live rent-free at Dad's, then pay off my half when he dies. You'd be tens of thousands of dollars ahead."

"I would be insane," Bryony said.

"Better crazy than poor."

Why did Mitch constantly insist she was on brink of financial ruin?

As she had earlier with her father, Bryony chose not to take the bait. She ended the call as amicably as she could, telling him she would buy something to donate for the sale and—knowing the lunch rush would be over—called Lillian.

Bryony repeated her phone conversation with Mitch,

anticipating her best friend would join her in being astonished, at least a bit peeved, over her brother's insensitivity.

Lillian's response missed the target completely. "You're going to donate store bought?" she asked. "Why don't you bake anymore? You love being in the kitchen."

"You know why I don't bake anymore," Bryony said.

"You still don't bake because of Nathan?"

"He said I was boring." Bryony couldn't believe she needed to repeat this to Lillian. "He said I was only good for dessert, and being with me made him fat. He said he wanted someone with an interest in heating up something other than the oven." Nathan, she discovered, had started seeing the snorkeling instructor before Bryony flew back on her own to Ohio. *Love at first sight*, he had called it. Bryony called it betrayal, and she was far enough past the acute grief of losing her mother to acknowledge the impact of losing her lover, too.

"Nathan was a jerk," Lillian said. "Throw him out of your mind, Bry. Get rid of him."

Perhaps if she had made the decision to kick him out before he left her first, Bryony would be able to do that. Being the one left behind made her a loser.

"Bry?" Lillian asked. "You still there?"

"Yes."

"Are you pouting?" Lillian asked.

"No," Bryony answered, but she knew she was.

"Bry," Lillian said in her Mom voice. "You've given up baking, your all-time favorite activity." Enunciating each syllable, she finished the rebuke with, "Get over him."

"Easier said than done." Bryony rested her forehead on the steering wheel.

"Who said life was easy?"

"Who said life had to be this hard?"

"It could get harder," Lillian said.

"Stop!" Bryony sat up and laughed. "You're not helping!"

"Just trying to be the voice of reason."

"Stop being so reasonable. Tell me my father and brother should understand a grown woman does not have to move back in with her father and care for him."

"They are being wholly insensitive and unkind," Lillian said.

"Thank you." Bryony sighed.

"Go home after work and bake something."

If living a contented life was as simple as the pleasure of making a perfect pie, Bryony's happiness bank would be bursting with wealth. But life wasn't that simple. There was no recipe for success and satisfaction. "Love you, Lil," she said.

"Love you, too, pet."

Bryony closed her cell phone, tossed it on the passenger seat, and headed back to the office. An apple and a snack pack of almonds in her purse would get her through the rest of the day.

LATE IN THE AFTERNOON, Bryony's coworker, Paul, popped his head around the corner. "Did you hear?" he asked.

"Hear what?" Bryony's eyes shifted rapidly as she compared the two screens in front of her.

Lightning flashed outside the window followed by deep, rolling thunder. Spring storms galvanized Bryony, especially during the work day when the bright, productive office softened threatening weather. She hunkered down, scrutinizing the screen, safe in the search for an elusive typo.

"Big news," Paul said.

"Hmph," Bryony muttered. Something somewhere in the account on her screen had not been properly transferred to the new software, and it threw off the sum by fifty-three cents. Unacceptable.

"Clyde sold the company."

Bryony swiveled her chair to face the man leaning into her

side of their shared cubicle, his hand resting on top of the divider. "Clyde told me he was thinking of selling," she said. "He said we'd all like the new buyer. We'll be fine."

Clyde Metcalf had started the accounting firm when he returned to Fieldstone fresh from Harvard, two years before Bryony and Paul finished high school. By the time they walked across the stage to receive their diplomas, Clyde had enough work to take on employees. Both Paul and Bryony started working on a Monday, still reeling from a weekend of graduation parties.

"How did you find out?" she asked, trying to soothe him. Paul adjusted at a slow pace. Updated software gave him hives. Bryony hoped a change in leadership would not upset him for too long.

"The new receptionist told me," Paul said. "She overheard Clyde talking to the new owner as he walked her out the door."

Bryony scoffed. "The new receptionist doesn't know her place yet." She would have a talk with the young woman later, but right now the elusive numbers glitch beckoned. Bryony swiveled back to the screen, determined to find the error before the work day ended.

"Clyde's a smart guy," Paul said. In her peripheral vision, Bryony saw him lean in farther. "He's getting out while he still has the stamina to enjoy retirement. I bet he'll buy a yacht and sail the Mediterranean."

"Lucky Clyde." Bryony scrolled both screens to the next set of numbers.

She knew little about Clyde other than his fairness as a boss. He had trained them from the ground up, paid for their associate degrees, and provided beyond adequate benefits. He kept his personal life private, having established separation of work and home life from the beginning. Bryony had no complaints.

"Lucky us, Bry," Paul said. "We've been here so long we can afford to retire. Aren't you itching to get out of here?"

"No." She itched to have Paul vamoose so she could solve the numerical mystery in front of her. As long as the new owner did not cut pay or benefits and allowed Bryony to do her job without micromanaging, she couldn't care less who stood at the helm. Her direct customers were her main focus.

"I'm ready for something new," Paul said.

Bryony turned only her head this time. "You're thinking about leaving?" Others came and went, but Paul had been a constant. "Are you serious?"

"You bet I am." Paul stepped around to her side of the divider and leaned against it, hands clasped in front of him.

"Doing what?" Bryony asked.

"Library Science. I can finish my bachelor's degree in anything and complete my MLS online."

She swiveled her chair again to face him full on. "You're quite serious about this, aren't you?"

"I am!" His grin matured into a full-fledged smile.

He'd talked about that for years, but she never thought he would follow through. Such a bold move had never occurred to her. And Paul, of all people, to consider an undertaking like that at his age both stunned her and unsettled her.

He continued to stand there, looking more confident than ever before.

"If you go, I'll miss seeing you around here," she said. Though a bit fidgety at times, he did his job with accuracy and speed. He had been the perfect colleague.

Paul unclasped his hands, crossed his arms in front of his chest, leaned down, and said, "You might not want to stay after you hear who bought the business."

"Who?" Whatever could Paul be thinking? Bryony had no enemies.

He straightened his back and pronounced the name of the rumored new owner with precision. "Charity Henderson."

Bryony paused, looked back at her screen, took a breath, pushed her chair away from the desk, and stood. "Excuse me."

After confirming Paul's assertion with Clyde, Bryony tendered her two-week notice in a brief resignation letter with no typos centered on a fresh sheet of plain white paper. Then, she called her best friend. Lillian lamented not being able to meet in the evening and begged Bryony to stop by in the morning.

❧

THE NEXT DAY before work, Bryony arrived at BeanHereNow alert and ready. She chose the table with red chairs. Red for two shots of adrenaline and a future with no plan. Bryony's mind was on fire. The vase in the middle of the table held fresh pink freesia and a few sprigs of baby's breath. Leafless thorny stalks with sharp tips would have been more apt.

Lillian moved toward Bryony's table from the back of the work area. Her husband, Rick, followed close behind, a white apron covering his shirt, plastic gloves on his large, strong, capable, brown hands. His real job was managing a construction company, but he pitched in to help when needed.

Stopping on the other side of the order counter, Rick asked, "Did you ask her yet?"

Without answering her husband, Lillian placed a mug of steaming coffee in front of Bryony, a bowl of strawberries in the middle of the table, and another mug in front of the empty chair opposite.

"What did you say, Bryony?" Rick asked, his eyes now directed at her, his brow furrowed.

Lillian went to the counter, stretched her arm across its surface, and put her finger to his lips. "Shh, baby, we haven't talked yet. Go back there and finish the sandwiches. I'll let you know what she says."

"Ask me what?" Bryony asked.

"My bad." Rick walked backward with his hands up. "Sorry to interrupt. I'll get back to my general man-duties while you two talk business."

"What's he talking about?" Bryony asked.

Rick resumed his stance at the table in the back of the employee work area. His arms moved as he assembled, cut, and bagged sandwiches. He raised his head to look toward them, and lowered it again when he saw Bryony watching him.

"I was wondering," Lillian said, lowering herself to the waiting chair. "It wouldn't be anything near what you're making now, but would you like to help out at the coffee shop until you decide what you want to do next?"

"Yes, I would." The answer came fast and hard. "I can start right away on weekends."

Lillian sipped from her mug and lowered it before saying, "You do understand the pay is not much above minimum wage, and we'd split the tips?"

"You don't have to pay me," Bryony said. Spur-of-the-moment job offer acceptances weren't her style. But neither were spur-of-the-moment resignations, and she had been awake all night wondering how she would fill her days. The offer was heaven-sent.

"I'm not going to let you volunteer, dear." Lillian bit into a strawberry.

"Whatever you want to pay me is fine."

"It won't be what you're worth, but I'll do what I can." Lillian turned to the work area behind the counter and announced, "You can come back over, Rick. She said yes."

Bryony heard a knife clatter to the floor and watched Rick skirt his work table.

"Great!" he said, gliding around the order counter and

rushing toward them. When he reached her, he patted Bryony on the back and said, "Welcome aboard!"

"He's happy because now he doesn't have to help me out so much," Lillian said. "Come here, baby." She put a strawberry in her husband's mouth. "There's your pay for all the ways you've helped over the years."

Rick chewed a few times and swallowed the fruit. "Don't let her overwork you, Bryony."

"No chance," Bryony replied. She loved to work. Whatever real work would come next, being at the coffee shop with Lillian would be perfect for the time being.

"Now go do your manly things," Lillian said to her husband.

"Aye aye, Sweetie Pie," Rick sang as he sailed back to his station.

"You two are awesome," Bryony said.

"We have our moments," Lillian said, a smug look on her face.

Knowing she did not face the abyss of an unknown future relieved Bryony to the point of being able to experience her body again. "I'm hungry!" Reaching for a strawberry, she realized she hadn't eaten since yesterday's apple and almond snack.

"Rick, honey," Lillian called out. "Please make a special bagged lunch for our new employee."

"Coming right up!" he called back.

Bryony put her hand on top of Lillian's. "Thank you," she said. "You have no idea how much this means to me."

Lillian placed her free hand on top of Bryony's. "I'll always be here for you, Bry. What are friends for?"

# CHARITY FOR CAL

*O*n the fourth day of June, Cal checked in at over a dozen graduation parties for his students. On the fifth day of June, he attended his own retirement party, organized by a committee of students and teachers, and held in the high school auditorium

Rudy went through the double doors first, waving Cal through and hanging back as Cal high-fived the aisle sitters on his way to the front of the full house. He took his place, center stage, in a recliner scavenged from the theater department's set collection, to listen to those who won the coveted speaking spots.

"Uncle Cal!" Hell-Oh called from the front row. A collective chuckle rumbled through the audience as her mother shushed her. Cal made eye contact with each of his family members as he quietly waved with waggled fingers and smiled greetings at them.

The principal gave a short introduction prior to calling up the first speaker.

So many current and former students volunteered that speakers had been selected at random. Knowing this vindicated

Cal for the torture he had inflicted on every single class he taught over the years. The nature of the torture had been public speaking.

Cal posited that being able to speak in front of a group strengthened democracy. Having witnessed a fair share of excruciating first attempts over the years, Cal often shared candidly about his own struggles with speaking.

His mother had helped him overcome a slight stutter when he was young by coaching him to recite the ABCs to her before he could read. When he could read, he read out loud to her every night. When she introduced him to other adults, she expected him to speak up, though he often stumbled through his words. She continued to work with him until the stutter all but disappeared, only surfacing in moments of strong surprise or deep uncertainty.

With a similar determination, he insisted all of his students develop skill in speaking to a group, no matter how awkward, shy, speech-challenged, or resistant the student might be. He never failed to see improvement, though some required after school tutoring, which he provided on his own time.

First speaker up was Chad, a tattoo-covered bass player who, in spite of being highly intelligent, barely managed to graduate.

"In ninth grade I had Mister Forster, and I hated him." Chad looked over at Cal, then back to the audience. "I hated him for making me stand up in front of the class. But one day he said, 'Get up there and talk about what you love.'" He looked again at Cal and smiled this time. "I gave a speech about music. It changed my life. Thank you Mister Forster. If I ever get a record deal, you're on my acknowledgement list. You rock, dude." He flashed a peace sign to Cal and bowed to the audience.

Everyone clapped as Chad left the podium, dyed black hair hanging in his eyes, a too-big black leather jacket slumping down both shoulders.

The rest of the randomly selected speakers stepped onto the stage one by one, fifteen in all, with no hesitation. Each told a story about how Cal changed their life in some way, small or large. Cal teared up a few times but managed to keep any drops from running down his cheeks. He wondered if retirement could ever be as rewarding as the fruits of his labor spread before him right now.

Finally, the only chosen speaker, Prissy Bangor, walked up to the stage. The entire auditorium erupted into applause. Attendees rose from their seats. Tears ran down Prissy's cheeks. Her willingness to show her vulnerability loosened the clamp on Cal's emotions. After they hugged, he noticed three wet dots on the back of her shirt. So much for getting through the day with his dignity intact, but the reason for his tears outweighed his need to appear stoic.

Starting in January, Prissy had organized a group of unlikely candidates to pierce their ears in memory and honor of her younger brother who died by suicide the previous fall. Half of the football team, all of the wrestling team, and every member of the Future Teachers of America endured a pierce—for some, their first—in one or both ears.

Standing on the podium, her hands gripping the lectern or moving notecards from one stack to another, Prissy described how she had lobbied at the local, county, and state levels to increase awareness of, and funding for, programs to prevent suicide. She credited Cal with her ability to speak to groups small and large.

Cal had promised to have an ear pierced if Prissy raised $5,000 for a local suicide hotline. He hoped his challenge would push her to exceed her original goal of $2,500. Donations had added up to over $6,500 and Cal purchased a one-carat diamond for each ear.

The moment to fulfill his promise had arrived.

As Prissy led him from the recliner to a straight back chair, she carried the cordless microphone with her and talked about how Cal had bolstered her belief in her ability to help others. After addressing the audience, she asked him to hold the microphone, cleaned his ear lobe, and said, "Don't worry, Mister Forster. I know what I'm doing."

Right before shooting the sharpened end of a gold stud into his lobe, she whispered, "Without you I might have ended up like my brother."

The post's stab went unnoticed, but he would forever remember the way her words pierced his heart.

"Oops," she said, dabbing at his shirt. "I got a tiny speck of blood on your collar."

"I'll wear it with pride," Cal said. After enduring the second poke, he hugged her again before she left the stage.

Cal spoke last. He had worked on his speech for two weeks. It ended up being less than half the length of the Gettysburg Address, and took under fifty seconds to deliver, about the same time allotted an Oscar winner.

"After my first day as a student teacher, my mentor told me I would never make it. I was too intelligent, too awkward, too arrogant, and too chummy. I never went back... to him. I found a new place to student teach."

The audience applauded.

"Never let anyone disparage you. Even if their assertions are correct—I am intelligent, awkward, arrogant, and chummy. And always remember you are nothing less than a unique, brilliant light. You are all stars in my universe, and my existence would be mournfully lonely if I had not met each and every one of you. Now go out and continue to make a difference in the lives of others. I am forever grateful for the difference you have made in mine."

The applause lasted for over four minutes, not a world record breaker, but likely the longest round ever heard echoing through the auditorium of Weber High School. Cal thought the event would end when the clapping stopped, but nobody wanted to leave. Two hours later, he shooed the last few out the door so the janitor could lock the building and go home to his family.

❧

FULL OF GRATITUDE, and exhausted by the emotion of the day, Cal retreated to the cement deck encircling the condo pool. From this day on, no calendar or daily schedule set by the school system would guide him, only the sun and moon. He supposed he would adjust, but right now the future felt—empty. Cal had no adult experience calculating time without imposed deadlines.

His cell phone rang, and Cal reached over to pick it up from the poolside table.

"Hey, Cal," a familiar voice said. "Am I interrupting?"

Rising from his reclined position, Cal sat sideways on the chair and switched ears. "Not at all, Charity. I'm just hanging out by the pool. How's Chuck?"

He had received a call the week before from Charity's daughter. She informed him Chuck had a heart attack followed by a procedure to unblock arteries. There had been complications. Charity had called since to update him on Chuck's condition. Cal appreciated being included, even more so when he learned Chuck had insisted he be informed. Their rekindled friendship meant as much to Chuck as it did to Cal.

He and Charity exchanged a few pleasantries. She asked about his retirement party and expressed regret for not being able to attend. She asked if Susie had been in touch. Cal said she had called a few times, and they had tried to find a time to get together, but they were both so busy. And finally, Cal asked about Chuck. Charity's voice had sounded strained throughout the call, and he worried she had bad news to share.

"The doctor told him to take off for an entire year," Charity said. "Actually, Chuck asked me to call you, and I know this is a huge imposition... he wondered if you would take his classes while he recovers. I hate to ask, Cal, but I know he'd rest easier if he knew he could count on you. I'm so sorry. We know about your travel plans." Her voice trailed off.

"Yes," Cal said. "Tell him I'll sub for him as long as he needs me." And just like that, his plans changed. He would start his journey closer to home and send pictures to his father from southern Ohio. The rest of the world would be there when Chuck was ready to resume working.

Charity sighed on the other end of the phone. "You don't know how good it feels to hear you're willing to come."

She had no idea how good he felt about having somewhere definite to go.

# BRYONY MEETS CHUCK'S SUB

*T*hree blocks from the high school, traffic crawled to a stop, then surged forward, stopping again in less than half a block. At first Bryony thought the jam must be related to everyone arriving at once, but then she moved forward enough to see a worker with an orange vest directing traffic.

Sweat darkening his T-shirt's underarms, the flagger held up a Stop sign. Bryony watched as cars traveled past in the opposite direction. Cool air recirculating through her car and closed windows blocked most of the smell from the fresh tar glistening in the morning sun.

The first day of school was going to be a hot one.

If the road work forced her to wait much longer, the large coffee sitting in her car console would be cold by the time she delivered it. The aroma of fresh-baked dough wafted from the passenger seat. Upon hearing Bryony's plan to celebrate the start of the school year with continental breakfast for her brother, Lillian added an extra dozen bagels for the office staff.

The flagger waved Bryony through. She steered around a clanging machine and into the driveway leading to the school.

Relieved to find the last open spot in the lane, marked "Visitors," she parked and loaded up her arms.

Nearing the entrance, a large red-headed boy with a larger bass viol almost knocked her over. Three giggling girls brushed by, disturbing Bryony's nervous juggle of bagel bag, latte cup, and overstuffed bronze shoulder bag. A tall, athletic boy wearing a school jacket held the door for her, but let go too soon when someone called to him from the parking lot. She managed to enter the lobby intact, with no spills, but her insides were jumbled.

Would she ever be able to enter this building without feeling like a piece of vine clinging to cracks in the wall? Had there been a high school contest for Least Likely to be Noticed, Bryony would have won. One teacher wrote in her yearbook, "You, my dear—unseen, unheard, undiscovered—are a treasure yet to be found. Your day will come." Within these walls, the timeline on when the "un" part of her life would end, and the "seen, heard, and discovered" part would commence seemed to stretch beyond her expected lifetime.

In contrast, outside the hallowed halls of her alma mater, Bryony had spent the last few months rediscovering lost—and uncovering hidden—strengths. After a series of pep talks from Lillian, four self-help books, and a barrage of TEDTalks by empowered women for women needing to be empowered, Bryony had made a few changes in her life.

She had written, "I am ready to blossom and bloom," in RedRose shaded lipstick across her bathroom mirror, and read the phrase out loud every morning. Meditation and lifting weights preceded her daily walking habit. She practiced yoga every evening. Five pounds of excess weight had evaporated into thin air.

All of these practices seemed to have resulted in substantive change in Bryony's persona, too. Her father recently asked if she had a nose job or dyed her hair because something about her seemed "different, less pinched." Lillian marveled at her ease with customers, and Bryony herself noticed feeling relaxed around people in a new way, almost like belonging somewhere.

But the biggest change was knowing that never again would a man become the focal point in the landscape of her life. She truly was fine being single. In fact, Bryony felt better than ever.

In spite of all that, being here, in the building she had fought hard to endure for four years, she wilted. Wall to wall, perfumed, upper-class adolescents bustled around exuding superficial confidence. Freshman struggled to open their lockers for the first time, their anxiety palpable. Bryony lowered her head and made a beeline for her destination.

"How nice!" Mitch said when she presented him with the goods she carried. "Let me introduce you to everyone."

"Introduce" was a funny word to use. Bryony had gone to school with the two women who covered administrative assistant duties, lived next door to the Assistant Principal, and had served coffee to the counselor and social worker less than an hour ago. But everyone played along as Mitch danced her around the complex of smaller rooms inside the glass door marked "School Office."

All eyes were on Mitch, of course, as he made a display of the effort his "little sister" made to kick off the year with community support. Mitch always garnered the attention—he always had.

After retreating to the largest room inside the office area, her brother closed the door and collapsed in his chair, sighing with dramatic relief. "I don't know if I have it in me for another year, Bry."

Bryony sat on the edge of a heavy coffee table, concerned. Typically, Mitch blathered on about how well the students responded to his discipline and the staff to his leadership. Mopey Mitch made no sense at all. Bryony inserted the tip of her finger into the potted plant beside her as she made eye contact with her brother to show she cared, she was here for him. She would tell him later he needed to water his plant.

"For instance," Mitch said. "Henderson is out for an extended cardiac rehab, and we have a substitute who might be here all year. He's a nice enough fellow, but"—Mitch raised his arm and made rolling movements with his hand—"he talks and talks and talks."

Brushing dry potting soil from her finger onto her skirt, Bryony searched for the right words. "Many people talk when they're nervous," she said. "You are his new boss."

She picked a dead leaf off the plant. She had heard about Chuck's heart attack. If he might be off all year, it must have been pretty serious. "How's Chuck doing?" she asked.

Mitch ignored her. "I met the sub for a burger last night. When I meet someone for burgers in the evening, the last thing I want to talk about is work. I thought I might soften him up a bit, make him feel at home, help him lose the professional facade of always showing how much you care about the kids, blah, blah, blah. But instead of loosening up, he asked about ways he might assist with extracurriculars."

"Sounds like maybe Chuck's sub cares about making a good impression," she said.

"Right!" Mitch said. "And talked until midnight!"

Should she send a card to let Chuck know she wished him well? "Sounds like the sub showed enthusiasm for his job."

"I didn't get to bed until after one!"

Bryony cocked her head. Mitch was whining! Unlike Chuck, whose temperament would have him taking his serious health issue in stride, Mitch moaned about a minor problem, which could likely be addressed with an earlier bed time. "Sounds like you didn't sleep enough last night."

"Right!" Mitch said. "You get it." He put his head in his hands. "I'll be sixty-six this year, Bry. Maybe I'm getting too old"—he swept his arm in a semi-circle—"for all of this."

"You'll feel better after a good night's sleep."

Bryony stood, preparing to leave. She didn't want to take advantage of Lillian's flexibility, and there would be plenty to do before the lunch rush. "Go to bed early tonight," she said as she inched toward the door.

"Mister Green?"

She turned toward the voice. A man she did not recognize peered around Mitch's office door and stepped in with caution. He appeared to be close to her own age, a few inches taller than her, trim, with short sandy-colored hair thinning on top. He wore glasses perched on the end of his slim nose, and his smile revealed bright white uneven teeth. He wore what passed for normal teacher fashion—navy blue pants and a pressed white shirt.

Her position blocked the man's view of her brother, and when she glanced back at Mitch, he mouthed, "He's the sub."

"Cal! Come on in." Mitch stood, his face shifting to a welcoming smile as he moved around Bryony and waved the man to enter. "Come in and meet my little sister, Bryony Green."

Mitch finished making the introductions. Bryony's face grew warm when Mitch, now situated behind the new teacher, made hand signals of a talking mouth as the teacher gushed a monologue of appreciations at Bryony for the warm reception he had received at the school and, in particular, for Mitch's hospitality.

Unwilling to join her brother in crossing the boundaries of civil conduct, and good taste, Bryony shifted her position to avoid seeing him altogether as she gave her full attention to the new teacher. "Nice to meet you, Mister Forster."

"Please, call me Cal." He extended his hand to shake hers, and the papers he held fluttered to the ground around his feet.

"Let me help," Bryony said, as the sub said, "Oh, dear," and they both leaned forward at the same time, butting their heads hard enough for Bryony to see stars.

"I'm so sorry!" they said in unison, rising as one.

"Ouch!" Mitch said. "I'll bet that hurt." He skirted his desk, sat down again, and began shuffling through papers.

Bryony looked at the sub as they both rubbed their foreheads. "I understand you're with us while Mister Henderson recovers from his surgery." The pain in her head dulled to a throb.

"Do you work in the building?" The sub clutched the disorganized papers in his free hand. "Because I've spent the last two days roaming the halls, meeting everyone I could, and somehow I missed you. Let me guess. You look like an artist, but I know you're not the art teacher. He's a scary looking fellow!" The sub raised his eyebrows, shuddered, and backpedaled, "But nice, so nice."

Bryony stifled a laugh. The art teacher was a large man with bushy eyebrows, a thick nose, and thicker lips, which never smiled. She knew he was not nice, and his students feared him. The sub was being kind.

The sub made comments, often insightful, about the other teachers he met. After a long-winded stretch, he took a breath and launched in for the home stretch. "I would say Home Economics for you," he continued, "but I don't think you offer Home Ec here, do you?"

The sub for Chuck Henderson had a quick mind, which covered a large swath of ground in a short time, like a hummingbird, Bryony's favorite of the winged creatures. She coaxed them to her yard annually with feeders and flowers. She couldn't help but like the man. He buzzed around inside her head, iridescent, magical.

"We offer Family and Consumer Sciences," Mitch said. "A great fit for my sister if she'd chosen a teaching career, but Bryony doesn't work here. She recently left a lucrative job as a bookkeeper to wait on tables in a coffee shop." Mitch rolled his eyes and looked back down at his desk.

"Oh!" the sub said. "I love coffee shops. Which one?"

Bryony pointed toward downtown with her thumb. "BeanHereNow, on Main Street."

"Bean Here Now," he laughed. "Reminiscent of Be Here Now, the famous book by Ram Dass, the title transformed from a command to a declarative statement, as in, 'I'm Being Here Now.' I like that."

Did he always talk so much? No wonder Mitch had a lousy evening. He liked being the center of attention, and Chuck's sub didn't seem like the kind of guy who would do all the listening.

"Okay you two," Mitch said. "Enough chit chat. I have to attend to the first fifteen crises of the day. Bryony, thanks for the coffee. Cal, what can I do for you?"

"I came in to give you these." The sub waved the wad of papers back and forth as he turned again to Bryony. "Nice meeting you. I hope we run into each other again."

"Good luck with the school year, Mister Forster," Bryony said.

She heard him call out as she walked to the outer office door, "Cal! Call me Cal, or I shall forevermore refer to you as 'Mitch's little sister,'" which made her smile.

Chuck Henderson's sub was funny, and nice.

Bryony left the office suite with as little disruption as possible to the staff, who were bombarded with student needs. She thought about Chuck as she navigated her way to the exterior glass double doors. She would ask later if the school staff had coordinated any ongoing support for him and his family. If so, she would slip in her thoughts and prayers there. Her contribution might go unnoticed, but she would know she had made an effort. Reaching out on her own at this point would seem strange. Chuck and she hadn't been friends for such a long time.

# CAL'S FIRST DAY

$\mathcal{C}$al watched the outer door to the office suite swing shut behind the principal's sister. "She works downtown at a coffee shop?" He shuffled the papers into a neat stack and handed them to Mitch.

"We've been over BeanHereNow," Mitch said. "Ram Dass, etcetera." He dropped the papers onto a pile of other, similar forms, and said, "If you don't need anything else right now, I need to prepare for my first address of the year."

"Sure, sure." Cal backed out of the office and turned to walk from relative serenity into outright chaos. He could see Bryony, her graying auburn ponytail swinging side-to-side as she opened the door to leave the building. He tried to catch up, but throngs of young people, all heading in the same direction, forced him into the school gymnasium.

Of course, this was where he was supposed to be now, not floundering after the first attractive woman to pop up on his radar since moving to Fieldstone a month ago.

Assembling here in this great hall would be the entire student body to greet the Freshmen, honor the Seniors, and pretend the older students would act as mentors to the younger ones throughout the coming year. Nice idea, but short on reality. Seventeen and eighteen-year-old students typically wanted nothing to do with fourteen-year-olds new to the school, many of whom were younger brothers and sisters.

Tiers of bleachers on the long walls of the gym awaited hormone-soaked bodies. The floor had been padded and filled with folding chairs. Knowing his main duty was being present, Cal took a seat in the back. He simply had to be here now. He would check out that coffee shop downtown as soon as possible.

During Mitch's speech, Cal took mental notes. Perhaps Mitch might be open to help the next time. His references were dated and the jokes a bit stale. As the program ended and the crowd dispersed to the hallway, Cal thought again of Mitch's sister.

Bryony Green's eyes were the color of tea shot through with a sunburst of amber. Did her dilated pupils indicate heightened interest? She retained her maiden name and did not wear a ring on her left hand.

She wore a simple brown A-line skirt and a crisp cream shirt, the long sleeves rolled up to halfway between her wrist and her elbow. She looked quite healthy with a posture indicating she had not given in to age. Her legs were covered in tights, and her shoes looked comfortable, not stylish. Did she always wear her hair in a ponytail? A bit juvenile for someone with so much gray, but she seemed to pull it off.

The delightful image of Bryony Green faded from his mind as he walked into his room to teach his first class.

"Who's up for learning about Marketing?" he sang out.

Thirty-five voices silenced, and seventy eyes watched him stride to the front of the room.

"My name is Mister Forster," he said, rubbing his hands together, "and we're going to have fun this semester!"

# BRYONY'S BUMBLEBERRY

he morning after her anxiety-provoking visit to the high school, Bryony prepped the drink area while Lillian attended to the oven.

"Remember when I told you about Chuck's sub yesterday?" Bryony asked. "I talked to Mitch last night, and he said the sub retired from teaching high school English in Cleveland, but he has a Ph.D." She finished filling the large metal urn with water for tea. "By the way, Mitch wants you to donate bagels for the Rotary meeting next week."

"What's he like?" Lillian asked.

Confused, Bryony answered, "You know what Mitch is like. Total cheapskate. I'm okay with you saying no, but I need it to not come from me." Her relationship with Mitch had always been strained. She never knew when he would turn on her.

"Not Mitch, silly." Lillian clanked a tray of bagels on the counter. "Chuck's sub."

The perfect answer popped into Bryony's mind. "You know what he's like? He's like razzleberry pie." She put a filter in a coffee pot and added scoops of ground coffee.

"And what goes in razzleberry pie?" Lillian moved around

Bryony to place a warm tray of bagels on the shelf against the wall.

"Raspberries and blackberries." Bryony held a second coffee filter under a dripping faucet to rinse off any loose paper fibers. "Or maybe bumbleberry pie."

"And what goes in bumbleberry pie?" Lillian swiped her hands across her apron and picked up a tray of napkin holders filled earlier. "Will you place these on the tables, please?"

"Will you finish setting up the coffee?" Bryony asked.

"My pleasure," Lillian answered.

Being with her best friend every day compensated for the low wages. Bryony lifted the tray from Lillian's hands and sailed it over the counter. "Bumbleberry pie has raspberries, blackberries, strawberries, and blueberries." She lowered the tray to the first table and began distributing the napkin holders.

"Sounds tasty," Lillian said.

Bryony brushed a crumb off the next table before placing the napkin holder.

"Is he married?" Lillian asked.

"I don't know, but maybe not," Bryony answered. She was almost done with the napkin holders. "When Mitch told me he rented the Wyan's old house on Parker Drive, he said, 'It's a lot of house for one person.'" Bryony plunked the last napkin holder on the last table and walked briskly back to the work area.

"Sounds promising," Lillian said.

"Why?" Bryony asked. She stooped to put the tray under the counter and stood up again.

"Well"—Lillian put her hand on her hip—"because he's all you've talked about since you came back from the high school yesterday."

"No, he's not." Bryony's cheeks burned.

"You're blushing," Lillian said.

"I'm standing in front of the oven," Bryony said.

"You can't fool me," Lillian said. "I think you like this Mister Bumbleberry who's new to town and conveniently—for all we know—not married."

"I need to unlock the door for the delivery truck." Bryony headed to the back of the shop.

"You need to unlock something other than the door," Lillian called after her.

THE MORNING RUSH lasted longer than usual, the day being warm and sunny. Bryony had no time to consider whether Lillian's accusation carried any truth, but the idea nagged at her as she poured coffee, plated or packaged bagels, re-stocked pre-made sandwiches, keyed orders into the computer, made change, and provided a credit card receipt when requested. Right on schedule, the customers slowed to a trickle. The three fixtures, Abby, Etta, and Mister Parker, arrived on time, ordered one coffee each, and took residence at their usual spots, predictable and silent.

After cleaning up the tables, loading the dishwasher, and prepping for lunch, Lillian and Bryony agreed on a short break.

"My feet hurt." Lillian put her coffee on the table nearest the cash register and furthest from the fixtures. "If anybody else comes in, you take care of them, Bry." She sat down.

"No problem." Bryony placed her cup on the table and sat down facing Lillian.

"I ran into Susie Quatman at the bank today. She's back in town for an extended stay, cleaning out her parents' house, putting it on the market," Lillian said. "She asked about you."

"Why?" Bryony asked. She hadn't seen or spoken to Susie in years, and then only to be polite at a class reunion.

"You know Susie," Lillian answered. "She asked about several people, poking around for trouble, looking for something to gossip about."

"I am not gossip worthy," Bryony said. Nothing about her would interest Susie Quatman, and Bryony planned to keep it that way.

"And what is up with your Mister Bumbleberry?" Lillian asked.

"He's not my Bumbleberry," Bryony said, though the heat in her torso might tell a different story. She squelched the feeling.

"Maybe he is," Lillian said. "Maybe he's the one."

"Stop it, Lil." Every time Bryony mentioned a man, Lillian was ready to marry her off. "I told you. I'm happy on my own. Not everybody will find their soulmate and live happily ever after."

"Rick and I aren't happy all the time," Lillian said.

Bryony raised her eyebrows.

Lillian smiled and sipped her coffee. "Okay, we're happy. But just because you haven't found your soulmate doesn't mean he's not out there. Give it a shot, Bryony. When's the last time you went on a date?"

"When I was fifteen," Bryony said. She went out with the boy three times before he dropped her for someone else. "I told you. I don't date. Dating is too uncomfortable."

"Right," Lillian said. "You met Nathan because he filled in when someone went on maternity leave, and you kept running into each other at the vending machine."

"And then we started having dinner together, as friends," Bryony said.

"And spending weekends together," Lillian added.

"And holidays." Bryony's mother had adored him.

"How could he prefer sun-scorched snorkeler to smart, sensational you?" Lillian put her hand on Bryony's arm.

"Maybe he preferred twenty years younger," Bryony said.

"Ugh!" Lillian lifted her hand and made a swatting motion,

as if brushing away a fly, a spider web, a foul smell. "Nathan is history. There's someone else out there looking for your future. Go on a date."

"I told you, I don't date." Bryony sipped her coffee while looking over the brim of her cup.

"Then go on a non-date. Are you telling me you haven't been interested in anyone?"

"Nope."

"Until Bumbleberry."

Bryony's cheeks burned again.

"See? Every time I mention him, you blush."

"Hot flashes."

"Call it whatever you want, I think you're interested in Chuck's sub."

"He's an interesting man." Cal Forster reminded Bryony of someone who might be seen on a stage or in a movie. His face was expressive, captivating. "Anybody who met him would be interested in Chuck's sub."

"Oh, I'm going to meet him," Lillian said. "I want to meet the man who sets your face on fire."

"He does not!"

Etta left her chair and approached the counter. She stood looking at the employee work area as if unaware of Lillian and Bryony sitting nearby. Bryony scooted around the counter and stepped up to the spot opposite Etta.

"May I have a second cup of coffee?" Etta asked.

"No problem." Bryony took Etta's cup, re-filled to one-half inch below the rim, and returned it with a wisp of steam curling up from the black liquid below. "Be careful. It's hot."

"Thanks," Etta said, placing a five dollar bill on the counter.

Pushing the cash back toward Etta, Bryony said, "Second cup's on the house."

"Then put it in the tip jar." Etta shoved the bill back to Bryony.

"Thanks!" Bryony said, but Etta had already turned her back to return to her seat.

When Bryony dropped the money into the tip jar, she noticed writing on it. She fished the bill back out, unfolded it, and read. *Relationship tip—Assume the other person likes you as much as you like them and act accordingly. If they don't like you, you have lost nothing. If they do like you, think of all you would have lost if you'd never tried.*

Bryony dropped the money back into the jar.

She did not engage in or condone magical thinking, and she would not be taking guidance from a tip jar. Besides, someone like Cal Forster would never be interested in someone like her.

# CAL STUMBLES FORWARD

*T*he second day of school had been a breeze. Cal stayed late to listen to a group of students who seemed eager to please while communicating their needs for extra help. Two said they had ADHD. Another, a shy senior named Todd, said he was dyslexic.

These kids were cool. So far, the greatest threats to Cal were falling asleep after lunch and remembering where he parked his car, though he did have an awkward moment with the principal right after lunch when he casually asked about his sister.

"Bryony?" Mitch had answered. "She's a little fragile right now. Let herself get all worked up about being dumped by a guy who seemed okay at first, but I never really liked him. She needs to get her life together. She's not in a good place, if you know what I mean." He'd eyed Cal with meaning.

"No worries," Cal had said. "Just curious." He followed up with a few questions about the sports trophies in the hallway display case which, yes, did belong to Mitch, and which Mitch did enjoy talking about in detail, including yards, touchdowns, rival games, game-winning plays, and championships. From

Cal's perspective, after the uncomfortable exchange about Bryony, they had shared what might be Fieldstone's version of a real bonding moment.

On his way to the parking lot, three students said, "Have a good evening, Mister Forster."

"I think I'm going to like it here," Cal said to himself as he hit the remote to unlock his doors.

The ride to his rented home took ten minutes. Bailey greeted him at the door, tail wagging, tongue hanging out.

"Hey, buddy!" Cal chuffed the dog under his chin and patted his head. "How was your second day of school?"

Cal answered for Bailey with a low growl. "I was a good doggie. Didn't eat the couch. Slept most of the day. Barked once, when the mailman rattled the box."

"Oh, you are a good dog," Cal said in his own voice again. "Shall we walk?"

He put on his walking shoes and secured Bailey's leash. "Let's go for a big walk, shall we?"

Since moving into the amazing brick Tudor at the beginning of August, Cal and Bailey had explored in all directions many times. Most of the houses in the immediate neighborhood were built in the forties and fifties, likely for managers of businesses which sprang up during and after the second world war.

A few blocks farther, he could see the effects of income distribution, siding instead of brick, smaller houses, some with no garage. Bailey visited every tree within three feet of the sidewalks crisscrossing the well-established neighborhoods. The trees were fat with years of sunshine and rain. Cement heaved up from strong roots below. Branches overhead provided shade and dropped various forms of seed pods, sticks, and leaves.

The ambience sure beat the sterile condominium Cal had purchased twenty years earlier in a Cleveland suburb. A former student now rented his condo as she completed her first year of teaching. He would be back there in June, but he was not wishing the time away. This place appealed to him. He liked the choice he made to come, the decision to rent a house instead of an apartment.

"Come on, Bailey," Cal said.

They arrived at the place where Cal would typically turn around, but tonight he crossed the street, continued down the block, and came across something he hadn't seen in years—a root beer stand with car window service.

"Bailey old boy," Cal said. "It looks like we just found our dinner!"

After ordering three hot dogs, a large root beer, and a to-go bowl of water, he and his dog took possession of the provided picnic table. Cal chopped up one hot dog into swallowable sized pieces for Bailey, and commenced to chow down on childhood memories.

"There used to be this great root beer stand close to our house," he said as he chewed. "I think I lived there until they closed down when I was twelve or thirteen. They sold frozen peanut butter cups. You haven't lived, Bailey, until you've worked your way through one of those."

He glanced down at his dog. Bailey's food bowl was empty, and he slurped at the water.

"Can't afford to do this too often," Cal said as he moved on to the second hot dog. "I don't even want to see the ingredient list for these, and the salt content's probably high enough to de-ice our entire driveway."

The carhops continued to wait on customers as Cal finished off his meal. He watched them walk with purpose to take the orders, return to the window, and carry trays or bags back to the cars. Someone had trained them well. Too bad the stand would be closed for most of the school year. Otherwise, he would have investigated placing a student there.

Depositing their trash in the plastic lined barrel, Cal thought about how many calories he had just ingested and decided on a longer walk. The town square was only a half mile or so farther on. He headed back to the sidewalk and said, "Let's explore new territory!"

Bailey wagged his tale and picked up speed.

"Good boy! New trees, new scents, it's a whole new world out there!"

Bailey agreed by lifting his leg on the next stop sign.

❧

DOWNTOWN FIELDSTONE CLUNG to its retail past with a diner, a gift shop, a florist, and a used book store. There were a few windows covered in brown paper with "For Rent" signs. Other storefronts housed a plumbing business, a bank, and BeanHereNow, the coffee shop where the principal's sister worked. The lights inside were off. The sign on the door said, "Closed."

"What kind of coffee shop closes at five?" Cal asked. "Lattes and bagels are twenty-four hour necessities."

He sauntered along the main street, looking up at the three largest buildings, all built in the late 1800s, a fact he learned by reading the historical plaques secured to each facade. Bailey stopped to lift his leg one last time on the second pass by the tree outside BeanHereNow when the door to the coffee shop opened and Bryony stepped out.

Surprised and delighted to see her, Cal said, "Hi!" as he stepped forward. The toe of his shoe hit the edge of a raised sidewalk segment, and he leapt forward to avoid falling, righting himself two feet too close to her brown eyes.

"Oh!" Bryony's hand flew up to her chest and she took a step back. "What are you doing here?"

Not the greeting he'd hoped for.

"Sorry," he said as he pulled back farther. "Didn't mean to startle you. Bailey and I were out for a walk."

She turned to fit a key into the lock and swiveled her head to look back at Cal. "His name is Bailey?" Bryony dropped the key into her bag and bent toward the dog. "Come here, sweetie."

Bailey wagged himself over to where she dangled her hand. He sniffed and licked and allowed her to stroke his back.

"You're a handsome fellow," she said before straightening her back and returning both hands to the strap of the purse hanging from her shoulder.

"Why thank you!" Cal said. "My parents thank you, too. When I was young, they were afraid I'd never grow into my ears."

Bryony crossed her arms. "I was talking to Bailey."

"I knew that." Cal stood at attention, his hands clasped in front of him, the leash dangling down from between them.

"So, what brings you here tonight?" she asked.

"Like I said, walking the dog."

"Right." Bryony nodded her head.

"Say, would you like to have a cup of coffee with me sometime?" Cal asked.

The minute he asked, he wished he had not. Whereas before he asked she seemed amused by him, now she looked at him with indifference, as if she had closed up for the night, maybe forever.

"Thanks, but no thanks," she answered. "By the end of the work day, I've had my fill of coffee."

Tugging on the leash, Cal said, "Of course you have." Bailey walked to his side.

She skirted around them both and walked to the sedan parked at the curb. "Enjoy your walk," she said, dismissing him with the perfunctoriness of the school bell signaling the end of a class.

"See you, Bryony," Cal said, the words coming out with a wistful sigh he hoped she had not heard.

"Bye, Cal," she said.

Cal smiled as Bryony opened her car door. Maybe he had a chance after all. She had called him Cal.

# BRYONY PLANTS HERSELF ON PURPOSE

At seven o'clock in the evening, Bryony sat down to watch a movie, a hot cup of tea cradled in her palms. She tried to settle into the cushions, but her legs were cramped, tense. She turned off the television, put the tea on the kitchen table, and slipped on her jacket. Maybe a walk would help.

Cal's appearance on the street earlier in the evening had startled her, and she had yet to settle down. He expressed interest, invited her for coffee, and she did what she had been doing for the past seven months of retreat and recovery. She shut down her feelings like a reflex.

Supernatural messages from the tip jar aside, how could Bryony believe someone like Cal Forster would be attracted to someone like her? Life seeped out of his every pore. What could he possibly see in her? Bryony closed her front door and walked out into the cool night air.

The yards in her neighborhood were narrow, the houses close together. Pansies and mums in purple, gold, rust, white, and maroon burst from window boxes or pots placed on steps. One eager neighbor had secured a cornstalk and a scarecrow to the porch post. She passed a few gourd displays, but no pumpkins yet. Bryony would buy one as soon as she could. She loved to carve faces, put candles inside, and watch them glow. She shoved her hands deep in her pockets and walked faster.

Maybe loneliness drove Cal to reach out. Mitch's introduction of her had not conveyed a resounding endorsement. He made her sound like a loser. Her brother had been berating her for months about her job change, but she had no regrets. If she were honest with herself, she should have quit Metcalf a long time ago.

For the past ten years or so, she had nursed a hollow feeling in her gut, boredom maybe, or feeling like she was missing out on some important life experience, but she had been too scared to try something new. Bryony should be grateful Charity's purchase of the firm gave the push needed to walk away from a job which had become routine to the point of being mindless instead of mindful, stress-enhancing rather than stress-relieving.

She stopped before stepping off a curb to cross a street, and waited until a car passed. A child looked at her through the passenger side window. Cute kid. Bryony crossed the street, aware of the car make and model. Way too expensive for her taste and budget.

Could she work for minimum wage at BeanHereNow until she retired? Probably, but it would not be a prudent decision. In addition to knowing a higher wage was a practical goal, she needed to create something of her own. She thought about the child in the car back there. She remembered when Lillian's children were young, the thrill of their sounds when she made them laugh. Tears came as she considered grieving the children and grandchildren she would never have. Too late for that. Maybe it was too late for most of what could have been.

A breeze lifted Bryony's hair and fluffed it about her eyes and nose. She reached into her pocket to extract a cloth band, gathered her hair, and fastened it away from her face.

She did mourn knowing she would never be a mother, but this energy swirling around in her gut, this urge to foster her own dream, seemed more like a dormant power than an irretrievable lost opportunity.

Maybe there was something she needed to do in the world.

But if so, what was it?

She didn't dream of being a librarian like Paul. She couldn't see herself opening her own tax service, which would have been the obvious next step. She loved working with Lillian. When she had learned the rudiments of cooking and baking in middle school, a door had opened, a gateway leading to sources of hidden power, almost like being in an office supply store, but with texture and aromas—and come to think of it—altogether different.

Office supplies anchored her. Kitchen supplies set her free.

Stopping at the edge of a field, she noticed for the first time how far she had come. She had walked clear out of town, past the car body repair place and the little Baptist church, past the development where the high-priced houses hid down a winding lane.

The air smelled more fertile here. Bryony took a deep breath, pulling the scent of dirt and corn and soy and hay into the bottom of her lungs, and exhaled slowly.

Why, when considering her options for the future, did Mr. Cal Forster come to mind? His mix of whimsy and male presence appealed to her, but any man in her life might fall for a younger face with a hotter body. She couldn't afford the risk again. In fact, she did not need a man at all. She needed a relationship with a goal, a purpose, something meaningful to her.

*Growing older allows you to deliver on dreams you only discover because you lived long enough to dream them.* Bryony had written that down on the inside cover of her checkbook while waiting to board the plane back to Ohio. In her mind's eye, she could still see the man who said it, and the woman leaning on his arm.

Bryony headed toward home calmer, more in charge. Whatever form this dream, this purpose, would take, the seed of inspiration had been planted. She was sure of that. And she would shield this tiny possibility from anyone who might stomp on it. Because he was a man, Cal Forster, as interesting as he was, could crush her dream before it broke the surface of her own awareness. Every other man in her life had done just that.

How could she expect him to be any different?

# CAL CONNECTS AT
# BEANHERENOW

*S*howered, shaved, and dressed for the day, Cal discovered the foil bag in the freezer he thought contained coffee was, in fact, full of dark chocolate chips. For a moment, he considered tossing a handful into his mouth, but knew he could not get through the morning without liquid caffeine.

He didn't have time to pick up a bag of beans and make a pot at home. The urn in the teacher's lounge looked like it hadn't been cleaned in years. Fast food drive-throughs out by Walmart were options, but their coffee tasted like sludge from the bottom of a pan used to strip paint off metal parts. He had never tasted the sludge, but he'd been in close enough proximity while working a summer job in high school. Bad coffee always took him back to every awful hour spent sweating through his shirt, his nose full of dirt and sludge smell. Cal jogged around the block with Bailey, put the dog back in the house, threw his briefcase in the back seat, and headed for town.

Arriving at BeanHereNow an hour before he needed to be at school, Cal started fifth in line behind a tall woman with a large poncho. Bryony stood behind the service counter, again wearing a crisp oxford shirt, pink this time, with a navy skirt and a flowered apron. Wisps of hair escaped the band holding back her hair. Her cheeks were flushed as she smiled and chatted to the customers, always moving, taking orders, filling them, collecting payment.

When he was third in line, their eyes met, and he smiled and waved hello. She seemed startled to see him at first, but raised her hand in recognition before returning her attention to the person next in line.

Another woman—her natural hair pulled away from her face with a colorful scarf—bussed and wiped tables. She and Bryony seemed to manage to keep things moving, but Cal could see where an extra pair of hands might change the pace to a friendlier, relaxed atmosphere.

The woman in line directly in front of him walked away holding her cup of coffee. Cal stepped up to the counter.

"Hi, Cal," Bryony said. She seemed confident, assured, in her element.

"Hello, Bryony," he said. "With this counter between us, no chance of me tripping on something and lunging at you like an ax murderer." The quip brought a wide grin to his own face.

Her countenance remained the same. "What can I get for you?"

"Um, I'll have a latte with a bagel."

"The milk frother broke ten minutes ago," she said. "We're offering coffee the old-fashioned way this morning."

"Old-fashioned works," he said. "And a bagel, plain."

When Bryony reached up for the bagel, he could see the muscles in her calves. Was she a runner?

She handed his bagel to him, collected a cup of coffee, ran his credit card, and dismissed him to greet the next person in line with the same warm smile and cheerful, "Hello."

Cal found an empty table and sipped his coffee, watching Bryony in his peripheral vision. She paid no special attention to his side of the room. He stopped looking for her to notice him and surveyed the rest of the shop.

Five tables with empty chairs were covered with used cups and napkins. The clutter reminded him of Leslie, the way her kitchen table would pile up over the course of the week with unsorted mail here, a few peppermint candies there, a stack of newspapers, unused plastic utensils still wrapped in cellophane, fast food napkins. He could never bear the way she tolerated disorganization. When he tried to help, she would playfully slap his hands, telling him to *stop*, calling him OCD.

Wanting to live with beauty and order in his life was not a mental disorder. People in general function better when they don't have to look for something every time they want to leave their house. How many times were Leslie and he late for a concert to accommodate a last minute search for her purse, or her keys, or her glasses? One time the lost item was her other shoe. As he recalled, she never found it.

His cell phone rang, and he looked at the number displayed, unknown to him, but with a Cleveland area code. He answered with, "Hello?" and prepared to hang up if the caller launched into selling something.

"Cal?" The voice sounded familiar and not altogether unappealing, a deep, feminine invitation.

"This is Cal," he answered, in line with his determination to never say "Yes" to unknown callers, a safety measure to ward off scammers.

"It's Susie. Remember me?"

"Susie, of course." He'd forgotten to put her number in his contact list, and he did that now as they exchanged pleasantries.

"You were the first person on my call list for the day, and I knew you'd be up early because you're teaching." She paused.

"Yep," Cal said. "I'm awake, alive, alert, and ready for action."

Susie laughed with that low, smoky sound. "I understand you're living in Fieldstone for the time being, and it just so happens I'm in town, too! Family business, but I have loads of free time, and I wondered if we could get together soon for dinner? A movie?"

The line for service extended to the door now, and another couple left a table loaded with their used dishes. Cal looked around. Who was in charge of clearing the tables?

"Sounds great," he answered. "Glad you called. Listen, I gotta run right now, but let's talk soon!"

"Great, great," Susie said, her voice sliding down the easy hill at Aspen. "Let's touch base later. Have a good day, Cal."

"Sure, Susie. Thanks for calling."

He snapped the phone shut as a slight young man with spiked blonde hair left the counter carrying a tray with a steaming cup and plated bagel. His eyes scanning back and forth, the young man stopped and started to place his order on a table still laden with the remnants of the last customer's meal, right next to Cal's table.

"Here, let me help," Cal said. He was out of his seat in a flash, clearing the table, stuffing used napkins in dirty cups, and gathering the cup handles in one fist. "I'll wipe it off for you."

Cal hurried to the counter and deposited the dirty cups there.

Bryony side-eyed him as she waited on the next customer. Her co-worker looked at him with an arched eyebrow.

"May I have a wet cloth to wash off a table?" Cal asked the co-worker. "I'm good at this kind of thing. Bussed many a table at a swanky restaurant when I was young. Those kind of skills stick with you."

"I'll do it," the woman said. She moved the cups to an unseen ledge below the counter and whipped through the opening with a damp rag. Cal returned to his seat and applied hand sanitizer from the bottle in his jacket pocket. Within a few minutes, the woman wiped the table for the young man, cleared four tables, and wiped those clean, too.

Cal gave her a thumbs up as she returned to her station.

Bryony's co-worker returned from behind the counter with a coffee pot and a fresh wet cloth dangling from her wrist. "Top it off?" she asked.

"Sure." He went to pick up his cup but bumped it with his fingertips, sloshing a brown puddle onto the tabletop.

"Oops," he said, reaching for her wet cloth.

She pulled the cloth out of his reach. "I can do it." She picked up his cup, wiped the table, and refilled his coffee in one graceful motion. "Thanks for the help," she said.

"Your manager needs to consider additional staff," Cal said. "You two are doing a great job, but you need help."

"I'll keep that in mind," she said. "I'm Lillian. Are you passing through?"

"I moved here recently. Teaching at the high school. Still getting to know my way around."

"Oh." The woman raised her eyebrows, glanced toward Bryony, and then returned her gaze to him. "I missed your name."

"Cal Forster." He held out his hand. "Nice to meet you, Lillian. Like I said, you two are amazing, but I think another pair of hands could increase your sales."

Lillian smiled. "Are you looking for a part time job?"

"Not me, but I run the work study program at the high school temporarily. If your boss is interested, I could come in and explain the program. It's a win-win for both the students and the work sites."

"Interesting," Lillian said. "Tell you what. Why don't you come back tonight, say around five o'clock, and you can tell us all about what you can do for us?"

"Sure," Cal said. "Who should I ask for?"

"Ask for me," Lillian said. "I own the place." She winked and carried the coffee pot back behind the counter.

"Cool," Cal said under his breath. If he could place a student there, he might have the opportunity to spend time around Bryony. And if she wasn't interested, sounded like Susie might be.

He wasn't looking for a girlfriend, but having an attractive companion, someone to pal around with, could enhance his connection to the community overall.

Maybe when he left Fieldstone to travel, his goal would be to create friendships wherever he went.

He liked the idea. "Travels with Bailey—The People We Met Along the Way."

Cal waved to Bryony before he left, but she was busy talking to another customer. He knew the perfect student for BeanHereNow, and this place would be great for that student, too.

# PIECE OF PIE

*I*n mid-afternoon, when she learned Cal would return at closing time to talk about the high school work study program, Bryony said she needed to leave early.

"You can't leave," Lillian said. "I need you here to clean up while I talk to your Mister Forster."

She winked when she said his name, and Bryony wanted to protest, but her thoughts and feelings were too jumbled to form a cohesive argument. So, she said the only thing she knew would make Lillian stand down.

"I need to go home and make a pie."

"It's about time!" Lillian said. "Bumbleberry?" Had her attention been directed at Bryony, Lillian would have seen the pained expression on her oldest friend's face. But her eyes were on the cash drawer, and so the confusion, the distress incited by Cal's attention, remained hidden. "Bring a piece for me tomorrow," Lillian said before retreating to her office.

Bryony busied herself with extra cleaning tasks and made it through the late afternoon rush with only slight trepidation that Cal would show up early. She left well before closing time, creating an assured clear distance between Cal's expected arrival and her departure.

Steering her car three blocks east, she pulled into the parking lot of Fred's, the sole independent grocery in town. Before the big box stores moved in, Fred's had serviced most of the town. Bryony remembered walking the aisles as a child, holding her mother's hand. Now, though without a hand to guide her, her feet still knew where to go. The smoldering wreckage of her confidence followed.

Why did Cal Forster's attention intimidate her so thoroughly?

Into the blue plastic basket on her arm she placed one pound of unsalted butter and one pound of flour. Fresh ingredients were vital. In the produce section she selected a dozen Jonathan apples and one lemon and headed for the spice aisle. Her cinnamon hadn't been replaced in years. When she had everything she needed to restore balance to her life, she headed for the checkout lane.

Regarding Cal, she was sure she was making something out of nothing. He'd run into her by happenstance that day he was walking his dog, not by design.

And what appeared to be interest in her was merely a reflection of how he treated everybody. He was just one of those people who appeared to like everybody, like that man on the beach in Florida. *He never met a stranger.* Her mother would have said Cal had the "gift of gab," something that did not come naturally to Bryony, and something she did not aspire to. She was happy to be learning how to enjoy her time behind the service counter, how to relax as she interacted with lines of customers and maintain a low-key, pleasant approach to meeting their needs. She had no illusion that someday she would be the life of the party.

At home, she unloaded the groceries from her canvas bag, washed her hands, collected the needed bowls, utensils, and measuring cups, and set to work. Cutting the flour and salt with butter and water, she mixed them until she could shape the dough and place it in the refrigerator to chill.

Chuck Henderson's sub began to fade into the background.

Thirty minutes later, comfy in worn jeans and a faded green T-shirt, Bryony sat at the table and began to peel apples. Some bakers recommend using a vegetable peeler, but Bryony enjoyed the challenge of inserting a razor-sharp paring knife just under the skin. Thin ribbons, red and smooth on one side, pale yellow and juicy on the other, curled around her wrist, leaving the apples naked, vulnerable, innocent.

She peeled them all, knowing all would not fit in the crust, but anticipating small, fresh, unbaked nibbles for the next few days, a tart wake-up in the morning, a sweet finish to a protein-laden lunch.

After filling a bowl with cored and quartered slices, she mixed in lemon juice and flour and set the bowl aside. Next, she cut butter into flour mixed with sugar and cinnamon. Dutch apple pie with a crunchy covering of sugary spiciness reigned supreme as the bridge between emotional discomfort and satisfaction with the day at hand, between hopelessness and knowing she could make good things happen in the world.

Bryony stepped to the refrigerator, pulled out the chilled dough, placed it on her lightly floured giant wooden cutting board, and rolled it with clean, deft strokes. Next, she folded the dough into quarters, picked it up like a newborn infant, placed it in the pie pan, and unfolded it to shape, prick, and flute until the dough rose to an even crest around the rim,

After pre-baking the crust, Bryony stood back to take a breath. This moment was her favorite, when the fruit, or minced meat, or custard filling, stood ready to meet the embrace of that which would hold it together for its short, thrilling life. The crust appeared to be perfect, the fruit healthy and firm, the topping a dull version of what it would become, a crispy sweet crunch crowning a baked wonder.

The moment passed. Bryony poured, topped, and popped the pie into the oven.

She was in the middle of mopping the table with a damp rag when her cell phone rang. She picked it up with her cleanest fingertips, noted the unfamiliar number, and answered the call with an inquiring, "Hello?"

"Hello, Bryony? This is Cal."

Bryony dropped the dough-splattered rag and watched it hit the toe of her shoe. "How did you get my number?"

"I'm sorry if I'm interrupting. Lillian gave your number to me and suggested I call. She's willing to think about having one of my students work in the coffee shop, but she wanted me to run the particulars by you, tonight if possible"—he took an audible breath—"because she said you would be the main trainer and supervisor. I thought she should talk to you first, but she insisted I call, said something about having to host a birthday party for her grandson tonight and wanting to move forward with my student as rapidly as possible. Am I calling at a bad time?"

He was a runaway train, but somehow Bryony kept up, excited and not scared, which terrified her. "Well, it's not a great time. I'm baking a pie, but—"

"Pie?" he interrupted. "Oh, I love pie. I hope it's apple because I'll eat any kind of pie, but apple is my favorite. You are going to offer me a piece? I can drop by any time, or we could meet somewhere. On second thought, if I'm being too forward, you don't have to give me any pie, especially if you've made it for someone else, but I'm trying to be polite here because I could really use a slice of homemade pie tonight."

She tried, but Bryony found herself unable to refuse. She found Cal attractive, charming, and a tad pathetic, which only made him more interesting, even if he did wholly intimidate her. "I suppose we could meet tonight—"

"How about now?" he interrupted again. "I'll bring over dinner, and we can have pie for dessert, if you're willing to share. Or you're welcome to come to my house. Or we could go neutral, meet at the library, a restaurant, a bar, but only a nice bar where you'd take a family because I'm not a fan of being in the vicinity of inebriated people who might pick a fight and force you to defend my honor."

Bryony laughed in spite of herself. "Give me an hour. The library sounds fine."

Sixty minutes later, Bryony entered the library and spotted Cal waiting in a corner in one of two low, cushioned chairs. He smiled and waved, his faded jeans and blue tucked-in T-shirt revealing a fit, toned physique. She didn't like how her own body responded to the sight of him sitting there, his expression welcoming her.

"I think this area is designed for children," she said when she was within whispering distance.

"I'm a kid at heart," Cal said, beaming up at her.

She sank into the seat beside him, her knees peaking parallel to her naval. "Really glad I wore jeans."

"This okay with you?" Cal sat lower than her, his knees up to the bottom of his rib cage.

"Is it for you?" she asked.

"I'm used to the children's section. Lots of time with nieces, and then their little ones."

So, he was close to his extended family. Bryony pushed past the thought. His personal life was no business of hers. "What do we need to talk about?" She'd tried to reach Lillian several times, but all of her calls went to voicemail. Maybe Lillian was too busy with a birthday party, but not likely. She had probably turned off her phone in anticipation of Bryony's protest about meeting with the man now sitting next to her.

She caught his fresh-from-a-shower scent and focused on his worn leather loafers as he explained about arranging for one of his students to work in the coffee shop. He laid out the details, the advantages to Lillian, the benefit to the students, the reduction in wage costs due to a funding grant, the hours the student could work, and the expectations placed on the supervisor.

Bryony's thoughts settled down as she listened to him, visualized his ideas, and—eventually letting her eyes drift upward—clarified her role in the overall plan.

"Essentially, according to Lillian, you'd be his teacher and supervisor," Cal said. "You would train him, analyze his strengths, his challenges, update me on needs so little problems don't grow into big problems, and write a brief report at the end of each semester. Nothing major, a paragraph or two. Hopefully, you'll keep him on after he graduates, provided you're both happy with the situation."

"I'll do it," Bryony said.

"Lillian thought you would," Cal said, and now Bryony felt embarrassed, on display and small, a pawn for Lillian's matchmaking strategy, but he didn't skip a beat. "Can I send him over Friday morning?"

"How about seven a.m.?" She picked up her purse, ready to cut and run.

"He said he's an early riser." Cal pushed himself out of the chair and stood.

Bryony rocked forward once and failed to escape the squishy clutch of the foam. "These were not designed for looking cool." Also, not designed for a quick getaway.

"Kids don't care about cool until they're too cool to sit in this area." He braced himself and stretched his hands toward her. "I'll help."

She tried again on her own and, failing, reached up. His palms were warm, soft, and his fingers gripped with assurance. As soon as she steadied herself on her feet, she withdrew her hands. He shoved his into his pockets.

They stood in awkward silence for a few moments, until Cal, with a mischievous glint in his eye, asked, "Where's my pie?"

The mention of pie caused a discernible shift in Bryony's sense of whether, or where, she belonged in the world. She had just spent a delicious evening reliving the sensation of how baking empowered her.

"In the car," she answered.

"What?" He pulled his right hand out of his pocket and gave a manual stop sign. "I was kidding. You don't have to give me a piece of pie."

"Couldn't bring it in the library." She strode toward the front door. "No food allowed."

"You don't need to do this." Cal's voice trailed behind. "I was joking."

"Mitch always says I can't take a joke. You said you wanted pie. I brought pie."

Cal followed on her heel as she led the way to her car. The evening air cooled her exposed skin. Autumn approached. She liked calling his bluff.

The remote chirped, and she opened the back door. A small plain brown box sat on the backseat. She picked it up and turned around to offer it to Cal. "I cut a large slice. Let me know what you think."

Lifting the lid, Cal brought the open carton to his nose and inhaled. "Oh, my."

He still stood in the parking lot, holding the pie, when she pulled out and drove toward her house.

Next time, she *would* make bumbleberry. A block from

home, Bryony opened her cell phone and hit the top number in "recent calls," knowing Lillian would answer this time.

"How did it go?" Lillian asked.

"You are not my matchmaker, Lil," Bryony said.

"Tell me what happened."

"I said yes."

"Yes to the student, or yes to Cal?" Lillian asked.

"I think it's a package deal," Bryony said.

Lillian squealed. "He's perfect for you!"

"He's a mess." Bryony turned into her driveway and hit the garage door remote.

"You need a mess in your life, Bry. You need a little wild to liven up the manicured life you've managed to put together for yourself, by yourself."

Bryony turned off the car. "What if he turns out to be more like an invasive weed?"

"He's a sweetie," Lillian cooed. "I can tell. Ask Mitch if Cal has a girlfriend."

"Mitch won't know." Bryony's brother could win at bar trivia, but he couldn't remember his own wife's birth date. "When did you know Rick was the one for you?" she asked as she unlocked the back door and walked into her kitchen.

"The first time I saw him," Lillian said.

Bryony sighed. She had skipped supper but experienced no hunger, a classic symptom. "See you in the morning, Lil." She walked to the hall and dropped her purse on the side table.

"You okay?" Lillian asked. "I was trying to be helpful. Did I overstep?"

"No, I'm just tired. I'll see you in the morning."

"Are you sure? Now I feel bad."

"Go be with Rick." Bryony forced lightness into her voice. "I'm fine."

Bryony ended the call. The bravado of forcing a piece of pie onto Cal Forster dissipated into exhaustion. She did like him.

And she did want to know if he liked her pie, if he liked her. She walked into her living room and fell back onto the couch.

Men were like pie—delicious, habit forming, and in the end, the reason a woman had to work hard to get herself back in shape.

Pulling the plush throw from the back of the couch, Bryony covered herself from chin to toe. The morning paper lay on the coffee table, still open to the horoscope she had read earlier. She extricated her arm, picked up the paper, and read again.

*Now is not the time to open yourself to possibilities from the outside. As the timeline of your life on Earth grows shorter, survival requires conservation of energy.*

Bryony needed to focus on what she herself could generate. The urge to root herself in a project pulsated, pulled her closer to the Earth, and promised to ground her in knowing her growing season had not come to an end.

She dropped the paper and pulled the afghan over her head while thinking of something she had learned in botany and never forgotten.

Some flowers, like tulips and poppies, demonstrate nyctinasty. They close up at night to preserve their strength.

Bryony snuggled deeper into the couch, surrendering to her own nyctinastic tendencies, peace pulsating down her neck, spreading across her shoulders and down her arms. In the garden of her soul, she remembered she was already planted. She knew how and where to find what she needed to grow. And she did not need Cal Forster, or any other man, to shine his light on her.

# CAL CONFIDES IN BRY

*T*he school day had ended. Cal sat with his feet crossed and propped on his desk, arms behind his head, his hands cradling his neck. "I think you'll like this setting."

Todd sat in a chair beside the desk, hunched over his books, his tennis shoes poised on their toes. He seemed like a good kid, but unsure of himself. Cal chalked it up to the dyslexia. When they met on the first day of school, Todd had said his elementary school teachers didn't recognize the problem for years. The kids had teased him, and his dad "blew up" when he learned his son couldn't read in third grade.

"Do I have to wear a uniform?" Todd asked.

"It's not a uniform kind of place. I'm sure a nice pair of jeans and a clean shirt with no rips or stains will pass." Cal pointed the pen in his hand at Todd. "Remember what we talked about in class? No T-shirts with slogans. No matter how much you think it's a neutral statement, inevitably someone will find it offensive."

Todd looked up. "That's the day I learned the word 'benign.'" He was a good looking kid, which would be obvious if he cut the hair hanging in his face. "I remember you said, 'No such thing as a benign T-shirt slogan.'"

Cal brought his arms forward and dropped his feet to the floor. "I'll bet most of the kids in the room had no idea what I meant. You were the only one who asked. Thanks for that."

"I like it when you use big words with us," Todd said.

Cal shook his head. Benign was not a *big* word in his estimation. Maybe he should have taught Kindergarten, instilled a love for an expansive vocabulary in those absorbent five-year-old brains. He closed his black planning book. "Be there at seven a.m. on Friday. Don't be late, and do not embarrass yourself or me. Neither would reflect well on your grade."

"It's pass, fail," Todd said. "You already told us if we, 'show up when scheduled, don't get fired, and don't end up being taken to jail for something illegal on the job,' we pass."

"You do listen well." Cal smiled. "Anything else on your mind before we blow this popsicle stand?"

"There is something I wanted to talk to you about." Todd lowered his eyes to the floor, then looked up. "If I tell you something, can you keep it a secret?"

"Does this secret include you planning to hurt someone else, or someone else hurting you or another person?" Some problems were best handled by the school counselor. Cal would listen long enough to steer the boy in the right direction.

"No, no." Todd shook his head violently back and forth. "Nothing like that."

"And is keeping this secret hurting you?" Cal asked.

"Yes, I think it is hurting me," Todd said.

"Then fire away."

"Funny choice of words," Todd whispered.

"What's the problem?" Cal put his hands back behind his head again. Sometimes students opened up when he looked less urgent, almost unconcerned.

"It's kind of complicated," Todd mumbled. "But I want you to know, just so I know I'm not hiding anything."

Cal nodded. "Go on."

"When I was ten, my older brother worked in a restaurant. He knew where they kept the cash, and he broke in one night to steal it. While he was there, he decided to treat himself to a burger, started a fire, and ended up confessing the whole thing to the nine-one-one operator." Todd raised his eyes with a look of expectation.

"Why are you telling me this?" Cal asked. Was the kid worried he'd repeat his brother's mistake?

Todd sighed. "Well, that's not the whole story. A firefighter fell through the roof and died. His kids were my age. My brother's in prison for a long time, and I"—Todd stood and paced to the window—"announced at the age of eleven, that I wanted to be a firefighter when I grew up. So, that's what my father expects now. Whenever people ask me what I want to do when I graduate, my father says, 'He's going to be a firefighter.'"

"And do you still want to be a firefighter?" Cal asked.

"No!" Todd answered. "Not at all. The coffee shop sounds great for now. I just don't know how I'm going to tell my father about the firefighter thing, and I'm worried he'll think that working in a coffee shop is about the least manly thing I can do."

Cal lowered his feet to the floor and put his fingertips on the edge of his desk. "Stand firm in the path of your own choosing. Don't try to atone for your brother's missteps. The truth is, you can't."

"What about my Dad?" Todd asked. "He got super depressed when James went to prison. He lost his job. We moved here to live with my grandparents for a while. When I started talking about being a firefighter, things got a little better."

"So, your father pinned his need for redemption on you? I think you'd do well to talk to the school counselor, but whatever you do, remember you're a good guy, whether or not your father feels disappointed."

Todd swallowed audibly and sat down again. "Thanks, Mister Forster."

"No worries, Todd. Any time." Cal picked up his planning book and put it in his briefcase. The boy's face said he wasn't done, so Cal settled back in his chair. "Got something else on your mind?"

"Yeah," Todd said. "There's this kid at school, Justin Hicks. The other day when I walked by him and his friends, I heard him say something about me being gay. I acted like I didn't hear, but I'm a little worried. Honestly, I'm terrified of those guys. I don't know what they'd do if they ever caught me alone somewhere."

Prissy Bangor's little brother came to mind. "Have you reported this to the principal?" Cal asked.

"Mister Green won't do anything," Todd said, then mumbled, "I think he's just like them."

"Do you mind if I have a chat with Mister Green?" Cal asked.

"I guess that would be okay," Todd said. "But leave me out of it."

"No worries," Cal said. "Justin is probably doing something similar, or worse, to others."

After meeting with Todd, Cal rushed home to take Bailey for a short walk. There were times when his job tugged at thoughts and feelings about his own life. In Cleveland, he always had someone to talk to when he needed to think out loud. When his relationship with Leslie ended, he still had Heidi, his father, Rudy, other old friends, a handful of trusted colleagues.

The Hendersons were his one connection in Fieldstone, and Cal did not want to bother them, though he perceived that, in addition to Chuck, Charity might be someone with whom he could eventually connect, trust. She'd called to check in with him several times since his move, offering whatever assistance she could provide, giving him tips about the town, other nearby locales, and regional sites. Someday he would reach out to either or both of the Hendersons, but not yet. He knew they were still deep in cardiac rehab with a side of professional health coaching, working as a team to bring Chuck back to full capacity.

He could, Cal supposed, videoconference with someone, but he preferred face-to-face contact, a 3D live experience a much better alternative to a cold, hard screen.

Only one person came to mind.

Assured his canine companion could stand another few hours of being home alone, he changed his shirt and headed back out.

There were three spots open in front of BeanHereNow. Cal chose the middle one.

Inside the coffee shop, he walked toward the sign reading "Order Here." Bryony took her position to wait on him when he was two steps away from the counter.

"Hi, Cal," she said. "What would you like?" Her expression seemed veiled, a bit shadowy.

"I'll have a burger with fries, and a Coke," he said, trying to break the ice, initiate a friendly conversation.

"And I've never heard that one before." Her smile looked impersonal.

"Rough day?" he asked.

"Ready for it to be over," she said.

"How about a cup of tea to go?" he asked. Maybe now wasn't a good time for her to listen, but here he was, his conversation with Todd still brewing, and a slew of thoughts and feelings rising to the surface, ready to bubble over.

"Coming right up." Bryony turned to reach for a paper cup

and lid. She filled the cup with steaming water from a red spigot on the side of a tall cylindrical silver pot.

"Todd's excited about working here," he said.

"We're excited about having him." Bryony set the water on the counter and put a basket of tea beside it.

"He's a good kid," Cal said.

Bryony nodded.

"Sometimes I'm happy I never had kids," Cal said, the pressure behind the dam of social propriety building. "Because I probably would have screwed them up. It's hard enough to be a good son."

This time Bryony's smile reflected understanding, which was all the encouragement he needed.

"Before I decided to come here," Cal said. "I was going to travel around the world, partly to get over a failed relationship, but mainly to be able to send back pictures and stories to my father because he was never able to travel. He never had a chance to do that because he had to take care of me and my sister. Dad didn't bat an eye when I told him I'd decided to put off the trip for a year, but he's ninety-six, Bryony."

She made eye contact with a hint of kindness, but no more encouragement.

He let go anyway, the words gushing, roiling at times, ending with, "The thing is, I love teaching. I might want to teach beyond this year, but if I don't travel soon, it might be too late. Dad was okay with the delay, but you can't imagine the time and energy we put into thinking about where I would go. He learned how to Zoom on the computer so we could see each other while I was on the road. I don't want to disappoint him, you know?"

"I need to wait on the customer behind you," Bryony said.

Cal whipped around and said, "Sorry," to the woman behind him.

The woman winked at him.

He turned back to Bryony, said, "Okay, well, thanks for listening. See you later," and walked toward the door.

Back in his car, Cal started to fasten the seatbelt when he remembered the tea. Still sitting on the counter, he had not paid for it.

He thought about going back in, but a quote, printed in large bold letters and taped to his dashboard, stopped him.

*Often when you think you're at the end of something, you're at the beginning of something else. —Fred Rogers*

Heidi had taped it there before Cal left for Fieldstone.

What if his new beginning was not a big adventure? What if he never stopped teaching?

He loved being an educator. He never wanted to retire. He only retired for his father. Cal disappointed himself to save his father from disappointment. That was the opposite of what he told Todd to do.

If kids like Todd were to walk through life without fear of disappointing others, they would need adults who were not afraid to face their own fears. The effective way to conquer fear was head on. Holding the steering wheel firmly with both hands, Cal felt sure of himself, in control of his future.

Before starting the car, he looked through the storefront window of BeanHereNow. Bryony wiped off a table, straightened chairs, and carried plates and cups toward the service counter.

"She must think I'm a total nutcase," he said under his breath.

§

BEFORE GOING TO bed he called his father.

"Hey, Pops, I've been thinking. I might want to come home when I'm done here and get another teaching job."

"Whatever makes you happy, son."

They moved on to other topics, Cal's announcement seeming to carry no more weight than his father's concern about the sanitary worker forgetting to push the empty waste can back up the driveway.

Cal ended the call with, "Thanks, Dad. Thanks for everything."

He slept better that night than in months.

# BRY'S FATHER TAKES A HIT

*E*ncounters with Cal ceased to be a mini crisis for Bryony. For the past three weeks, he had shown up at the coffee shop during the morning rush. Bryony refrained from asking about his strange behavior the day after Lillian manipulated her into meeting him at the library. There were no more occurrences related to ordered and forgotten drinks or staring at the door of the shop from the driver's seat of his car. People usually behaved strangely when they were having trouble, and she didn't know Cal well enough to ask.

Todd caught on fast. Training him had been a breeze, and his presence eased the workload to the point where Bryony felt less drained when her shift ended. She hadn't seen her father in days. Tonight she had stored up enough positive perspective to risk another visit.

As had become routine, Bryony found her father sitting with Alma in the hallway's little alcove. Today Alma wore red polyester pants and a white cotton shirt with red, white, and blue horizontal stripes accentuating the roundness of her belly. Bryony's father wore a new shirt, plaid with turquoise and pink.

"My granddaughter tells me she knows you," Alma said.

"Abby says she sees you every day at the coffee shop you work in."

"Making food for complete strangers and cleaning up after them," Bryony's father said.

Bryony turned away from his bitter tone and smiled at Alma. "Abby's your granddaughter? She comes in every day. Her crochet work is beautiful."

"I taught her how to crochet when she was eight. Can't do it myself anymore. Darned arthritis!" Alma held up both hands, each with a set of fingers sporting enlarged joints and twisted shapes.

"Everybody has something to complain about," Bryony's father said. "Bryony complains I favored Mitch. Mitch complains he feels responsible for Bryony. They don't seem to notice I'm stuck in here with a bunch of old people who do nothing but eat and watch TV all day."

"You're certainly in a gnarly mood today, Mister Green." Alma smiled at Bryony. "We both know he merely pretends to be an old grouch, don't we dear?"

"Why does Mitch feel responsible for me?" Bryony asked.

"Because he's your brother," her father growled. "Why wouldn't he? You're not married, you live alone, and you don't have any kids. Whatever you get when I die won't be enough to live on for the rest of your life. Mitch has a right to be concerned."

Bryony's father crossed his arms and hunkered into the couch, his eyes on the television.

"Don't mind him, dear." Alma put her hand on Bryony's arm. "He lost the Bingo coverall this afternoon to Charles."

Bryony patted Alma's hand before moving to a chair beside her father. She hadn't seen him in such a foul mood for quite a few weeks. The administrator had a favorite line she often repeated when Bryony had gone to her with concerns. *Play to his strengths, Bryony.*

Settling into the cushion, she reached out and put her hand on his arm. "Daddy, I have a new role at the coffee shop. I oversee a high school student in a work study program. Any advice for managing people?" Her father had supervised people before he retired.

Her father answered, his voice dripping with sick-sweet sarcasm. "I have a new job, too. I'm being an old guy in a home for the lost and forgotten. Do you have any advice for how I can live the rest of my boring, miserable life?"

Bryony removed her hand and backed up a hair. That had not gone well. What next? She didn't have to deliberate for long because suddenly Alma whomped his arm.

"Albert Green," Abby Dunaway's grandmother said. "You are being an old grump. Now look at your daughter. If you don't have anything constructive to offer, smile and say, 'Good luck, honey. I'm sure you'll do fine.' You don't have to be so mean, especially to your kids."

Bryony froze. She had never heard anyone verbally rebuke her father, let alone hit him. She watched as he turned to Alma, menacing her with a cold hard stare. Alma didn't flinch. She kept her hand on his thigh and glared back. When Alma didn't back down, he turned to Bryony, the hostility draining away, replaced with what looked like amusement.

"Bryony, dear," he said, honey dripping from his words. "Good luck." He turned back to Alma. "Was that okay with you?"

Alma giggled as she swatted Bryony's father on his belly. He chuckled and hugged her.

The rest of their visit was strained for Bryony. Alma did most of the talking, while Bryony's father sat and listened, or looked out the window. He seemed relaxed, a subdued large game animal. Unsure when he would pounce again, Bryony guarded her words, but the attack never came. After an exhausting twenty minutes of anticipation, Bryony stood and announced her departure. Alma thanked her for visiting.

Bryony's father said, "Bye."

She walked away in wonder. Her mother had never talked back to her father. She trained Bryony to keep peace, to overlook taunts and teases. Hard to imagine anyone could tame her father's wicked understanding of how to treat a woman, especially someone like Alma. On the surface she seemed bubbly and warm, but Bryony had witnessed a bit of molten rock boiling below. Alma might be the volcano that would forever change the terrain of Bryony's father's behavior.

After pulling out of her parking spot, and before making it out of the parking lot, her cell rang. She pulled to the side of the driveway to answer.

"Did you remember to order extra bagels for the band boosters?" Lillian asked.

"Yes," Bryony answered. "Lil, you're never going to believe what happened just now."

"What?" Lillian asked.

"Dad started in on me, and you know what Alma did?" Bryony savored the telling of what she witnessed.

"She dumped him!" Lillian said.

"She hit him, Lil! Not hard, but hard enough to get his attention. And you know what he did?"

"He hit her back!" Lillian said.

"No," Bryony said. "He didn't hit her. He backed down."

"He did what?" Lillian asked.

"The thing is," Bryony said. "That's the first time I ever noticed how scared I am of strong men."

"Not all strong men should be feared," Lil lectured.

"I know." Bryony was quick to respond. "But I realized I always pick uninteresting men because they don't scare me. In response to them, I become uninteresting, and they dump me."

"You're catching on to what I've been trying to tell you," Lillian said.

Bryony rolled her eyes. "See you in the morning, Lil."

"Goodnight, Babe."

Everything looked different on the drive home. The steel gray sky excited Bryony. The red and orange leaves were not merely waving in the wind—they were dancing. And when she pulled into her driveway, her house was not merely a place where she could store her belongings and sleep well at night—it was fertile land, a launching pad, a point of embarkment, which might take her to adventures she hadn't even dared to dream.

And then there was Cal.

# CLEVELAND CALLS

*R*ight before his cell phone rang, Cal had settled into his favorite kitchen chair to enjoy a few bites of dessert. He pulled the phone out of his pocked to answer the call.

"Cal?" His sister's voice started low and swooped high, ending in a strong melodic question mark. She sang the same tune when she asked, "Is that you?"

"No." Cal made his voice low, gruff. "This is Bailey. Cal broke the rules and taught me how to talk." He closed the lid on the half-eaten pint of ice cream and stowed it in the freezer. Thank heavens for Ben & Jerry!

Heidi sighed. "Cal, when are you coming home? The grandkids miss you."

"Ahh," Cal said. "How are my seven little munchkins?" He rattled off their nicknames.

"Their parents hate those names."

"But the names are apt, and the kids love them." He settled back into the chair.

"The kids love you," Heidi said." Come home this weekend. You promised to visit at least twice a month."

Cal ran his hand through his hair. "I'm sorry. This weekend is homecoming, and I've been asked to chaperone the dance. I meant to make it home over Labor Day, but I needed the weekend to get to know the town a little."

"You haven't met anyone special have you?" Heidi's voice forewarned disapproval.

Bryony came to mind, but he answered, "None of my students seem interested in a guy who's less than a decade away from Medicare."

"Not funny, Cal. I'm serious. You cannot fall in love with someone who doesn't live in Cleveland. Got it?"

Cal rubbed his forehead. His sister hadn't wanted him to travel any distance, yet still complained when he decided to stay in Ohio and teach for another year. Nothing would suit her but him being close by, permanently, or at least until their father was gone. Cal understood. However, he couldn't be in two places at one time, and he was committed for the year.

"Cal?" Heidi said. "Are you still there?"

"Still here and promising to visit asap. I know I'll be there for Thanksgiving."

"Thanksgiving!" Heidi said. "You have to at least be here for Halloween! You've never missed a party."

"I'll be there," he said.

"Promise?" Heidi asked, the tone of her question promising hell-to-pay if he failed to follow through.

"I promise." They ended the call after Heidi extracted three more cross-my-heart-and-hope-to-die promises to make it home no later than Halloween, sooner if possible.

As Cal cleaned up his dinner dishes, memories of Leslie bubbled up. She had not been the love of his life. He knew that from the beginning. But the truth was, he missed her. During their time together, she had become part of his routine, in spite of the ways she did not fit for him. They had enjoyed daily contact. She had been his sounding board, his buddy, his confidante. More than missing her, he realized, he missed that. He missed having someone who had his back.

He needed to stop missing what he had with Leslie because she had never been what he wanted. He wanted more than a companion. He wanted someone like... why did the principal's sister keep popping into his mind? Granted, Bryony Green could make a mean apple pie, but if he dated anyone, they should be firmly established in the place to which he would return next June. And clearly, her brother was not in favor. Mitch Green's message had been straightforward. *Stay away.*

Checking his contact list, Cal was pleased to see he had saved Susie's number after she called the last time. He wondered if she was still in Fieldstone. And if so, would she be returning to Cleveland when she left? He'd give her a call sometime soon. But not tonight. Tonight he would clean out the dog's bowls, maybe clean the bathrooms, or find something to glaze over in front of the television.

# BRYONY FALLS

From the parking lot, Bryony saw a multitude of people milling around a mountain of combustible material. Tradition designated the last Thursday in September as kick-off day for Homecoming. Activities to reunite Fieldstone High alumni with each other and to connect them to current students commenced with a bonfire. The evening event had grown over the years, and now included a food truck rally, vendor booths, and three hours of stage performances by local entertainers. Bryony joined the throng slogging through wet grass from an earlier downpour and heading toward the conical pile awaiting a lit match.

Halfway there, she found herself side-by-side with Charity Henderson. Per usual, Charity looked like a million bucks, which was probably only half the estate value she had inherited from her parents.

"Hello, Bryony," Charity said. "I heard you're working with Lillian now."

Was she goading her? Bryony chose to not take the bait. "I heard about Chuck's heart issues. How's he doing?" she asked, the hairs on her neck raised, her jaw clenching.

"Better!" Charity answered. "Thanks for asking."

Nearing an appropriate place to veer right, Bryony started to say farewell when Charity spoke again.

"You're missed at Metcalf, you know. If you ever want to come back, there's a place for you there." As a teenager, Charity Beaman had possessed the enviable ability to appear completely sincere while rocking an inner sneer. Apparently, time had not diminished that capacity.

"Thanks, I'm happy where I am." As Bryony moved away, she called back, "Say hello to Chuck," and then turned her attention forward, trying to let all that had passed stay in the past, where it belonged.

Lillian, Rick, and their brood greeted Bryony with a swarm of hugs. As usual, the sons soon left to join old friends for a game of touch football, while the in-law daughters dispersed together. Grandma and Grandpa would watch the grandkids.

"Rick, will you take the kids over for candy apples?" Lillian asked. "Bryony and I want to wander around and say hello to folks."

This, too, followed their established tradition, but Rick never complained. He kissed his wife on the cheek and instructed his six grandchildren to pair up and hold hands before steering them away. "Meet up at the lighting of the fire?" he called over his shoulder.

"We'll be there!" Lillian answered.

He moved on, clearly in charge of his half dozen with humor and smiles.

"You're lucky," Bryony said. "Rick is an angel."

"Don't let him fool you," Lillian said. "He's a man. And because he's a man, he often requires the same kind of effort required of children and grandchildren—basic training in courtesy, hygiene, and safety."

"But he's a good one." Bryony watched as Rick stood in line at the candy apple stand, his arms reaching out to gather his progeny and protect them. "You know how lucky you are, right?"

"I do." Lillian gazed after her husband. "He's my rock." She turned back to Bryony and asked, "Where should we go first?"

"Vendor booths," Bryony answered. "Maybe next year we offer coffee and bagels?"

"You think you'll still be with me next year?" Lillian linked her arm with Bryony's and led the way. "I hope so, but only if that's good for you."

"You're always good for me," Bryony said. She didn't bother telling Lillian about the brief encounter with Charity. Lillian had never quite understood.

Bryony and Lillian met in seventh grade, their friendship emerging when paired for a party-making project in Home Economics. From that moment on, they had been the best of friends, in spite of their inherent differences—Bryony being the quiet, shy one, and Lillian being the life of the party—and in complete agreement about all things, with the exception of their opinions on the popular girls.

Bryony could never quite convince Lillian of the damage done by Charity, Susie, and their little squad of backbiters. Lillian seemed impervious to the impact of their antics. In this area of life only, Bryony had suffered alone, but in all other ways, the two had been each other's champions.

Now they stood together, forty-two years later, in front of a booth selling brownies and cookies.

"Remember those little pies we made for our Home Ec project?" Lillian asked.

"Of course I do." Bryony had stayed up all night modifying the recipe until the tarts were as close to perfection as possible.

"What would it take to start making those for the coffee shop?"

"Me, cloned," Bryony said.

Lillian laughed. "I could use a few more of you in my life."

They sauntered together, stopping to chat with old friends and new customers, when someone tapped Bryony's shoulder.

Cal Forster stood beside them, a worn purple leash drooping between him and his big, curly haired dog. "What an event, huh? I had no idea. This must be bigger than the Fourth of July!"

"Don't bet on it," Lillian said. "You haven't seen our Fourth of July."

A small show of fireworks exploded in Bryony's brain. She leaned down to ruffle the fur around the dog's head, to tamp down unbidden, unexpected excitement.

As Lillian and Cal exchanged small talk, the intensity of their interaction crescendoed. Lillian's voice gained volume. Cal's perpetual patter ramped up to full speed, witty remarks inserted with strategy and skill. Lillian's laughter peaked three or four times. Bryony looked down at Bailey. He cocked his head at her, as if to say, *I'm not sure what that's about either.*

She leaned over and patted his head again. The dog's hypnotic response to her touch indicated she didn't have to be entertaining or interesting to make a strong, healthy connection with another living being. She wished people were as easy.

"You are a treasure, Cal," Lillian said. "My husband will love you."

"Hopefully not more than he loves you," Cal said.

Lillian chortled again and turned to Bryony. "Do you mind if I take off for a bit? I need to catch up with Rick and the kids."

Disoriented for a second, Bryony wondered if Lillian remembered it had been her idea for Bryony to attend every year. She started to protest, but Lillian was already moving away. This was a first. In the past, Lillian had always insisted they stay together for the entire night, citing it as one of the "signature events" of their friendship, like a commemorative holiday or a wedding anniversary.

Added to the surprise of Lillian's turnabout, Bryony now faced Cal's unbridled energy without a buffer. She stood alone, exposed to his attention, no counter between them, nothing in common but his student, and she could think of nothing new to say about Todd.

Silent, Cal clutched his dog's leash. What was he waiting for? Usually he could say more in five minutes than she could respond to in a week.

Rainbow fabric wound around Bailey's neck. "He's festive," Bryony said. Talking about his dog seemed like a safe subject.

"We're both allies." Cal smiled.

She squatted to greet the dog and rub his ears a third time. "Nice seeing you again, Bailey."

"You two are old friends, having met downtown when you thought I might be stalking you." Cal stood at attention, a wry smile on his face.

Bryony stood. "I never said I thought you were stalking me."

"Oh, that must have been the other woman I met the first day of school who undoubtedly thought I walked by her workplace the next evening to meet her again."

Cal grinned, and Bryony felt confused. Was he now confessing he had intended to run into her that night?

"Fancy a walk about the to-do?" The gleam in his eyes was youthful, not lethal.

The nervous knot in her stomach eased. Her shoulders dropped. She hadn't noticed they were tense. "Lead the way," she said. Not much could happen in the midst of hundreds of other people.

When he came into the coffee shop each morning, Cal talked to Todd, or Lillian, or anybody else who crossed his path. He shared funny little stories or turned a moment into a reason to laugh. Here and now, he appeared less urgent, and she appreciated his calmer tone, but her insides still threatened to turn into a jumble.

They sauntered past the performance stage.

"Todd is working out great," Bryony said. "He comes in every day now, and I started training him on the computerized receipt system and cash drawer."

She realized she already mentioned Todd's excellent performance to Cal earlier in the day and started to apologize for repeating herself, but Cal interrupted. "He seems happy to be there."

They walked toward the vendors' booths, words tumbling out of Bryony's mouth because silence seemed awkward. "He told me about his dyslexia, but it doesn't seem to interfere with any of his job duties at this point."

"I have great faith in the young man," Cal said.

"Do you monitor all of your students as much?" Bryony asked.

"Let's not talk shop," Cal said.

Now what? She would have to endure walking beside him, conversation not an option to mitigate the impact of his presence on her because she couldn't think of anything other than Todd to talk about. *Please, God*, she prayed. *Do not let me do or say anything half as crazy as what I am feeling.* So thrown off course, confused.

They were headed straight for the fifteen foot pile that would be ignited at sundown.

"How much wood do you suppose they've managed to collect in that pile of brush, logs, pallets, and other dunnage?" Cal asked. "That is one impressive pyre."

"What's dunnage?" The question slipped out before she could check herself to hide her ignorance.

Cal answered in a relaxed, even tone. "Dunnage refers to all the different kinds of packing materials used to secure loads for shipping."

Rather than leave her with a sense of insecurity about not knowing, his simple answer seemed to settle her emotions. Her body again started to relax. "How do you know that?" She had observed twice his having to explain the meaning of his words to others in order for them to see the humor in his jokes. Cal seemed to be full of obscure bits of information and knowledge.

"Crossword puzzles? Novels? Dictionary addiction? I don't know."

"Sometimes I'm not quite sure what you're talking about." Like earlier, when he made the joke about stalking her.

Cal laughed. "Story of my life." They walked in silence a few more steps, then he stopped and looked at her. "Would you like to take a spin around the block, escape this madness and have a friendly chat without interruptions?"

Every day, she had renewed her decision to not be pulled into her attraction to him. She had expected him to lose interest, but he didn't seem to be going away any time soon.

Was he seriously flirting, or flirting with being sincere? Maybe if she understood him better, she would be able to relax around him. Reluctant, but willing, Bryony said, "Okay. Let's take a walk."

"Really?" Cal asked. He seemed surprised and unsure of the idea now.

"You weren't serious?" Was this another bring-me-a-piece-of-pie moment? "Were you blowing smoke?"

"Yes!" he said as he fumbled with Bailey's leash. "Um, no! I mean, no, I wasn't blowing smoke, and yes, I was serious. Ab-absolutely. Let's go!"

He had stammered. She'd never heard him do that before, and suddenly he became far less intimidating, but—she reminded herself—she was not interested. Not interested as they walked toward the parking lot full of cars, trucks, and SUVs. Not interested as they approached the road, the resurfaced asphalt still black with bright paint lines.

Neither of them spoke until they reached the sidewalk. Bailey sniffed the grass in the tree lawn, and they fell into an easy pace.

"Tell me something I don't know about you," Cal said.

"You don't know anything about me." The smell of his aftershave and the way his arm brushed against hers elevated her interest. Her mind fought hard to not notice.

"I know you work in a coffee shop," Cal said. "And I know you quit a lucrative job, and I know your brother doesn't support your decisions, and I know you're an excellent teacher and mentor."

Bryony grew uncomfortable, warm. "Sounds like you only know the good stuff. Not a fair and accurate way to assess someone." She bit the inside of her lip. What was she saying? He was lovely to say such nice things about her.

"So, I'm asking," Cal said. "Tell me what I don't know. Who is the real Bryony Green?"

"Not fair," Bryony said. "You go first. Tell me something I don't know about you."

"I think you know a lot already," he said. "You know I teach, and I have a dog, and I'm new in town. I could tell you many superficial facts, but let's start with the deeper stuff. Agreed?"

"Okay." She had never met anyone like Cal before. She knew that already.

"I find it hard to forgive adults who hurt my students," he said, "and I become clumsy and awkward when I'm around attractive women."

Why, oh why, had she pulled her hair into a ponytail tonight? She looked down and let the few stray locks hide the flush heating her cheeks and burning through her last remaining bits of courage. "You like flirting with women." Was he looking at her? Did he see her discomfort?

"No!" he said. "I hate flirting. Is that what you think I've been doing? Oh, geez. Not how I want to be perceived at all."

His answer scared her. He wasn't flirting? What was he saying? Her thoughts tumbled forward, out of control. "What brought you to Fieldstone?" she asked, trying to steer the conversation back to a safer lane.

"I have an old friend who lives here," he said. "He asked me to...."

Car tires screeched in the road beside them, and a horn blasted. A streak of feline dashed from the road across the sidewalk. Bailey barked once and charged after the cat. In doing so, he pulled Cal into Bryony, which knocked her off her feet. She landed in a muddy area with Cal dragging across her legs until Bailey broke free and ran with all his might after the cat, toward the crowd, leash flying behind him.

"Are you hurt?" Cal asked, breathless. He struggled to stand up, muddy water dripping from his hands and arms.

"I think I'm fine," Bryony answered.

Cal's head jerked in the direction of Bailey's flight.

"Go," she said as she brought herself to a sitting position. "Go find Bailey. I'm fine."

"You're sure?" Cal asked, jogging backward toward his disappearing dog.

"I'm fine. Go."

Cal took off at a run while Bryony moved to her feet. Her right leg and the entire back end of her jeans were soaked. Mud covered her hands, and her wrist started to hurt. Maybe she had jammed it trying to break her fall, or maybe she fell on it.

Reaching up, she touched the muddy mess in her hair. She had left her purse in her car so she couldn't use her tiny mirror to survey the damage to her face. When Bailey took off, his leash had scraped across her nose and chin. Those areas would be explored later. She didn't want to touch any exposed skin because her hands were caked with dirt.

Face pointed downward, Bryony walked back to her car. She didn't want to alarm anyone who might see her. She was halfway home when Cal called.

"Where did you go?" he asked. "Are you okay?"

The concern in his voice tugged at her. "I'm fine," she said. "No worries. I'm going home to shower and call it a night."

"I'm so sorry." He sounded truly distressed.

"I'm fine."

"Are you sure you're okay?" he asked again.

"I am fine," Bryony answered, and to deflect his concern, asked, "Did you catch Bailey?"

"Bailey won the lip syncing competition when he stormed the stage during a painful rendition of Cindy Lauper's, 'Girls Just Want to Have Fun.' I caught up with him before your brother could sentence him to a lifetime of detention."

Bryony smiled. "He's okay?"

"Mitch reacts with strong emotion to surprises, not what one would expect from a high school principal. I think he'll be okay once he calms down. "

Bryony smiled again. "I meant Bailey. Is Bailey okay?"

"Oh! Bailey's fine, a true hero to all the kids who like to pretend homecoming is one big joke." Cal hesitated. "Are you sure you're okay?"

"For the last time, yes. I am okay."

"Good," Cal said. "That's good. I hope we can try again soon, to take a walk, I mean."

Bryony's heart blipped. Shortly before Bailey crashed their moment, Cal had said something about not flirting with her. Did he mean his intention was genuine?

"Sure," Bryony answered.

They said goodbye and ended the call, but her phone rang before she had time to put it on the seat beside her.

"Look," Cal said. "I forgot to tell you something. Bailey offered to pay for any clothing that was torn or otherwise ruined by his unbecoming behavior. He's really quite distraught and asked me to extend his most since apologies."

Bryony laughed. "Tell him I'm fine. Nothing was damaged."

"Well, thanks for walking with us, and I do hope we'll be able to try again some time," Cal said.

"We'll see," Bryony answered, smiling.

As soon as they ended the call, her cell rang again. Without looking at the caller ID, she answered with lighthearted indulgence. "I'm fine, Cal."

"Me, too," Mitch said. "But your friend, Mister Forster, made a fine mess of the festivities. I heard you were with him. What's going on, Bry?"

"Nothing," Bryony answered, her courage crashing. "His dog chased a cat. I fell in the mud. I came home." She parked in front of her garage and turned off the ignition.

"Are you dating him or something? He's not a good match for you. Cal's a go-getter. He likes action. Did you know he was voted Teacher of the Year twice by the state teachers association?"

"What's that got to do with anything?" Bryony asked.

"He's not like you. You're quiet, reserved," Mitch said.

"Boring?"

"I didn't say that." He didn't have to.

"One of his students works in the coffee shop," Bryony said. "We talked about the student."

"Listen, Bry. If you're ready to date again, I have a few ideas, much better suited for you than Cal Forster."

Bryony bit her lip before saying, "I'm not dating Cal Forster, Mitch."

Mitch started to say something, but Bryony interrupted. "How about a few pies to share with the office staff?"

"Pies?" he asked. "Nice idea! While you're at it, make extra for the staff lounge. I'll need about ten. Okay?"

"Anything you want, Mitch."

"Gotta go. They're lighting the fire. Hot time in the old town tonight!" Mitch ended the call without saying goodbye.

Bryony exited the car with care. Her leg hurt now, and the side of her face throbbed.

When she was in high school, Mitch had steered her away from the guys who he thought would be bad for her. Now he worried about men who were too good for her. Her ego joined her leg and face.

By the age of over fifty-five, one should not be controlled by the opinions of others. She was, she reminded herself, a strong, independent woman. Lillian reflected her strengths back to her every day. When would her father and brother see her in the same light? And if they never did, why let their opinions matter?

Peeling her clothes off on the small enclosed porch, Bryony walked through her house in her underwear to the bathroom, one of the many perks of living alone.

A hot shower revived her mood.

Wrapped in a clean fluffy white robe, she padded barefoot into the kitchen and cut a small sliver of peach pie. Seating herself at the table, she drew one leg up, placed the sole of her foot on the chair, and rewrapped the robe, cocooning herself as she slid the fork though fruity filling.

The memory of Cal's arm brushing against her sleeve lingered with the peachiness sliding over her tongue and down her throat. He'd called back and said he wanted to try again. The idea ran through her mind, sweet, delicious, and maybe not entirely terrifying.

# CAL GOES ABOVE AND BEYOND

$\mathcal{T}$odd's appearance in Cal's classroom at the end of the school day came as no surprise. He stopped in at least once a week.

The young man settled into a chair facing Cal's desk. "How are things going with you and Miss Green?" Todd asked.

"Too personal, dude." Why was he asking? Maybe Todd saw them at the bonfire. Cal moved a paper pad and pen to a desk drawer and locked it. "I'm your teacher. We have to maintain a certain level of professional distance."

"Would it be too personal to ask for fashion advice?" Todd asked.

"Fashion? Check this out, Todd." Cal swept his fingertips from head-to-toe. He tried, but wearing khakis, a shirt, a tie, a semblance of color coordination, and clean socks were the sum total of his dress-for-success efforts. "Am I the guy you want to ask?"

"Your style"—Todd spread his fingers in Cal's direction—"appeals to me more than this." He mimicked Cal's head-to-toe finger sweep down his own attire.

Cal surveyed Todd's faded shirt and baggy, ill-fitting jeans, the cuffs resting on worn, canvas shoes.

"Anyway," Todd said. "I wasn't so much wanting to ask about what to wear as where to find decent clothes at a reasonable price. I'd like to look better when I go to work, but I can't afford what appeals to me."

"Again, I am not the obvious person to ask, but it just so happens I do have an idea about where you might look for help. There's a consignment shop in the basement of the Methodist church that specializes in work clothes."

"You've been in town for what, about two months? How do you know this place when I've never heard of it?"

"Mister Henderson left a resource list."

"Sounds great," Todd said, his voice flat. He sat in a chair, stretched out his legs, and crossed his feet.

"But?" Cal asked.

"But I feel a little uncomfortable about going to places like that."

"Places like what?" Cal asked.

"Like secondhand stores. Dad says they're for poor people."

Cal scoffed. "Haven't you heard of retro?"

"What's retro?"

Cal sighed. "Do you want me to take you there?" Most people lacked an understanding of how far teachers would go to help their students.

"Yes, thank you!" Todd sat straighter in the chair. "When are you available?"

"How about now?" No time like the present. He would stop by the house to let out Bailey for a few minutes, and meet Todd at the church.

$\&$

TWENTY MINUTES LATER, Cal and Todd browsed shirt and suit racks, and stacks of men's jeans and pants. Todd picked out eight items. Cal added an additional ten. After trying on all eighteen, Todd picked three pairs of black pants, two pairs of jeans, six shirts, two ties, a suit jacket, and a pair of black boots.

"Since when did work clothes include jeans and 'skinny' sizes," Cal asked the woman at the cash register.

Glasses perched on the end of her nose, the cashier re-tucked the bottom of her pale blue acrylic blouse into a navy skirt. "Since after you and I were too old to wear them well." She turned her attention to Todd and said with her nasal voice, "Young man, you have made wise decisions there. Where are you working?"

"Downtown at the coffee shop," Todd answered.

"May I suggest you consider black patent loafers, without socks?"

"No socks?" Todd asked.

"I know!" she said. "Sounds bold, but with your build and those nice tight pants, going sockless will seal the deal. Of course, no socks means buying foot covers hidden inside your shoes, and going into colder weather might not be the right time to experiment, but come next March, April, remember what I am telling you."

"Thanks." Todd received change for the money he had laid on the counter. "Thanks a lot."

"Come back any time, and bring your Dad, too." She glanced sideways at Cal. "You might want to consider a little sprucing up yourself."

"Oh, I'm not...." Cal started to say.

"Great idea!" Todd said. "Thanks!" He handed a bag to Cal and picked up the other two. "Let's go, *Dad*."

In the parking lot, Todd hooted as he took the third bag from Cal. "Awesome, Mister Forster! She thought you were my father. Wild."

"Wild, yes." Cal unlocked his car door with his remote. "I'm happy she didn't assume I was your grandfather."

Todd walked backward toward his car, brandishing the three bags with raised arms. "I can't thank you enough."

"Glad I could help." Cal waved goodbye as he continued to walk to his car. Glancing at his watch, he knew he'd missed the chance to stop by the coffee shop before it closed. How long should he wait before asking Bryony out again? His sister would not be happy if she knew he was interested in seeing someone from Fieldstone, and dating the principal's sister did fall right on the line of suitable women, but he couldn't stop himself from thinking about her.

Today was too soon. He knew he should wait and give her some time to recover from the fiasco with Bailey.

He chuckled when he recalled being referred to as Todd's dad. No doubt, Todd's real father was missing out on a great kid. Cal hoped the man would wake up soon. The boy needed someone to step up for him.

When Cal told Mitch a student had complained about Justin Hicks bullying him, Mitch said, "Not much we can do. Boys will be boys." Mitch's response had shocked Cal. He had asked if there was an anti-bullying policy. Mitch answered a phone call, shooing Cal away with his hand, saying, "This is going to take a while."

Bryony Green's brother was a piece of work.

But Bryony Green was starting to look more and more like an exquisite example of feminine humanity. Exquisite, but also fairly guarded. Considering the potential fallout from her brother, and the fact that she lived hours south of his homeland, he should stop thinking about her, but he could not.

Just how soon would be too soon to ask her out?

# BRYONY'S STUDENT TURNS THE TABLE

$S$leep and dreams gave way to imagining the pies Bryony would make for Mitch's staff. She lay in bed thinking through a list of ingredients and formulating a schedule to make room for purchasing fresh products, while leaving time for serenity in the kitchen. When her mental pad indicated completion of the planning process, she showered, dressed, and readied herself for the work day.

A pink glow lit up the eastern horizon. Bryony sipped the last of her tea and set the cup in the sink. She should take advantage of these mornings, when the cooling air whispered the arrival of bitter winds in a month or so. She shrugged her shoulders into a light jacket. She had just enough time to walk to work.

Stepping carefully down the steps from her side door, she tested her leg as she did every morning. So far, last Thursday's fall had produced only a large bruise, but no lasting effect. All muscles and bones seemed to be in good working order. She set off at a brisk pace.

What a hopeful time to be outside. The air smelled crisp and clean. Streetlights shone on leaves still green, but dull now, awaiting their autumn palette. Bryony loved fall and its evocation of new-school-supply memories, every year a fresh start.

Arriving at the coffee shop a few minutes early, she found Todd waiting beside the front door.

"Good morning, Miss Green," he said.

"Good morning!" Bryony did a double take and clapped. "Wow! You look stunning." The young man wore a black jacket over a crisp T-shirt with tight black pants and leather boots rising to mid calf.

Todd blushed.

"You look like a pop star! And I love your new haircut."

"I cut it myself," he said.

Bryony inspected his face. "Do I see a bit of black eyeliner?"

"I tried to be subtle. Mom asked me at breakfast if I was getting enough sleep."

How could anyone mistake eyeliner for dark circles? "Your mom doesn't wear makeup, does she?" Bryony asked.

"No," Todd said. "Not even on special occasions."

Her own mother had worn little makeup throughout her life, but Bryony could think of few women who never added a dab of color here or there. She used a bit of concealer every day. If women did, why not men? "You look fantastic. Lillian will love it."

"I was afraid it wasn't professional enough."

"It's perfect for the coffee shop."

"Mister Forster helped me pick out the clothes."

"He did?" she asked.

Cal had been in the coffee shop several times since their mutual mud bath, but he and Bryony had interacted very little, she being too busy with work tasks, he chatting with whoever waited in line with him or sat at the table beside him. She'd rarely met a more friendly, social person. Come to think of it, she'd never met anyone as engaging as Cal Forster.

Together, she and Todd turned on lights, prepped sandwiches, set up the coffee, and placed napkins on every table.

As they finished the usual start up tasks, Todd turned to her and said, "My brother's in prison. He broke into the restaurant he worked at to steal money and accidentally started a fire. A firefighter was killed when he fell through the roof while trying to put out the fire."

The sentences had come out one on top of the other, a scramble of imagined action evoked by the telling of his story. "I'm so sorry," Bryony said, unsure if that was an adequate response.

"I wanted you to know. Mister Forster encouraged me to not keep it a secret, to tell people I can trust, and I think I can trust you."

"Thank you, Todd." Bryony gently laid her hand on Todd's arm. "Your trust is a gift to me."

Lillian arrived, dropping her purse on the counter. "What did I miss?" She gave Bryony a sideways hug and hit the start button on the coffee makers.

"Nothing," Bryony answered.

Todd mouthed, "Thank you," from behind Lillian's back.

Lillian, too, praised Todd for his new look. He tried to brush off the compliment, but Bryony could see the delight in his face.

This boy had a future, no matter what Mitch said, and Mitch had said plenty on a phone call the night before. *Watch your back, Bryony. He can't cut school work. And there have been family troubles, really serious troubles. Don't let your guard down.*

Lillian would have scolded him, saying something like, *Everything came too easy for you, Mitch,* but Bryony had remained silent, unwilling to challenge the big brother who coached her to excel only to belittle her when she tried. He demonstrated no empathy for his own sister. Why would she expect anything different from him when it came to boys like Todd?

The morning rush commenced and ended like clockwork. Cal, as usual, made his daily witty remarks, added a compliment about Bryony's smile, stayed a bit longer than usual, and gave his customary wave goodbye before he walked out the door.

Todd stayed longer than usual, too. He said a teacher's meeting had pre-empted classes for the day. Midmorning, he and Bryony sat together at a table near the counter, taste testing a new line of teas Lillian wanted to offer.

"This one hurts my stomach," Bryony said. "Too spicy."

"Try this one." Todd pushed a small cup across the table.

Bryony sipped. "Lemony, I like it." She sipped again.

"Have you ever talked to Mister Parker over there?" Todd asked. "He's like the smartest guy I ever met. I sat with him one day last week. We talked about an assignment I have for U.S. Government. He could reel off dates and names and tell stories without using his smart phone!"

"I'm impressed." Bryony had never had a conversation with Mister Parker lasting longer than the time it took to fill his order or refill his cup. Todd's attention to the retired gentleman further validated her perception about the boy's character.

They made their way through the other flavors, debating the qualities of this line of tea products versus the line they were already selling. Bryony wanted to revisit Todd's morning pronouncement, but didn't want to push. She would wait for him to bring up the topic again. In the meantime, she fell into asking the same question she was asked too many times as a senior in high school. "What do you want to do when you graduate?"

"I have no idea," Todd said. "Maybe college, something with computers, or something in the food business. I like working here. I do *not* want to be a firefighter."

She knew he must be referring to the brief confession from earlier in the day, but when he failed to say more about that, she asked, "What do you like about working here?"

"The people mainly," Todd answered. "Being forced to be friendly at seven a.m. changes the rest of my day. I've made a few new friends at school because I started treating my classmates like customers, you know, smiling first and asking them about their days."

Bryony smiled. "A great life lesson." And one she, too, had learned from working at BeanHereNow. Small talk came easier to her these days, as well as initiating a greeting when passing someone on the sidewalk, or at least offering a smile.

"What did you want to be when you were in high school?" Todd asked.

The question startled her. High school had ended so long ago. But she liked being asked because in asking, Todd had put them on equal footing, and in some ways that made sense.

"I wanted to make pies," Bryony answered. "I wanted to make every kind of pie ever made anywhere on Earth. I remember going to the library after school and searching for information about pies all over the world. It took months—we didn't have the internet then, you know—but I compiled a list of one hundred and thirty-seven pies. My goal was to make one pie every Saturday until I completed the entire list."

"Did you?" Todd asked. "Did you make all those pies?"

"No." Bryony finished off the last tea sample. "My dad didn't mind as I worked my way through the common fruit pies— apple, cherry, peach—you know, the standards. But when I moved on to the savory pies and requested a moderate financial investment from my parents to buy pigeon meat, Dad put his foot down. He said I was spending too much time in the kitchen."

"That was mean."

"I blame myself," Bryony said. "I should have started with something less exotic, a shepherd's pie, minced meat."

"So you gave up?" Todd asked.

"Something like that." After her father exploded, she had run to her room in tears. Her mother followed close behind promising secret support, begging Bryony to not give up, but unwilling to stand up to the man who would ultimately be funding the project. In the end, Bryony vowed to make her own money and pay for the ingredients herself. She couldn't remember why or when she gave up. The dream just slipped away without any further fuss.

"I like the teas we already have." She gathered the cups and put them back on the tray. "What do you think?" she asked as she rose from her seat.

"I think you should finish the pie list," Todd answered.

His firm tone surprised her. Bryony lowered herself back down to her seat. "Now?" she asked. "Why?"

"Because it's never too late." Todd took the tray from her hands as he stood and carried it behind the counter.

The strength of his conviction stayed with her throughout the workday.

In the evening, Bryony climbed the stairs to the second floor of her cozy cape cod. Though she rarely needed to go up, she kept the floor vacuumed and stored items dusted. For years she had hoped to one day finish off the upstairs, turning it into a couple of bedrooms for children, but that plan had included a completely different look on the main floor. There would have been a wedding album on the coffee table in the living room, his and hers toothbrushes in the bathroom, and a box of checks for a joint account in the desk drawer. Those dreams, too, now abandoned, the half story remained a large open area with a wide-planked floor and slanted walls of brown paper backing for fiberglass insulation between exposed rafters.

The boxes she had moved from her parents' home after her mother died were placed together in one location. They had been stacked in her old bedroom, and her mother had often urged her to take them when she was ready. Still feeling not ready, Bryony used a utility knife to slash the clear packing tape holding the lid flaps down on all three boxes.

The first box held sewing supplies. Her mother had been an avid seamstress and quilter. The contents of the box must have been her way of trying to pass on to Bryony the joy found in those activities.

The next box contained kitchen supplies, duplicates of objects stored in drawers downstairs, but these reminiscent of Bryony's childhood. She couldn't part with them. Her grandmother had been the first to use the potato masher, red paint worn away to reveal a wooden handle

In the third box, Bryony found leftover contents of her childhood bedroom. She had boxed them up herself and left them behind when she moved out in her twenties.

A green Girl Scout sash lay on top, all the appliqué patches she earned still whip-stitched in place. Bryony fingered each embroidered symbol signifying an achievement—this one for hiking, the next one for health aid, another for art. Twenty-four patches altogether murmured quiet pride and nostalgic hope for her future life.

Beneath the sash lay tennis trophies. Bryony had forgotten the strength and accuracy of her playing, all the wins she collected in high school.

Packed among the trophies were pressed flowers from high school dances. She had always attended with girlfriends, and her mother had supplied the wrist corsages. Bryony put those in a pile to throw away. No point in hanging onto reminders of not being able to attract a date.

At the bottom of the box she found the reason for her search —the list of pies.

Lifting the booklet out of the box, she ran her finger over the poster board cover. Large lettering on the front spelled out "Bry's Pies." Vines and leaves wrapped around the legs and curves of each letter. She opened to the Table of Contents listing the one hundred and thirty-seven typed recipes she had collected, then leafed through the first few pages.

Every recipe had been illustrated. The drawings surprised her. She could barely remember creating them. She must have spent hours hunched over the details at her desk, filling in shapes with a black pen, choosing a floral design for one, a geometric pattern to border another.

Noted at the bottom of each page were the references where she had located the recipe. All these years later, she found herself impressed with the young woman who put together the book she was now holding. That young person possessed the ability to think through a project, gather her resources, apply determination, and add artistic flare.

Her fourteen-year-old self's drive impressed her fifty-seven-year-old self as she continued to scan the book. When she turned to the last page, she found a note. *Bryony, I always knew you would make it to the end. Congratulations, Darling. Now, clean up the kitchen and makes plans for your next project. Love, Mom.*

Her mother must have written that before Bryony stopped baking the pies. Bryony had never read the note because she had never made it to the end of the book. She gently placed the book on the floor, lowered her head, and wept. Giving up on that dream had initiated the habit of giving up on herself.

When the tears ended, Bryony closed the boxes and pushed them against the wall. Carrying the book in both hands as she descended the staircase, she didn't know what her next project would be, but she was ready to finish the one she had started over forty years ago.

# CAL'S FIRST BRUSH WITH SMALL TOWN POLITICS

*C*al's colleagues continued to tease him about Bailey's appearance at the Homecoming bonfire through the following week. Today's rendition started with the art teacher calling from across the teacher's lounge, "Hey, Cal! My students are redesigning cover art for music. Think your dog would be willing to pose for *Appetite for Destruction* by Guns and Roses?" The art teacher's jowls shook as he guffawed, and the others present joined in with subdued laughter.

"I'll have my dog's agent call your agent," Cal answered. "But rest assured, my dog comes at a very high price." He closed his planner and stood. "You all have a fulfilling rest of the day." Before leaving the lounge, he added, "Remember, we're shaping the minds which will fund and provide care for our twilight years."

As he walked away from the lounge, he considered that Bailey's antics had cost him dearly indeed. Cal had missed the chance for an honest conversation with Bryony. Every time he saw her, he wanted to learn something new. In the past few days, she had been polite with him—in spite of the fading bruise on her cheek and the slight hitch in her step—but she continued to treat him with an attitude of cool customer service reserve. When he had apologized again in person, she had said, *No big deal. Nothing broken but my pride.* Another reminder of her humble nature. Bryony appeared to be nothing like her brother.

Musings about Bryony and her numbskull brother gave way to the scene outside a wall of windows opening onto the school courtyard. Full grown ornamental trees lined the perimeter, their leaves tinged in brown, a few on the ground. Soon they would burst with fall color.

"Mister Forster?" Todd stepped in line with Cal's stride. "Can I talk to you this afternoon after class?"

"Sure," Cal said. He glanced down at Todd's new boots, and then up at the rest of his outfit. "Nice duds."

"Thanks." Todd smiled.

They finished the walk in silence.

"Hello, hello, hello!" Cal called out as he walked in the room. The buzz in the room quieted. The students faced forward, sitting in jagged rows with desks and chairs at odd angles. A few stood against the walls.

Cal had informed them the first day of school that he found straight lines oppressive, and he would be beyond grateful if the students could find their way to destroy the order of the desks, as long as they could face the front without straining their necks. Students often fell in line behavior-wise, he had learned, when they were allowed ample leeway posture-wise.

That first day, when a student named Marabelle asked if she could stand up for class, he gave his blessing. *Of course you can,* he'd replied. *I had a friend with low back problems who stood wherever he went, except in cars, as doing so would be both dangerous and impossible.*

*Except for midgets,* Tom J. had said.

*That's not politically correct,* Peter P. had called out. *You're supposed to say Little People.*

The remarks had led to a long discussion about proper

language and respect for others. Cal had been able to lay down guidelines for classroom conduct by tweaking the comments made by the students themselves. The spontaneous discussion thrilled him. Empowering students as much as possible laid the groundwork for a classroom environment rich with enthusiastic engagement. At least that's how Cal saw it, though the teachers in adjoining rooms complained about the noise level.

This day passed with no new complaints from neighboring classrooms. Todd returned as the last stragglers from the final class of the day left the room.

"Pull up a chair," Cal said. He straightened a pile of essays, each one titled "Why My Vote Counts," clipped them together at the top, and stuck them in the back of his planner.

Todd placed a chair beside the desk and sat down, while Cal collected a pile of copied documents verifying voter registrations, also clipped them together at the top, and added them to the back of his planner, its binding strained against the added bulk. Reconsidering, he took out both sets of clipped papers and put them in his brief case, along with the planner.

In addition to the board-approved content of the class, Cal had added a bonus-points opportunity for anyone over eighteen who could prove they had registered to vote before the deadline for the next election. Those under eighteen could earn points by writing a two-page, double-spaced essay about the history of voting rights in the U.S. Today he had collected both proof of registration and essays. He would be busy this weekend.

"What can I do for you?" Cal asked. "Your hair, by the way, looks nice." The new cut opened up Todd's face, allowing others to see his eyes.

Todd brushed his hand above his ear. "Thanks. Miss Green said I look better with less hanging down."

"And she's right!" Cal flashed on having seen Bryony early that morning, her hair pulled back with a green ribbon, her respectful response when one of his students had complained about the coffee being too strong. She'd merely apologized and provided a fresh cup, as she should have, deepening his respect for her, and his interest in her.

He sat back and asked, "So, what is it you wanted to talk about?"

"I mostly wanted to check in with you," Todd said. "How are you doing?"

"I'm good!" Cal answered. "You?"

Todd fidgeted in his chair and cleared his throat before raising his head to make eye contact. "I heard my mom talking to her friend who works in the school office—and this is between you and me—but the principal has been mad at you ever since your dog crashed the Homecoming bonfire celebration. And yesterday he started getting calls about you helping students register to vote."

The newsflash made Cal bristle, but his irritation had nothing to do with the purveyor of the information, though there were concerns there, too. "Maybe you shouldn't be telling me about conversations you overhear. Think about the ethics of doing that."

Last week he had introduced the subject of ethics. This week they had covered ethics in business. Cal liked exploring both the value and challenges of living in a wealthy nation. Who profited? Who suffered? The class discussions were heated, passionate, mind-blowing at times.

"Well," Todd said. "I wanted to check in and make sure you weren't going to get fired or something because you're the best teacher I ever had."

"No worries," Cal said. "I haven't done anything worthy of being fired, and from now on, please honor your parents' privacy. Anything else I can help you with?"

"Whatever happens," Todd said, "I want you to remember,

overall the people who live in this town are good, but prone to cronyism and gossip."

"The latter of which you have aptly demonstrated." The boy's use of language often caught him off guard. What other talents lay dormant in his young mind?

Todd blushed. "Yeah, I guess so. I should have listened to my grandpa. He always said the way to stay alive is to keep to yourself." He assumed a voice of authority. "Do good quietly, and keep the conversation superficial. We're doers, not talkers.'"

"But talking is doing," Cal said. "How can people transcend superficial relationships without talking? That's why people with hearing loss learn to communicate with their hands. Language connects us." He opened his desk drawer and dropped two pens into the front well designed to hold less than he collected there. "How have things been for you at home?"

"Better," Todd said. "I told my mother about not wanting to be a firefighter. She told me not to tell my Dad, and when I graduate, to"—he assumed the authoritative voice again—"'get the heck out of Dodge. Go east, or go west, young man. You'll be happier.'" He dropped his shoulders. "The idea of going away makes me sad," he said in his normal voice. "I don't want to leave here."

Cal chose to think Todd's mother was trying to protect her son. "I'm sure she means well. Have you talked to the school counselor yet? Even if your father is disappointed in your life choices, maybe you can still stay right here, have a good life."

"I don't know," Todd said. "But at least half of my parental load is informed."

"And good for her for not giving you a hard time." The reported response by Todd's mother relieved some of the concern Cal had for Todd, but his father sounded fragile. "Trust yourself to know when and with whom you want to be open, honest, and vulnerable."

"Oh, and I told Miss Green about my brother, too."

"Wise choice. What did she say? I mean, how did she respond?" Cal winced at how quickly the questions came out, and at how much they sounded like, *Does she like me?*

"She was nice. Said she was sorry about what happened." Todd stood and pushed the chair back into the crooked lines of desks filling most of the room. "I'll let you know if I hear anything else about you. Oh, wait. Telling you wouldn't be ethical. If I hear any gossip about you, I'll keep it to myself."

"A plus!" Cal said.

Todd strode out of the classroom. Cal sat for five minutes mulling over the implications of the boy's inappropriate disclosure, then picked up his briefcase, and headed for the hallway.

The door to the office suite was unlocked, though ancillary staff were absent. Cal marched straight to the open door labeled "Principal." Generally, Mitch seemed to leave the school grounds soon after the students departed, but today he remained at his desk, hunched over a document, pen in one hand, head cradled in the other.

"Mitch?" Cal said as he knocked. "Okay if I come in?"

Mitch looked up, dark circles and bags under his eyes. "What can I do for you, Forster?"

"Um," Cal started.

Anger had propelled him forward, but now that he had arrived at his destination, his mind worked to sort out a rational way to start what could be a difficult conversation. Was Mitch really still mad about the Bailey incident, or did he see Cal leave the bonfire area with Bryony? And what was that nonsense about voter registrations?

"Just wanted to check in about anything I should be aware of," he said. "Um, you know, make sure I'm not missing any important deadlines, breaking any codes of conduct." *Or otherwise pissing you off and, if so, why don't you say it to my face?*

Mitch closed his eyes, placed an open palm across his

forehead, and massaged from his eyebrows to his hairline three times before answering. "Right now I can't think of anything but this damned report that's due tomorrow." He took a deep breath and blew it out. "Hasn't been a great day."

Cal waited a beat, his irritation calming further, before asking, "Anything I can do to help?"

"With this?" Mitch dropped his pen on the document. "Not unless you have a time machine and can drum up a few hundred votes for the last election."

"School levee?" Cal asked.

"People who can't afford children should not have them," Mitch said.

"Children are the future of the whole community," Cal said. "Better funding sources would make sense."

Mitch raised his eyes, smirked, and flashed a peace sign. "Power to the people."

Cal took a calming breath and let it out slowly. He'd come to get some straight answers from Mitch about the gossip Todd had relayed, but Mitch was not in the mood for straight talk. Was he ever? Looked like Cal would have to do an end run.

"Anyway"—Mitch looked down at the document—"I've got to finish this before I go home, and then I have to dig up a new trivia partner before Friday night."

"Trivia?" Cal asked, his interest piqued.

Head snapping up, Mitch asked, "You play?"

"Sure," he answered. "And I play to win."

"And do you? Do you win?" Mitch asked, his eyes taking on a wildness, like one possessed.

"More than I like to admit," Cal answered. "So much in fact, if I reel off the list of prizes won, feels like I'm bragging."

"Seriously, Forster," Mitch said, practically salivating. "Are you champion material?"

Who knew that trivia would be the bait to lure Mitch into what might be a softer, kinder, more fraternal kind of interaction. Cal decided to give him a little more line, let him struggle a bit before reeling him in.

"I wrote the book on how to be the big winner," Cal said.

That was true, though it was more pamphlet than book. He'd handed out copies at a Halloween event last year at the Cleveland pub where he'd played trivia every week. Intended more than anything to serve as a party prop, a door prize, he had signed copies, which gave it a book-like launch. And the eight stapled pages did contain some rather pertinent advice, like, *Stop watching television, get off your arse, and take your lazy brain to the library.*

Mitch started to smile. "Will you sub for my partner?"

"Always the sub, never the regular," Cal said, a bit coquettish.

"I am serious," Mitch said.

"I think you said that already." His whole reason for the office visit subverted by the topic of trivia, Cal was starting to enjoy seeing Mitch squirm.

"Will you partner with me?" Mitch asked. "Friday nights, eight o'clock, sports bar on Taft."

"How many people on the team?"

"Just me, and you if you'll join me," Mitch answered, quick to add, "I could do it by myself, but I like sharing the grand prize."

Then why was he so desperate to have a partner?

Before answering, Cal made a show of deliberating, putting his finger to his chin, checking the calendar on his phone, then shrugging his shoulders as he said, "Sure, I have nothing better to do with my time."

"Great!" Mitch rose up from his chair to slap Cal's upper arm. "Good to have you aboard. Now go home to that raggedy mutt of yours."

"Friday night, then," Cal said as he walked backward to the door.

"And leave my sister alone," Mitch said. "She's just getting over the last one." Though smiling, he had balled his hands into fists, placed them on the desktop, and leaned forward on his knuckles. "You don't want to add to her pain."

"Funny way to start a partnership," Cal said, too wise to engage further. He only smiled, tipped an imaginary hat, and left the office.

So, Mitch Green and he would start seeing each other every Friday night. Well, if he was going to spend that much time with the brother, maybe he could find a way to get to know the sister. Might Bryony Green like him well enough to follow through on another walk? And if she did, what payback might her brother dish out?

"Let it go!" Cal said under his breath, and a song began to play in his head.

Hell-OH! had invited him to watch Frozen eight times before he moved to Fieldstone. He had stayed with her, beginning to end, until he knew all of the songs and most of the dialogue by heart.

He missed the little munchkin and looked forward to seeing her and the rest of his family in a few weeks. Should he hire a magician for the Halloween party? Something monstrously large would be a hit. A bouncy house? No, those things were prone to flying away. He would come up with something. Maybe he could dress Bailey as Cyndi Lauper and put an iPod on his collar with a tiny speaker. Cal burst out laughing at the image in his mind, and then wondered, *Does a man's laughter make noise if there's no one else in the parking lot to hear him?*

# BRYONY'S YES

For the second day in a row, Todd arrived for work looking like a cover model for GQ. Did he want Bryony to continue to gush over him every time, or react with a subdued acceptance of his new look? She settled on, "You look nice today."

"So do you," Todd replied.

"Thanks." Bryony tucked her hair behind her ear. "Hey, Todd, I want to thank you for encouraging me about the pie list. I'm taking your advice. I'm going to finish the list."

Todd looked taken aback. "I don't remember any adult ever doing anything I thought they should do."

"I hope I'm not the last," she said. "Because you have good ideas."

"Thanks." Todd reached for his apron. He put the neck strap over his head, and as he tied the longer straps around his waist, said, "Hey, Miss Green, if you want to make a pie with a pigeon in it, and you need some taste testers, I'm game."

"I heard what you said." She pointed at him and smiled. "Pigeon meat? Game?" She liked Todd, liked working with him, and was grateful to Cal for bringing them together.

They finished setting up all of the tables with time to spare. Bryony headed to the ovens. Todd stationed himself at the counter to stock the tea basket.

They were quiet for a few minutes before Todd said, "Mister Forster's the best teacher I ever had."

Bryony popped a tray of bagels into the oven without comment.

"Ask anybody in any of his classes," Todd said.

"What makes him the best?" Bryony asked. She reached beside Todd for a towel to wipe down the oven door, and he moved away to allow her easier access.

"He asks about our interests and incorporates them into his lectures," he said. "And he talks to us like we're real people."

"I like people treating others well, too." She finished shining the stainless steel surface and tossed the towel into the bin between the refrigerator and storage cabinet.

"Mister Forster likes you."

"What?" Bryony stopped moving.

Todd leaned against the counter, crossing his arms at his chest and his legs at his feet.

"I can tell by how he looks whenever he comes in here. He likes you. When I told him I'd told you about my brother, he said, 'Wise choice.'"

There were so many things wrong with this conversation. Todd should not be talking to her like this. And she should not have such a strong response to what he said. Her heart rate increased. Heady confusion came as her thoughts bathed in euphoria mixed with rising trepidation.

She ignored Todd's comment and readied the cash drawer for the day, counting money being the best way to calm herself.

Todd was quiet for a minute or so before saying, "I wish my father was like Mister Forster."

His words surprised her. She stopped counting and looked at him. "Why?"

"He seems to care about everybody," Todd said. "And I'm not just talking about students. He talks to the janitors, asks about their families, remembers the details so the next time he sees them, he can ask, 'So how's it going with Jay's broken leg?' or, 'Did your Lorissa win the contest?'"

"How do you know what he says to other people?"

"I pay attention," Todd answered quickly. "Most of what I've learned about how to get along with people came from noticing how others get along well."

"Okay." Bryony looked sideways at the young man. "Maybe that sounds less stalkery now."

"Anyway," Todd said. "I think you deserve someone like him, Miss Green. You two deserve each other."

"What?" She stumbled over her next words. "Mister Forster and I aren't… we don't… we hardly know each other."

"You can change that," Todd said. "You should get to know him."

"You and I shouldn't be talking about this." How had this happened? Maybe she had not been such a good choice as a supervisor. She should have established better boundaries, been less empathetic, a more decisive authority figure. "You need friends your own age."

"You need to give Mister Forster a chance."

"I agree!" Lillian emerged from the back of the store.

Of course she would show up right at that moment. Lillian had a way of turning up at opportune times, usually like a guardian angel, occasionally more like a plucky, annoying sprite.

"When did you get here?" Bryony asked.

"You didn't hear the back door? You two must have been so wrapped up in your little tete-a-tete you didn't notice me back there."

"I think Bryony should ask Mister Forster to go on a date," Todd said.

"Oh, happy day!" Lillian clapped and looked upward. "Someone else agrees with me."

"This is no business of yours," Bryony glared at Lillian as she tied on her apron. "Or yours," she said, glancing at Todd. She didn't like them ganging up on her.

"I'm sorry, Miss Green," Todd said.

"Apology accepted. Would you please unlock the front door now?"

&.

BREAKING WITH HIS routine, Cal had not shown up for his morning coffee, and Bryony decided to walk home before the after-school crowd arrived to ensure she would miss him then, too. She knew she would be hyperaware of how Lillian perceived her every interaction with the man. She would feel awkward, and it would show. Lillian might take that as a sign of her interest in Cal. He might, too, and she wasn't ready for any more encouragement from Lillian or confusing comments from Cal.

Why did being attracted to someone have to be so confusing, agitating, threatening?

She remembered the revelation she'd had about her father the day Alma socked him in the arm. Maybe it was that simple. Maybe she'd been raised to fear strong men. And maybe Cal was one of the strongest men she'd ever met. Not in terms of athleticism, though he did seem fit. His strengths were his mind, and his obvious love for people in general, and his sense of humor.

A blue sky with wisps of cloud backdropped the traffic light as she approached the intersection. She glanced at the car stopped at the red light allowing her to cross. Cal drove a similar car. She made eye contact with the driver. The young man behind the wheel met her eyes and smiled. She replied with a brusque tip of her head and looked forward, a slowly curving Mona Lisa smile on her lips . She had wanted it to be Cal.

The realization came like a puff of smoke that faded as fast as it appeared.

Two blocks from her house, the cell phone in her pocket buzzed. She pulled it out and flipped it open, familiar with the number.

"Hello?" she answered.

"You weren't in the coffee shop, and I wanted to talk," Cal said.

"You wanted to talk?" she asked.

"Yes," he said. "I need to go over forms for the program."

Bryony held the phone tight to her ear. "Are they important?" They must be if he couldn't wait until tomorrow.

"Forms have no inherent importance, but we must fill them out," he said. "We could meet somewhere for dinner, and I could, uh, hand them over. I mean, I haven't eaten, and you probably haven't either."

Was he asking her for a date? Had Lillian or Todd said something to him?

"Can it wait until tomorrow?" she asked.

"No," he said. "Dinner cannot wait until tomorrow. That would make it breakfast. I never skip a meal."

She smiled, and though unclear about his intention, the inclination to accept his invitation overcame her worry about whether she was ready to explore a relationship with any man, and whether she could trust this man in particular. "Meet me at the coffee shop at six-thirty."

They ended the call after Cal assured her he would be on time, not too early, not late at all, and dog free.

Within sight of her house now, she visualized her closet. Should she wear a dress? No, she should wear a pair of pants and a nice sweater, business casual. Because he had said there were forms to sign.

Wearing a dress would send the wrong signal, telling him she wanted it to be a date, and she wasn't ready to declare herself open to that, not to him, nor to herself.

But later, when she stood naked in front of her closet, still damp from her shower, she forgot all about business casual and pulled out a dress that flattered her curves and made her feel pretty.

# CAL CRACKS THE DRESS CODE

"*I* feel like a girl." Cal stood between his closet and his bed.

Sitting on the floor beside him, Bailey thumped his tail.

"What should I wear?" Three shirts, still on hangers, covered the bottom half of Cal's bed. "Pick one, buddy."

Bailey dropped to his belly and put his lower jaw on the floor between his paws.

"You're no help. You always wear the same thing." Cal scanned the closet again and returned to the three on his bed. "Blue to match my eyes, brown to match hers, or classic black?"

Bailey rolled to his side and stretched his legs.

Cal returned to his closet and moved the shirts left to right again, one by one. "No, no, no, no, no, no, no, definitely not, Hawaiian's too casual, no tees—" followed by eight swishes of metal across metal. "Okay, the suitable options are on the bed."

He returned to the bed and picked up the black shirt Heidi had gifted to him for Christmas last year. Maybe it would bring him luck. He put it on, pairing it with a newer pair of black pants and a tie with blue and brown swirls on a black background.

"This color combination covers all the bases," he said as he knotted the tie and patted down his hair. "And I'm wearing these." Cal picked up the tiny box from the shelf beside the medicine cabinet. Inside lay the diamond studs.

He never wore them at school. Earrings would have attracted too much attention. Conservative dressers received less scrutiny, and the appearance of conformity allowed for leeway in teaching methods.

Arriving promptly at the appointed time, Cal saw Bryony through the front door glass of the shop. Before he had the car all the way into the parking space, she had thrown a lacy black shawl over a black dress, stepped out onto the sidewalk, and locked the door behind her. He would not be escorting her to the car or opening the door for her, at least not yet.

"Okay, Bryony," he said under his breath as he put the car in park. "You're in charge."

Bryony opened the car door and lowered herself into the passenger seat.

"You look nice," he said.

In fact, she looked and smelled heavenly. Her hair fell in soft waves around her shoulders. An herbal scent filled the car, reminiscent of a field of wildflowers, out of sight and out of reach, but hinted at by the wind.

"So do you," she said.

"We match," Cal said.

Her head and shoulders shifted toward him. "Aw," she said. "Nice tie." She moved her gaze to one side of his head, and then the other, frowning. "What are those?"

"Are you referring to my high cheekbones, or the masculine angles on each of my jawbones?"

"Has Mitch seen those earrings?" she asked.

"This is the first time I've worn them outside the house since moving here. I generally put them in at night before I go to bed. I was advised to wear them daily so the holes in my ears wouldn't close up. What do you think?" He turned his head side to side, modeling Prissy's handiwork.

"I think they look good, but you might want to keep not wearing them to school." Bryony lowered her head and dropped into a serious tone. "Mitch lobbied for the gym teacher's resignation when she had her nose pierced."

"And she left?" Cal asked. "With no fight?"

"Oh, I think she negotiated a pretty package." Bryony sat back in her seat and buckled her safety belt.

*Pretty package.* Women were sometimes referred to with the phrase, and while Cal routinely railed against such open displays of sexism, he couldn't help feeling like the phrase fit nicely when he recalled his fall with Bryony, their brief togetherness of being tangled in Bailey's leash. Cal had wanted to stay there, wrap his arms around her, unwrap her reserve and find the places where she could warm up to him, feel safe with him.

"Cal?" Bryony asked.

"Hmm?"

"Are you ready to go?" She settled into her seat.

The truth was he didn't care whether they stayed or left. He could sit in the car with her all night, as long as they were together. But he knew she wasn't ready, and he also knew he wasn't confident about his long term prospects. If they ended up dating, it would be casual, something easily ended without anybody crying or wishing they had never started it in the first place. Maybe this was a bad idea, this dinner date initiated by none other than him, Cal, the challenging child, the manic man, the friendly fool.

"Cal?" Bryony asked again.

"Where are we going?" he asked.

The way he asked must have conveyed more than he meant to reveal because she turned to look at him, chewing on her lower lip before answering. "A little place on the edge of town. I think you'll like it."

Did she have any idea how appealing she was? He wanted to reach out and touch her face, just to make contact, to connect with the slightest hint of intimacy. Instead, he put the car in reverse and said, "Lead the way, Ms. Green."

She directed him to a state route exiting the town and heading east. Less than a mile from the city limits, she directed him to turn right into a gravel lane winding down a steep hill with trees arching overhead. He parked beside a low brown building with a silver metal roof. A sign hung above the door. Dewey's Diner.

Bryony exited the car before Cal could walk around and open her door.

When he joined her outside the car, she asked, "Where are the forms?"

"Oh, rats! I forgot them."

Bryony smiled. "Are there forms, Cal?"

"There are always forms, Bryony, but the truth is I wanted to have dinner with you."

"You could have asked if I wanted to go to dinner."

"Would you have accepted the invitation?"

"Probably not." This time her eyes lit up when she smiled.

The diner sat on the edge of a large pond. Ducks swam near the edge. Children stood on a small landing over the water holding small paper cups. They picked what looked like dried peas and corn out of the cups and tossed them onto the surface of the water, squealing as the ducks raced over to pick up the food with their broad beaks.

"I hope those children are not feeding our dinner," Cal said. "Tell me duck's not on the menu."

"No duck," Bryony said. "Chicken, beef, fish. You're not vegetarian, are you?"

"I could live off vegetables every day of my life if I needed to. I love vegetables in all their shapes, sizes, and colors, my favorite being the kind grown underground, the root vegetables, potatoes, turnips, parsnips, and so on. But since other varieties of food are available, I'd have to say I am equally fond of all the groups. Grains, fruits, oils, meat. Call me city-grown, but while I'm open to the full range of culinary options, I don't want to eat the family members of ducks who have been fed in my presence."

Over-talking balanced his physical energy and helped him focus. In fact, his mother taught him to manage himself when he was young by reeling off stream of consciousness. The practice kept him in line, its effectiveness revealed tonight in the reduction of his preoccupation with a desire to kiss Bryony Green.

"Ready to go in?" Bryony asked.

"This looks great. I'm starving." He followed her to the side of the building and in through a door with worn paint.

The interior offered low lights, an odor reminiscent of the era prior to the statewide smoking ban, and the aroma of fried food. Three men sat at a bar, their bellies hanging over their belts, each one caressing a tall brown bottle, their eyes directed at an entertainment news program on the television. Not the romantic setting he would have chosen. Cal wondered if the ambience reflected her interest in him. If so, he would have to rate her interest at the low end of the scale.

Bryony led him to a table for two in front of a huge, bowed window overlooking the pond. She sat down and gestured toward the seat opposite. "Is this good for you?"

"It's fine." He sat, unable to not compare Dewey's to the places he would have introduced to her in Cleveland. His choice would have been upscale, trendy, foodie, fun. Should he be offended she put so little effort into picking a better spot?

"Hey, hon." A waitress approached the table, her faded black polo shirt stuffed into worn jeans with unbelted loops at the waist.

"Hi, Maggie," Bryony said. "How's Howard?"

"Better," the waitress answered. "He's home now, but it might take another six weeks before he can work again."

"Who's cooking tonight?"

"Jimmy was supposed to, but he got the flu, so Lillian's back there."

"Oh." Bryony seemed surprised. "I wondered why the coffee shop hadn't been properly closed out for the day. Tell her I'll go back and finish after I eat."

"You will?" Cal had imagined they might spend a longer evening together.

"I'm sorry," Bryony said. "I should have introduced you. Cal, this is Maggie. Maggie, this is Cal Forster. He's subbing at the high school while Chuck Henderson recovers. Maggie's an old friend of mine, Cal. She and her husband own this place."

"My husband, Howard, is recovering from a double knee replacement," Maggie said. "Bryony and Lillian have been helping out with the cooking." She put her hand on Bryony's arm. "Bless you, hon."

"I don't do much," Bryony said. "I call around to organize a schedule for cooks."

"Well, I couldn't have done it without you and Lil." Maggie brought the pad up, poised to write. "Now what can I get for you two?"

Cal picked up the menu as Bryony answered.

"Two baskets of chicken, fries, and coleslaw. I'll have water, no ice. What do you want to drink, Cal?"

She had ordered for him? "Um, water's fine," he said.

Maggie snatched the menu out of his hand and replaced it in the stainless steel holder attached to the tray for salt and pepper shakers.

A bit disoriented, Cal wondered if he had fallen into an episode of Andy Griffith. Everybody seemed to know each other, help out when times were bad, and he was a heel for comparing Dewey's to upcoming urban eateries. The two kinds of venues were like grits and spring rolls, in a world wide enough for both.

Before Maggie could leave, and because he wanted to make amends for his unexpressed, shameful, insulting thoughts, Cal said, "Listen, I hope your husband has a quick and full recovery. If you're interested, I teach the work study program at Fieldstone High. I have a few students who might benefit from working here."

"That's a great idea." Bryony put her hand on his arm for a moment. "Why didn't I think of it?" She removed her hand and turned to Maggie. "The student he placed with Lillian is a Godsend."

Warmed by her touch, Cal fell into a quick overview of his program, after which he and Bryony tag-teamed on the impact at BeanHereNow. Bryony focused on the business benefit. Cal extolled the positive effect on the student placed there. Hard to miss how well they performed as a team.

"Okay." Maggie nodded her head, looking from Bryony to Cal. "We could talk about that."

"I'll drop by tomorrow," he said. "Is four good?"

"I'll be here. Thanks." Maggie smiled, accentuating the wrinkles at the outside corners of her eyes, and the darkness of the delicate skin above and below her eyes. She left the table and disappeared through a door beside the bar.

"Thank you, Cal." Bryony said. "I should have thought of the possibility myself. Todd's been a dream for us."

"I think he'd say the same about you."

She countered quickly with, "How's school going?"

He'd seen her do that before, dodge compliments, hide from attention.

"School is good." Cal didn't want to talk about school, but

school was safe, and she seemed to need safe, so he gave her twenty minutes of coverage. She asked the right questions. He elaborated and made her laugh, and her laughter made him warm inside.

He knew he'd rushed her on the night of the bonfire, but thinking she might be more ready now to let him in, he said, "Tell me about you, Bryony." He wanted to know everything.

"Not much to tell," Bryony said. "I'd like hear more about you."

"I think I'm having a déjà vu," Cal said. "Haven't we done this before, and didn't it lead to a mud bath and bruises for you, public ridicule for me and my dog?"

"Bailey's nowhere near." Bryony said. "I think we're safe. Tell me about you. Why did you take the job here?"

"Don't you want to know if I've been married, have ten kids, and date dozens of women at a time?"

She put her hands in her lap. "Or start there."

"I retired last spring and came here for one year to fill a need." Might as well get that on the table right away. He would be around no longer than next June. "I've never been married, have no kids, and date one woman at a time. I haven't dated anyone since my last breakup. I'm not rebounding. I am certifiably single, and interested in you, Bryony, though I have to warn you, like I said, I will be leaving no later than the end of the school year. So, in all fairness, I need to say I'm looking for a dating friend, not so much a girlfriend." He waited only seconds before saying, "God, I love seeing you blush."

Her hand flew up to her hair, tugging a lock down until it ended, and her fingers slid off. "I don't like blushing."

"Most people don't, and I've never understood why because it's the most endearing sign of being fully human. People who don't blush can be monstrous." He waited a beat before saying, "Your turn."

Bryony smiled and shook her head at him. "Okay, me. I don't

know what I'm doing here. I was going to wear pants, but I wanted to look nice for you, and now I feel overdressed. I like to make pie. The last man I was with told me I was boring, and dumped me for someone younger." Her pace picked up. "You seem to like me, and that scares me. I'm not looking to date anybody. You're an unwelcome surprise"—she paused, lowering her head—"that I say yes to. Something about you makes me say yes." She raised her head, her voice becoming stronger. "And did I mention I like to make pie?"

Flummoxed, Cal considered he had never dated anyone who matched his ability for openness and honesty. Most of the women he dated offered verbal resumes, reeled off family trauma, or settled for being coy and *no need to talk about little old me.* Bryony's answer showed a kind of vulnerability that matched his own.

He replied with the first thought that came to mind. "Your pie is wonderful."

They went back and forth a few more times. She seemed to be able to keep up with his teasing remarks, and parried with a few of her own. Bryony exceeded his expectations in so many ways.

After what could have been twenty minutes or two hours—awareness of time suspended by the flow of their conversation—Bryony looked behind Cal. "Here comes our food."

Cal moved his arms away from the table as Lillian slid a red plastic basket of fried chicken with french fries and a small dish of coleslaw in front of him. She placed a similar basket and bowl in front of Bryony, and a wicker basket of dinner rolls, a plate of butter pats, and a bottle of ketchup between them.

"Need anything else?" Lillian asked.

"Bigger pants?" Cal said.

Lillian laughed. "You're too skinny anyway, Cal." She walked away, winking at Bryony, who seemed to be doing everything she could to avoid noticing.

Bryony picked up a french fry and bit the end of it. "I always take at least half of it home."

"Bailey will be having chicken for breakfast." Cal picked off the breading and tasted the meat.

"Good, isn't it?" Bryony asked.

"It is!" Cal answered. "But not as good as that pie you made. How did you learn how to bake like that?"

Between bites, she shared the story of her plan to make pies from around the world, giving up, and then, thanks to Todd's encouragement, finding the list of pies again with a note from her mother. She ended with, "I like to bake pies. Sweet or savory, I like pie."

"Sounds like an advertising jingle." He ate another french fry. "You have ketchup on your chin." He almost reached out to wipe it away for her, but the act might be perceived as too intimate.

She brushed her chin with her own napkin.

"What a great story," Cal said. "So, you're going to finish the list? I mean, as Todd pointed out, you have to make the pies now, right?"

"Yes," Bryony said. "I'm going to make all of the pies on the list."

"That apple pie you made was really exceptional. Have you ever thought of selling them?"

The idea seemed to shake her up a bit.

"I don't know," Bryony said. "It's a big step."

"Every big step is preceded by smaller steps. Sounds like finishing the list is a great start."

"Maybe…."

If she were his student, he would dig into her resistance, find the nugget of fear or negative thinking holding her back, and help her flesh out a business plan. But she wasn't his student. And he had an idea Bryony Green would not want to be probed or analyzed in any way, shape, or form. She had a strength about her, but also a fragility. He liked both of those qualities.

They were real, honest. His desire to know everything about her grew stronger every time he saw her, but he wanted their connection to unfold organically, to not be pushed by artificial timelines like the end of a date, the completion of a school year, a deadline on his tenure in Fieldstone. He considered he might someday soon find himself in some kind of emotional trouble with her, but it was the most appealing trouble he could imagine. Why would he stop now?

They talked through the rest of the meal, Bryony not shy with him anymore. She was funny and kind and interesting.

Maggie brought doggie bags. Bryony insisted on paying. She said she was doing it on behalf of the community, for his service to their young people. Other than the Hendersons, nobody had shown as much appreciation since his move there, not even Mitch when they went out for burgers.

When he pulled into a parking spot in front of the coffee shop, Cal quipped about her being unable to invite him into her house for a drink after he walked her to the door. Instead, he suggested he could accompany her into the coffee shop and make a pot of decaf while she cleaned up.

"I'm fine," she said. "I'll work faster on my own. Thanks for dinner." She climbed out of the car.

"That's it?" he asked.

She bent down, said, "Goodnight, Cal," and shut the car door.

He watched her walk across the sidewalk, unlock the door to the shop, turn on the lights, and give a little wave before closing the door behind her.

All he wanted to do was follow her inside, watch as she worked, and spend time with her.

"What an interesting woman!" Cal said. He drove home, chastising himself again for his petty judgement about her choice of dining places, trying to remember word for word everything she had said. Had she really called him an unwelcome surprise right before saying she couldn't help but say yes to him?

Bailey demanded a walk the minute Cal entered his house. He leashed up his best canine friend and trotted out the door with him.

"Bailey old boy," Cal said. "I met someone." Bailey sniffed the telephone pole in the tree lawn.

"Remember the woman you knocked down when you were in pursuit of a cat, right before your stage debut?"

Bailey trotted to the next pole.

"She's kind of awesome. Not hard to look at, the right age, not married, intelligent, kind, funny." Gene Kelly singing in the rain came to mind. Cal laughed and clicked his heels once.

Surprising he should have such strong feelings about someone who was practically a stranger. He had never believed in love at first sight, but if he had to name the feelings Bryony inspired, he would have to say the phrase might be apt. Funny this should happen to him for the first time in his fifties.

Bailey finished up with another pole and moved on to a bush.

"The problem, Bailey, is geographic."

Bailey sniffed a spot, inspected it again, and moved on a foot farther to do his business.

Cal pulled a plastic bag from his pocket and slid it over his hand to pick up the pile.

"What a load of crap," he said. "Why couldn't she live closer to Cleveland?"

# BRYONY'S WELCOME SURPRISE

*T*ables gleaming, bread racks clean, BeanHereNow stood ready for the next morning. Bryony finished counting the money and zipped it inside the bank bag. Taking the bag to the drop off slot at the bank so late in the evening involved risk, but leaving it in the shop overnight seemed riskier.

An easy solution to her unease about the deposit would have been to have Cal walk with her to the bank, but she had needed the evening together to end. He would have been a complete distraction from the tasks she completed in less than thirty minutes.

He outtalked any man she knew, which she was starting to like very much. He seemed to appeal to all kinds of people, which she also liked. His imperfections, like his annoying way of not giving up, seemed almost perfect.

She shook her head, smiled, and picked up the money bag. He was too good to be true.

With her shawl draping her shoulders, Bryony carried the deposit bag to the front door. Her cell rang and she put down the bag to fumble in her purse for her phone. Eager anticipation of a call from the man with diamonds in his ears turned to annoyance when she saw Mitch's name flash on her screen.

"Bry!" Mitch said. "What's up?"

Her brother never called to chat. Bryony sat in a chair and sighed. "What's wrong?" Something with their father? He seemed fine the last time she saw him.

"I hear you had dinner with Cal Forster," Mitch said.

"What?" Bryony looked up. Rain pellets hit the window with vigor, and a car passed by the shop. "Who told you?"

"Does it matter?"

Her heart rate increased, pumping up a sense of being caught in the act. She closed her eyes. Would she ever be able to do what she wanted to do without feeling like she required permission?

"I think I told you before," Mitch said. "You might want to steer clear. Besides not being a good fit for you, he'll be gone at the end of the school year. Even if Henderson doesn't return—I shouldn't be telling you, so don't tell anyone—funding for the program will likely be cut."

"Why?" Bryony sat up straighter in the chair and turned to look at the service counter. "Todd's working out great for us. He's a good kid, and I think the experience here has helped him."

"Not my call," Mitch said. "It's all about money, money, money, and the school board has the final say."

"But you have influence," Bryony said. "Can't you talk to them, lobby for Cal, I mean for the program?"

"What's it to you?" Mitch asked. "Don't tell me you're serious about him." He snorted a laugh. "Have you noticed he has pierced ears? He is so not your type."

Of course Mitch would have noticed the holes in Cal's ears. Mitch missed the important facets of a person, and noticed the features he could criticize or ridicule.

"Cal's a nice guy," Bryony said. "He already told me he's only here until June. If he asks me out again, I'll go. And if he doesn't ask me, I'll ask him." As much as she would like that to be true, she knew she overstated her courage. Arguing with Mitch had never been her strong suit.

"Bry, Bry, Bry," Mitch said. "You're not hearing me. I'm not trying to tell you what to do. I'm trying to protect you."

"From what? From finally doing what I want to do, even if you don't like it?" Her neck grew hot and sweaty.

Surprise exploded through the phone speaker. "What are you talking about?"

"Do you remember when we were young, and I wanted to date Buz Culpepper?"

"You mean the guy who drove the motorcycle and wore chains on his neck?" Mitch issued a guttural sound of disgust, and said with sarcasm, "He was a winner."

"Buz started a software company. I saw an article about him online. He has a beautiful wife, grandchildren, a vacation home in Colorado, and his employees love him."

"You're kidding," her brother said. "That guy? Unbelievable."

"People are more than what you can see on the outside, Mitch. I have to go." Bryony snapped shut her phone, the finality pitched too high, too sharp, over too soon. If only cells came with real receivers, the old-fashioned kind you could slam down for maximum effect.

The ringer sounded.

She flipped open the phone and held it to her ear, ready for open combat, though she shook inside. "What?"

"Yikes," Cal said. "Do you have my name in your contact list? Because if you do, and if you knew it was me, I'd say by the tone of your voice you're not feeling too great about having dinner with me."

"I'm sorry." Bryony rubbed her forehead. "I thought you were—oh never mind."

"You okay?" Cal asked.

Remembering her conviction with Mitch, Bryony answered, "I'm glad you called. I enjoyed being with you."

"Good to know," Cal said. "Because Bailey insisted on a longer-than-usual walk, and we ended up here."

"Here?" Bryony raised her head to see Cal peering in through the door. Bailey sat beside him, both of them drenched.

She closed her phone and dropped it into her purse before grabbing her keys and stepping to unlock the door, concern for both of them eclipsing her trepidation.

"Come in, come in!" she said.

"No," Cal said. "Because the minute we step inside, he'll shake, and you'll end up with wet dog hair plastered ten feet in every direction. But if you're ready to leave, and you could let us use a few towels, we could dry off and allow you to give us a ride home."

"Of course!" She left the door open as she hurried to the store room for towels.

Though she had ended their dinner date stiff and unresponsive, he came back. Any tension from the argument with Mitch, any nervousness about noticing how much she liked Cal, melted in the warmth of knowing he liked her enough to come back.

"You're okay with this?" Cal asked as he ran the towels over Bailey's fur. "He might leave wet places and fur in your back seat."

"Yes, that's fine, not a problem," she answered. Fur on the upholstery would remind her Cal had come back. She might never vacuum the back seat again.

Cal smiled up at her. "Is that your car?"

"Yes." She pointed to the blue Malibu parked in front of the store. She hit the remote to unlock the doors, pulled her shawl over her head, and started to lead Cal and Bailey out the door.

Cal stopped. "Isn't that your purse on the table over there?"

"Yes!" She stepped back to retrieve her purse and the bank

deposit, led them out, and locked the door behind her. "I have to drop this off at the bank on the way. Do you mind?"

The rain slowed to a sprinkle.

"Do whatever you need to. We're along for the ride." Cal smirked. "After all, we are the 'unwelcome surprise' here."

For the umpteenth time since meeting Cal, heat flooded Bryony's cheeks. "Please forgive me," she said. "I don't know why I said that."

They walked to the car, neither of them hurrying.

"It's not the first time I've heard it," Cal said. "That's how my mother described me for the first ten years of my life."

"Is that true?" Bryony asked.

"No, but it was a great one-liner." Cal bumped her ever so lightly with his arm.

She wanted to bump him back with more oomph, but she settled for simply noticing the heat generated by his touch. It spread through her entire body, and she turned to him, a flower turning toward the sun, to say, "Tell me more about your mother."

# CAL CALLS AGAIN

*a*fter Bryony dropped them off, Cal went into the house and immediately called her. She answered after one ring.

"Are you still driving?" he asked. He wanted to hear her voice again. The short conversation in the car as Bryony drove him home upped both his interest and his confidence. For every answer he gave, she found another question to ask.

"You know I am," she said. "I'm a block away. Did you leave something in the car?"

"No," he said. She sounded happy, not annoyed. A good sign. "Are both of your hands on the wheel?"

"I have you on speaker."

"Good." He had nothing to talk about. He merely didn't want the evening to end. "You shouldn't talk on the phone while driving."

Bryony laughed. "Why are you calling, Cal?"

He was calling because, geographically challenged or not, he wanted to be as close to her as he could be. "Would you like to go on a non-date Saturday night?"

There was a pause before she answered. Had he pushed his luck too far?

"Any paperwork involved?" she asked.

Cal breathed out. "I can bring something to grade if it makes you happy."

"Not necessary." Her voice was warm, confident. "Yes, I will have dinner with you on Saturday night."

"Pick you up at five?"

"I'll be ready," she said.

Heidi would give him a hard time, and he might regret this decision to follow his heart and not his head, but he couldn't stop himself. Bryony was to his whole being, what the shoe insert was to his knee pain, what vitamin D was to his immune system, and what a low fat diet was to his cardiovascular system. She made everything feel better, function better. He would never write any of that on a Valentine's Day card, but if he did, Bryony was the kind of woman who would understand.

Feeling pleased and hopeful, Cal showered and threw on a pair of socks, some old jogging shorts, and a tee under a thick, lined sweatshirt. He had just settled into his favorite reading spot when his phone announced a caller. Mitch.

"Seriously?"

Bailey raised his head, his ears perked, his eyes alert.

"Thanks for being here, buddy." Cal rubbed Bailey's head with his foot and poked the green button with his middle finger.

"Hey, Mitch. Looking forward to Friday night. You're not backing out on me, are you?"

"What? No, are you?"

"Absolutely not. I'm stoked. Ready to wipe the floor with those other teams. They don't stand a chance against us." Cal raised his fist and pumped the air mouthing, "Woot woot!"

Bailey barked.

"I like your style, Forster, but I didn't call about trivia. I called because it has come to my attention that in spite of my best efforts, you have not stayed away from my sister."

Mitch's tone was subdued, heartfelt, probably due to his interest in not losing Cal on Friday nights.

"You're not hearing me, Cal. Bryony is special, not like other people. She's easily hurt, and not able to deal with the world as it is, and she hung up on me tonight! She's never acted like that before. The best thing you can do for her is leave her alone."

Was Mitch Green even talking about the same person Cal had just spoken to less than an hour ago?

"Look, Mitch," Cal said. "While I respect your concern for her, I think you don't give her enough credit. I think Bryony can make her own decisions, but if it eases your mind at all, I want you to know that I have no intention of hurting her."

Silence met his response.

Bailey remained on guard, ears up, eyes bright and searching Cal's face.

Finally Mitch spoke, unable to keep the menace from his voice. "You'd better not, Forster. See you at school tomorrow."

# IS BRYONY ROOT-BOUND?

*S*aturday morning baking produced a perfect sugar cream pie. In the afternoon, Bryony carried it out to her car and drove to RestHaven. On the way into the building, a man in a Bengals shirt asked if she was delivering pies to everyone. He was one of the friskier residents. She smiled and kept walking.

Her father and Alma sat together in the alcove, reading the newspaper.

"It's about time you came for a visit," her father growled.

"I missed you, too, Daddy." Their relationship had changed. His surliness held less bite.

"Nice to see you, honey," Alma said. She wore a pink dress, the hem falling to right below her knees, white anklets, and bright white sneakers with big pink dots.

"Love your shoes," Bryony said.

"Aren't they fun?" Alma giggled. "My daughter loves to shop, and she knows how much I love polka dots. I'd take a pair in every color."

"What do you have there in your hand?" her father asked.

Bryony held out the pie, uncovering the top as she extended her arm.

"Sugar cream pie?" he asked. "You'll shoot my sugar sky high."

"You're having trouble with your sugar?" Bryony asked. Nobody had mentioned it to her.

Alma pinched his thigh. "Now you stop. We're about the only two around here who don't have our fingers pricked every day." She inclined her head toward the pie. "Are you going to share some with me?"

"I guess so, if you'll stop with the pinching," Bryony's father said.

Alma laughed and brushed the back of her hand across his shoulder. "Don't be a baby, Albert." She looked at Bryony and said, "I'll go get plates. Will you have a piece with us, dear?"

"I'm good," Bryony said.

Alma was her father's girlfriend, there was no doubt now. Her pinches were love bites, to be sure. And her father's complaints were about needing to be heard, not about defending himself. If anything, the subtext of his comments were along the lines of begging Alma to keep touching him.

While Alma collected the plates, Bryony and her father reviewed the long list of his oft repeated complaints. The cost of living there, the food, the other residents, the staff, the cable TV, the lack of privacy, and the presence of the big friendly mutt who everyone but her father adored. Halfway through his tirade, he yawned, and Bryony realized he was becoming bored with his own bad mood.

Alma returned with plates, napkins, forks, and a pie cutter.

Bryony sliced into the pie, placing a perfect piece on each of the two plates, while Alma recounted the delightful events of the past week, extolling the many virtues of life at RestHaven.

How Bryony's father had managed to snag the attention of

this easy-to-please elder defied logic. Hopefully, a more appealing man would not come along. Her father would never admit it, but if Alma defected, he would be devastated. Bryony was sure.

"Oh, honey," Alma said after the first bite. "I've never tasted anything so heavenly, and I have tasted many a pie. Where did you learn to bake?"

"She taught herself," her father said.

Did she hear pride in his voice? Bryony mumbled, "Thanks," caught off guard by the rush of emotion evoked by her father's show of appreciation.

When they both finished their last bites, neither leaving crumbs, Alma gathered the plates, utensils, and napkins before scurrying off with a promise to return with coffee.

"The woman reminds me of a tree rat," her father said. "Always moving. Doing this. Doing that."

"You like her," Bryony said.

"Yes," her father said. "And I find her exhausting."

"Daddy," Bryony said, moving to sit beside him on the loveseat. "You said something a while back, and I wanted to ask you about it. You said Mom was selfish. What did you mean?"

He jerked toward her. "I never said that."

Bryony took a breath and waited.

"Selfish is a harsh word," he said. He turned away to stare out the window across the hall. "Your mother wasn't selfish. But once you kids were born, I hit the back burner and stayed there until the day she died." His eyes grew hazy. "I miss her. But I've been missing her for a long time."

This admission on his part broke the family rule. Nobody in Bryony's family ever talked about their feelings without blaming the person in front of them. Again, a surge of emotion filled her chest, but she didn't want to interrupt him by drawing attention to herself. As much as Bryony cherished the gift of his honesty, he gave the gift to himself, too. She wanted him to experience the full impact of what he was doing, what he was saying.

"We used to dance every Saturday night," he said, turning back to look toward Bryony. "Before you kids came along."

"I didn't know," she said, hoping he could not hear the catch in her voice.

"She was a real hoofer. She danced with a troupe to entertain GIs when she was in high school." His eyes were softer than she had ever seen before.

"I remember," Bryony said. "There were pictures."

"Here we are!" Alma announced. She closed the distance between them, setting a round tray on the coffee table. "I brought the whole pot," she said. "And a cup for you, Bryony. Would you like some?"

"I need to go." Bryony stood, clutching her purse.

"Thanks for the pie," her father said.

Alma slapped his thigh. "Now that was the nicest I've seen you be to her."

Bryony's father grinned and shook his head.

Bryony saw nothing, heard nothing, as she made her way back to her car, her mind absorbed by the shift in her father's behavior, the perspective he shared.

Perhaps her mother was not the saint she had imagined. Maybe once her mother found security in marriage, she abandoned the man she married, the man she was supposed to love, honor, and cherish until death. If her own mother could turn a marriage sour, how favorable were Bryony's chances of making a relationship work?

Thinking about Cal burdened her now. She might pull off a date or two, but she had no idea about how to be in a healthy relationship.

Her phone buzzed with an unknown caller, and she answered anyway because she needed distraction, or connection, and even a robocall might do.

"Bryony?" The female voice was familiar, but Bryony couldn't place it with a name or face right away.

"Yes?" Bryony answered.

"This is Charity, Charity Henderson." She need not have said her first name twice, or even included her last name. There were no other people named Charity in Bryony's life. Bryony's inner guard rose to attention.

"Yes?" Bryony asked. Why was she calling?

"Is this a good time?"

Was there ever a good time for Charity? No, but Bryony was raised to be polite. "Sure," she answered.

"I'm sorry to bother you," Charity said. "But I've been thinking about this for quite a while now, and I wondered if you would consider coming back to your old job? Paul left, you know, and we have not been able to replace either of you, and, well, I think I may have bitten off more than I can chew." Unlike the head cheerleader who had rallied the fans to support all of the high school sports teams, Charity's small laugh conveyed nervousness, maybe even neediness.

Charity Beaman Henderson needed Bryony's help? This was a first, maybe a one and only. Bryony had the oddest sensation —perhaps for the first time in her life—of being in a position to make someone else squirm. Now was her chance to exact revenge.

The fleeting feeling dissipated rapidly, replaced by a more self-serving thought. She could go back to her old job, her comfort zone of boring routine, where her days were laid out in predictable patterns, and there was no need to push herself to be friendly because numbers never complained, and her income didn't rely on tips.

"I'd offer a raise, of course," Charity said. "And we could discuss an enhanced benefits package."

Why was Charity being so nice to her?

"I'm honored you would think of me," Bryony said. Her

inner avenger grimaced. One should never show weakness to an enemy.

"I know this is out of the blue," Charity said. "And I don't expect you to answer right now, but would you think about it? Call me next week?"

"Sure," Bryony said. "Thanks for calling, and tell Chuck I hope he's doing well."

"He'll appreciate hearing that. Thanks, Bryony. Let's talk soon."

Bryony drove home in a daze. Charity had sounded friendly, sincere. And her offer tantalized. She could go back to her old job, fall back into her comfortable, familiar routine, build an even stronger retirement portfolio, take herself on vacations— anywhere but the beach. Mitch would get off her case. Her father would be pleased. What would Cal think?

Funny that she cared what he would think when they were barely dating, but she did.

# CAL'S DATE SIZZLES & FIZZLES

*O*n Saturday evening, Cal pulled into Bryony's driveway. Again, he was right on time. He hoped she would appreciate his promptness because Bailey had given him such a hard time about leaving.

The houses in Bryony's neighborhood had developed their own personalities over the years. The neighbors on her right had a second floor over the garage. The neighbors on her left had a complete second floor on their house. Across the street, a glassed-in porch covered the front of the house. Bryony's house appeared to be architecturally unaltered, but bore signs of excellent care.

Taking his time, Cal walked to the front door. The sidewalk was edged to perfection, the bushes along the foundation freshly mulched. Colorful mums bloomed in large pots filling the spaces between the larger plantings. Did Bryony pay someone to do her yard work? Did she do it herself? He liked the idea of her working out there, her hair pulled back, dirt on her knees and hands.

He pressed the doorbell with his left hand as his right reached over to touch a pansy petal in a window box. They were silk. He smiled. His mother would have done something similar.

In less than a minute the door opened, and Bryony stood before him, dressed for anything other than digging in the dirt. She wore a green dress with black polka dots, black leggings, and a soft black sweater. Her hair lay around her shoulders. Her face appeared younger, and Cal realized she wore makeup. Yeah it hid a few wrinkles, but her face was beautiful au natural.

She ushered him in, saying, "Let me get my coat."

A hint of perfume, almost like she wasn't wearing any, gently touched his nose as he helped her into her coat. He wanted to pull her close and bury his face in her hair, but he knew she wasn't ready for so much affection. Was he?

For the few seconds it took Bryony to collect her purse, Cal stood at the front door and glanced around her home.

There were potted plants everywhere. Hanging in front of windows, placed on every available horizontal surface—the mantel, tops of bookcases, tables—and on the floor, growing from large ornamental pots set on slightly elevated wooden surfaces.

Before him stretched a narrow hallway leading back to a bright yellow kitchen. He saw a kitchen table with a wooden bowl full of fruit.

A stairway on the left had a runner with a deep red, blue, and gold oriental design. A gallery of family photos climbed the wall to a door at the landing above.

Through an open door on his right he saw black and white photographs on a dark gray wall, a black leather chair, a floor lamp, and light gray carpeting.

Everything seemed to be in order, and her home had a peaceful, serene atmosphere. He wondered if she had cleaned up any clutter for him. When he first met Leslie, he never would have guessed she generally lived in chaos.

"Ready!" Bryony stood before him, keys dangling from the

same fingers clutching a black purse, not the one he'd seen her carry in the past. Her worn everyday bag looked like it could hold everything she might need to make a pie on the spot. This purse was small and shiny, like her shoes. He took in every detail, the whole auburn, black, and green picture of her standing there dressed up for their first real date.

Bryony dropped her head and raised it again, her eyes wide. "Did I overdress?"

"No," Cal assured her. "You look wonderful."

Her smile returned, and he stepped out onto the porch ahead of her so she could lock her door.

They ate at a Chinese place on the edge of town. Dinner conversation was lighthearted. He liked how she kept up with him, and how she could quiet him down with silences that didn't come off as censure.

When they arrived at the cineplex, Bryony insisted on paying since he had covered dinner. She also insisted he choose the movie. Had he been alone, Cal would have chosen the animated science fiction saga, but he picked with Bryony in mind.

As the movie unfolded, an older married couple faced disappointments and rekindled their relationship. Cal relaxed into his seat, less interested in the Oscar winner on the screen, highly aware of the woman by his side. He didn't put his arm around Bryony's shoulders or try to touch her hand as she reached into the popcorn box wedged between them. She would let him know when she was ready.

He noticed her tears when the movie ended.

Walking from the bright lights of the theater lobby into the equally lit parking lot, Bryony said, "It was just as powerful the second time."

"You saw it already?" Cal asked. Who paid to see a movie twice, like he did?

"Last weekend," she said.

"Why didn't you say something?"

"I thought you wanted to see it."

Cal smiled. "I did, but true confession, if I'd known you already watched it, I would have picked Alien Space Battles."

Bryony grinned. "I wanted to see Space Battles, too, but I wasn't going to question your choice, especially since I made you choose."

"You sat through *Waving Hello* again for me?" he asked.

She shrugged.

"And even though you knew the ending, you cried." He sometimes cried at movies, always when a child or animal was hurt. "What made you cry?"

"Happy endings make me cry," Bryony said. "No matter how many times I see them."

He should have known.

"I'm not ready to call it a night," Cal said. "Where's the late night hot spot for dates that don't want to end?"

"Dewey's?" Bryony asked.

"Dewey's it is."

Mitch had been cool when they ran into each other on Friday. If none of his spy ring recognized them at the Chinese restaurant or movie theater, surely someone at Dewey's would. Cal would deal with her brother on Monday. Tonight was all about Bryony.

When they arrived, she allowed him to open the car door for her. Cal took her arm as they walked across the gravel to the door.

This time the waitress was young, vivacious, and blonde, in both hair color and stereotypical behavior. And he knew her because he had placed her there two days ago—Marabelle Piper, the student who preferred to stand during class.

Marabelle seated them at the same table they had occupied earlier in the week. She giggled every time she said something, no matter how inane. She touched Cal's forearm twice, as if they were old friends. And she barely looked at Bryony at all.

Bryony ordered a decaf, and Cal followed suit. Marabelle returned within minutes, carrying steaming fresh brews, her attention again lingering solely on Cal. Choosing Dewey's had been a mistake. He never would have agreed if he'd known she was on the schedule. He assumed she was feeling nervous and overcompensated with familiarity. He could relate, but he could not let her behavior go unchecked. He would talk to her later to discuss the importance of ensuring each customer enjoys the sense of being valued by the one serving them.

When she finally left, Cal dismissed her from his mind and focused on Bryony. "Is this our table now?" he asked.

"Seems so," Bryony answered.

Her words were encouraging, her tone not so much.

"I like this table," she said, looking away. "I like the lights on the water."

"What did you like about the movie?" Cal asked.

Bryony continued to gaze out the window, and Cal started to ask again. Before he could, she took a breath, turned back to him, and said, "I like the idea of people being together for fifty, sixty years, and staying in love."

He couldn't read the look on her face, but before he had time to wonder what it meant, she asked, "How old were you when your mother died?"

Funny question, but he answered with ease. His father had taken both Heidi and him to therapy to help address their grief. Cal harbored no leftover, complicated feelings. "I was eleven. Mom was fifty-three. I was a bit of a later-in-life surprise for her and dad, though welcome, or so she said." He was referencing the statement Bryony had made about him being an unwelcome surprise, trying to get a rise out of her, but she seemed to miss it.

"How's your father doing?" she asked.

"He lives alone in the old homestead. A bit worrisome. He's fallen a few times, but he doesn't want to move."

"Oh, my," Bryony said. "But your sister lives in Cleveland. Does she help?" The distance in her eyes faded. She seemed interested in him again, her attention back at the table.

"She does. Heidi is ten years my senior. Lucky for me, she's produced a slew of lovely children and grandchildren who claim me as their uncle and grand-uncle extraordinaire. They were quite angry about my moving here, and not quiet about it."

"Sad and sweet at the same time." Bryony smiled. "But you'll be moving back at the end of the school year."

"I have no solid plans at this point," he said, for the first time realizing a longer stay in Fieldstone was not out of the question. The truth was, he could do whatever he wanted, stay or go wherever he wanted.

She nodded, smiling, and he was utterly taken in by her appearance, her presence, the warmth he experienced when he looked in her eyes. She was someone he could stay for, but before this thing with Bryony went any further, he had to ask. "Do you ever dream about moving away, maybe finding an island getaway, hanging out on a beach, or jetting off to South America?" How serious was Bryony Green about staying put? He knew he was moving a bit fast to ask, but he didn't want a repeat of Leslie.

"Beaches…." Bryony said, her smile fading again, her voice trailing off.

"You know, the good life. Retire in a warmer climate. Work on the tan. No strings, no ties, day in, day out, fun in the sun?" He knew he sounded like an infomercial, but he had to ask.

"Um, I used to vacation in Florida." Her right hand pushed her hair behind her ear.

Cal could not get a read on her response, so he pursued the topic again. "Brazil for instance. You could start a whole new life in Brazil. You could bake pies in Brazil."

"You know, Cal…." Bryony's face appeared drained of color. "I have a headache coming on. Mind if we cut this short? I'll do better tomorrow if I take something and go to sleep."

"No problem." A headache would explain the way she had been fading in and out since they arrived. "I've had a migraine or two in my life. Do you get them often?"

"Not a habit with me, but I know better than to ignore them." She was up and out of her chair before she finished her sentence.

Cal left money on the table and followed her out the door. She said little on the way home, and he tried to be quiet. He remembered what headaches could do to him, and he didn't want to add to hers. After pulling into her driveway, Bryony opened the door and stepped out of the car before Cal could turn off the engine.

"Thanks. I had a good time," she said, shutting the door a bit harder than necessary and walking herself to the front door.

Stunned by the abrupt ending to what he had considered a propitious beginning, Cal watched until she turned and gave a quick wave before closing the screen door behind her.

He pulled out of the driveway and headed home, but his mind remained on Bryony. Should he be concerned about her? Sudden headaches could be a symptom of a serious medical condition. Should he call her?

Cal circled the block. As he approached her house, he could see lights on in the living room and toward the back of the house. She was okay. He was being overly concerned. Calling her would be a bit too much.

He drove home thinking about how he disliked the way she had clammed up. He would have liked staying with her, even if she felt unwell. If he needed help, she might be the first person he called for assistance. Cal considered the enormity of that assumption. He wanted to see her as available for him because that left him less lonely, when in fact he knew so little about her.

For instance, he had learned earlier this week that she spent time helping her friends Maggie and Howard. What other commitments soaked up the time and attention of Bryony Green?

Starting a relationship with another human being was hard.

He did, he reminded himself, have one uncomplicated connection.

Bailey had no secrets. Bailey made his needs known and appreciated every attempt to provide for those needs. When he had no immediate needs, he napped.

At least his dog would be happy to see him.

# BRYONY WILTS

Sluggish, Bryony dragged herself into the shower on Monday morning. Sunday had been a stay-in-bed-and-read day ending with her first attempt at Shaker lemon pie, number twenty-seven on the list. She'd been skeptical, unsure how sliced lemons in a pie with a top crust would stack up to the more common custard-with-meringue version of lemon-based pies, but as with every other pie on her list, this one surprised her.

The marriage of sweet to tart worked. Her stomach—fully linked with her brain in the scaling of relationship satisfaction when it came to ingredients—would have rebelled against too much of either. But while her gut aced pie testing, she couldn't get a read on how to think about Charity's offer or the date with Cal.

He had texted once, asking if she was okay. She had answered with a brief, "Resting," and hoped he would get the hint. He must have because he didn't text again.

Stepping out of the shower to buff dry with a fluffy orange towel, she thought again about the disaster Lillian would reference as a "first date" with Cal. It had all seemed perfect until the saucy new waitress practically sat on Cal's lap as she took their order. And then Cal launched into asking about retirement to a beach location.

Bryony stood at the sink, looking in the mirror. She could have been honest with him. "I was offended by the waitress's behavior," she could have said, and, "No beaches for me."

If sandy shores were a requirement, he could have politely seen the evening through and never asked her out again. Being honest with him might have left her feeling intact because she would have asserted herself. She would have been proud she took a stand. Instead, she had collapsed into herself like she always did.

Maybe she always would. Maybe she should accept Charity's offer. Maybe she belonged in a swivel chair all day long, her eyes locked on a computer screen. She didn't need a man. In particular, she did not need a man who would upend her life, expecting her to fly off and retire to a South American beach.

Fully attired for the day at hand, she entered the kitchen for a quick bite, still coaching herself, reasoning herself into acceptance of the inevitable.

Cal needed a woman with adventure in her spirit. He needed someone like… every woman who came to mind would be a better choice. Anyone would do for Cal, anyone but Bryony. At this delayed stage in her life, discovering her own desires and setting her own expectations required constant attention. Bryony had no time to live up to someone else's. And she had no intention of moving away. She liked Ohio. She liked Fieldstone. She was going nowhere because being here now was good enough for her.

She opened the refrigerator door for the carton of orange juice. The pie, minus one piece, sat on the top shelf, a reminder of her commitments—to complete the pie list, and to piece together her life based on her own thinking and inclinations. She'd think about Charity's offer later.

When life serves you lemons, make Shaker lemon pie. The thought made her smile.

By the time she arrived at the coffee shop, her thoughts were less unsettled, her heart less erratic, her legs less heavy.

"How did the first date go?" Lillian asked.

"Fine," she answered.

"Fine?"

"Yes, fine." No need to argue about semantics. Lillian would label the event however she wanted. "We ate at the Chinese place, went to a movie, and had coffee at Dewey's."

Bryony put her purse under the counter, went to the back of the work area, and washed her hands. When she returned to the counter, she picked up a stack of napkins and headed out to check the tables.

"Will you stop?" Lillian intercepted and took the napkins from Bryony's hands. "Talk to me, Bry. How did the date go?"

Bryony dropped her shoulders and tried to stare Lillian down. Stare downs had never worked in the past either. In one motion, Bryony pulled a chair away from the nearest table and plopped down. "It was wonderful," she said. "Until it wasn't."

Lillian grabbed a chair and scooted in beside Bryony. "What happened?" Overhead lights glistened off tinted lips.

"What color is your gloss?" She pointed to Lillian's lips. "It matches the purple in your shirt."

"It's not purple—it's eggplant." Lillian's lips went pouty, and her nose wrinkled. "Don't change the subject. Tell me about your date with Cal."

Bryony laced her fingers and placed them in her lap. Her carefully constructed bravado slipped further. "I had so much fun getting dressed," she started. "He picked me up and looked at me like I was beautiful."

"Did you hold hands?"

With a heavy sigh, Bryony said, "No." Painful to admit even to herself, she had wanted him to touch her, but she had been too shy to let him know. "I don't want to talk about it." She stretched her neck to one side, the other, down, and back.

"What happened?" Lillian asked, less insistent, tender now.

As little as Bryony wanted to relive the overall experience, to not tell Lillian would be worse. Lillian would not rest until she understood why there would be no further dates.

"We had a great time at dinner," Bryony said. "He picked the movie and chose what he thought I would like."

"The one starring Pierce and Sullivan?"

Bryony nodded.

"That was sweet of him," Lillian said.

Sweet, yes, but that wasn't the point. Bryony pressed on. "We went to Dewey's after the movie, and everything was going well until the blonde snorkeler—I mean waitress—threw herself at him, and he asked about whether I ever considered retiring to a beach home. The whole mess with Nathan—and every failed relationship before that—came flooding back." Bryony paused and smiled. "But I'm okay. I realized again this morning, I'm good alone."

Lillian leaned in. "You do know that waitress is Mark and Sherry's granddaughter. And I'm pretty sure she's all invitation, no action. Sherry was the same way when she was young. Remember? All talk and bouncy walk."

Now Bryony realized why the waitress seemed so familiar. Knowing she was Sherry's granddaughter completely wiped out her resemblance to the snorkeling instructor. The waitress was her flirtatious grandmother reborn. And the truth was, Cal had not given the girl any indication of interest. If anything, he had looked a bit horrified.

But there was the invitation to think about retiring south. And if Cal was serious about Florida or becoming an expat, she might as well give up now. "There will be no happy ending for me." Bryony reset her shoulders before declaring, "And I'll be okay without one."

"You do this every time," Lillian said.

"Do what?"

"Run for the hills."

"I'm not running anywhere," Bryony said. "I'm sitting right here, right where I belong, not running." At least for now, but would she run back to her old job? Falling back into her old life would be so easy, seductively comforting. She wasn't ready to discuss that with Lil.

"How did the date end?" Lillian asked.

"I said I had a headache and asked him to take me home."

"Maybe it wasn't a total disaster." Lillian leaned forward again and patted Bryony's arm. "I have a feeling he won't give up easy."

Bryony picked up the napkins and stood to argue her point of view. "Last week he suggested I think about starting a pie business, and on Saturday night he asked if I was interested in retiring outside of Ohio. As if a person my age can start a business, close it or sell it in a few years, and start again somewhere else. Obviously he doesn't take me seriously, just like Dad and Mitch."

"Are you thinking about starting a pie business?" Lillian asked.

"It's just an idea. I probably won't. But that's not the point. The point is, he didn't take me seriously."

"Hold on, Bry." Lillian reached up and snatched the napkins, placing them on her lap. "He's asking you about your future plans." Bryony tried to retrieve the napkins. Lillian blocked the attempt with both hands and a half turn. "How do you know he's interested in a beach house? Maybe he was making small talk. You watched a movie about a couple at the beach."

"Can I get back to work?" Bryony asked, irritated with Lillian's sensible analysis.

"Don't take this wrong," Lillian said. "But while I love every inch of you, you're too hard on people, including yourself. You like this man, maybe more than you have liked any other man."

"I know." Bryony sat down again and buried her face in her hands. She did like Cal. She dropped her hands and looked at her friend, searching for support. "But why would I consider a serious relationship at this stage of life when I could start my own business." Or work for Charity. Ugh. Too many options now.

"I love my coffee shop," Lillian said. "But it's no substitute for family."

"Easy to say when you're the woman who has it all." Bryony put her elbow on the table and laid her temple on her hand, propping her head. "I don't have a family. Maybe having my own business could be my comfort in old age." Could working for Charity last into her post-retirements years? Maybe. Bryony knew a CPA who had continued to work into her early nineties.

"You can't snuggle at night with fiduciary success." Lillian stood, put the napkin stack on the table, and pushed her chair in. "But have it your way. Look at your dad. Maybe you'll find an Alma, or an Elmer, when you're old and gray."

"I'm already gray, partially." Bryony used her free hand to sweep her bangs to the side.

"And so incredibly cute and adorable!" Lillian pinched Bryony's cheek as she walked back to the work area.

Her best friend ended all disagreements with a joke or a compliment. Bryony sighed, picked up the napkins, pushed herself out of the chair once again, and refilled the napkin holders. She wished she could be more like Lillian. Calm when calm counted. Feisty when a fight arose.

Never an obvious fighter, Bryony's way of staying alive was slow and steady, the ability to thrive in unlikely places. She was the dandelion sprouting up between cracks in a sidewalk.

Her mood improved as the morning commenced. By the time the first rush ended and the fixtures settled into their spots, Bryony stopped worrying about Cal Forster and put herself back in the rhythm of the day, the tempo set by choosing a CD of background music featuring Lillian's favorite female jazz singer.

As she returned to the work area after cleaning a few tables, Abby stopped her.

"Miss Green?" Abby said. "I almost forgot to ask. My grandmother lives where your dad lives, and she said you brought in a sugar cream pie."

"You're Alma's granddaughter, right?" Bryony asked.

"Yes!" Abby lit up. "I am! Grandma said you make the best sugar cream pie she's ever eaten."

"I haven't had a piece of sugar cream pie since my wife died," Mr. Parker said, lowering his newspaper, his eyes misty.

"I wondered," Abby said. "Could I buy one from you for Grandma? I'd like to surprise her."

"You don't have to pay me," Bryony said. "I'll bring one in next week."

"Me, too?" Mr. Parker asked. "But I'm gonna warn you, if it's anything like the ones my wife used to make, I won't stop with one."

Bryony smiled. "I'll bring one in for you, too." She glanced over at the third fixture. Etta continued to stare at her laptop screen, tapping on the keys, engrossed in whatever she did every day. Bryony deliberated about offering a pie to her, too, but chose to not interrupt. Something about Etta scared her a little. She didn't want to bother her unnecessarily.

# CAL PERSISTS

*A*fter texting once, Cal had decided not to bother Bryony anymore on Sunday. Instead, he visited with his father on Zoom, and called Heidi to talk about Halloween plans.

On the videoconference, his father complained Heidi would worry him to death about the ways he might die if he insisted on living at home alone.

On the phone, Heidi complained Cal's absence put her in the position of bearing full responsibility for ensuring their father's safety. She provided a sample of what—Cal assumed—she fed to her father on a daily basis. *What if he fell? What if the house caught on fire? What if someone broke in and hurt him?*

*What if he hired someone to help?* Cal had asked, but Heidi shot down the idea as it hung in the air still touching his lips, countering with, *What if the paid caregiver rips off Dad? What if they hurt him? What if they marry him?*

The last suggestion made Cal laugh so hard Heidi couldn't help but laugh, too, while continuing to insist those kinds of things happened all the time. *Read People Magazine or Star,* she had said, making him laugh all over again.

All of the love and laughter had given him a good night's sleep.

On Monday morning, he woke with one mission in mind, to stop at BeanHereNow to see Bryony. He waited until after school, so he didn't have a deadline to meet. When he entered the coffee shop, he strode to the counter. Bryony finished with the person in front of him, and Cal started to ask how she was feeling, but stopped when she looked at him.

"What will you have?" she asked. She looked pale. Maybe the headache had hung on.

"I guess I'll have a latte." He waited until she turned her back to make the latte before asking, "Is everything all right?"

"As good as it can be," she said. She set the steaming cup on the counter and snapped the lid on it.

He pulled his wallet out of his back pocket and found his credit card. "Are you sure?"

She forced a mechanical smile. "Peachy."

He held out the card. "What's up, Bryony?"

Lillian appeared at Bryony's side and snatched the card from Cal's hand. "Bryony seems distracted today, Cal. Why don't you two have a seat over there and chat for a few minutes? Maybe you can help her focus."

Bryony started to protest, but Lillian lowered her chin and raised her eyebrows. Cal had never seen a more perfect version of, *Not another word out of you.* Bryony seemed to understand as she raised her hands, palms toward Lillian, in a clear response of, *Okay, I surrender,* and led the way to an empty table in the far corner of the shop.

When they were both seated, Cal decided to wait for Bryony to explain. Whatever was going on, she did not want to talk about it. He would not push her.

He didn't have to wait long.

"There was a guy," she began.

"Is he still around?" Cal asked. Mitch had mentioned

someone dumping her—idiot—but maybe she was dating someone else now. He had considered asking, but saw no signals to indicate there might be another guy.

She shook her head. "No, he's not around, at least not here. As far as I know, he is far far away, and I'm happy he's gone." She seemed to lighten up.

Cal relaxed.

"He's not around because he broke up with me last year." She paused there, lowering her head, but raising her eyes to indicate implied meaning. "After he met someone else at the beach."

"The beach?" Cal asked.

"The beach," she repeated.

Shrugging his shoulders, Cal gestured confusion with his hands and said, "I don't get it. He was a jerk. What does that have to do with me?"

"Are you planning to move south someday?" Bryony asked. "Do you want to retire to a life of hanging out on a beach?"

"No, why?" Perplexed, Cal wondered if Bryony had confused him with someone else. "I don't hate going to the beach, but it's not one of my favorite spots. I'm more of a woods and rolling hills kind of guy."

Bryony leaned forward. "So, why did you start asking me about Brazil?"

"Right." He had raised the question, hadn't he? "I'm sorry, Bryony. I should explain."

He told her about Leslie, how she had asked him to marry her after announcing her plan to move to Brazil. "I thought she was joking at first," he said. "But she had planned it all out. She had studied Portuguese for a year without telling me."

"Why didn't she talk to you about her plans earlier?" Bryony asked.

"She said she wanted to surprise me," Cal answered.

"Brazil's a big surprise." Bryony seemed more at ease, the blood returning to her cheeks, turning them to a soft pink.

"She bought an engagement ring for me," Cal said. "We were standing on the edge of the football field on graduation day. She opened a velvet box to wave a shiny silver ring with a huge diamond under my nose."

"Sounds like a bit much," Bryony said.

"It was hideous," Cal said.

"Did she go?" Bryony asked.

"Oh, yes," Cal answered. "But she's not down there anymore. She came back in six months, sick of the weather, homesick. She wanted to resume our relationship."

"And you didn't?" Bryony asked.

"No," Cal said. "I was over it. Remember when I told you the one thing I can't forgive is when someone hurts my students?"

Bryony nodded.

"I guess another is when people I should be able to trust lie by omission. Leslie betrayed me when she didn't tell me about her plans. I was totally blindsided. My buy-in was assumed, an afterthought, if thought of at all. I don't have room in my life for one-sided relationships anymore." Cal glanced at his watch.

"Do you need to go?" Bryony asked.

"No, no." Bailey could wait a bit longer. "So, now you know the bizarre reason for my beach question, a kind of preemptive strike at the possibility of another nutcase like Leslie." He winced. "Oh, that sounded terrible." He put his hands over hers. "I promise you, you don't strike me as someone who would turn out like Leslie."

Bryony smiled. "I understand." She didn't move her hands, which Cal took as a sign that they were past this latest glitch. "I guess I should explain my strong reaction."

"I'd like to hear." He smiled encouragement.

"The guy," Bryony said.

"The guy who dumped you at the beach."

"Yeah." She laughed. "It sounds kind of pathetic now, but we were together for a long time, and then he left me for a young gorgeous snorkeling instructor—who, by the way, bore a strong resemblance to the waitress last night, at least in low lights—while we were on vacation in Florida."

"No!" Cal said, overstating his disgust, making her laugh, mentally noting again the need to address Marabelle's behavior.

"Yes!" she said. "He did." She withdrew her hands to comb stray hairs from her face. "And the thing is, now I'm glad he did because he'd talked me out of baking. He said I was making him gain weight."

"How could he blame you for that?" Cal asked. "Were you force feeding him while he slept?"

"No." Bryony laughed again. "But seriously"—she sobered her face—"he reminded me a lot of my dad and Mitch. I guess I'm used to the men in my life telling me to stop doing what I love."

"Wow," Cal said. "Talk about family dynamics."

"Cal." Bryony looked directly into his eyes. "Only teachers and counselors talk about family dynamics."

"And yet we are all affected." Cal wanted to reach out again, but moved his hands to his thighs, forcing them to stay put by drumming his fingers.

"I don't want you to get the wrong idea about Mitch," she said. "He's a good man, but I feel like I don't exist when I'm around him. Like there's only enough air for him. Like I'm suffocating."

"Don't let him smother you, Bryony. There's room for both of you in the world."

She sighed. "He'll try to discourage me if I decide to do something daring, like start a pie business. He's so negative about me taking risks, doing what makes me happy."

"Being negative about pies is like being negative about puppies," Cal said. "You should never listen to people who aren't mad for puppies and pies." His hands started to rise, but he pushed them down again. "Listen, don't let Mitch or anybody else smash your dreams. Let the world hear from you, Bryony. You'll never know where the pies will take you until you bring them to fruition."

Bryony shook her head. "Worst pun ever, Mister Forster."

"I am so happy you noticed. Your ability to catch on quickly encourages me to continue to ask you out. So, what do you say? Try again?" he asked.

"I'd like to," Bryony answered.

Lillian appeared at the side of the table, sliding Cal's credit card in front of him. "You two okay now?"

"Yes, Lillian," Bryony said.

"Thanks," Cal said as he palmed the card.

"My pleasure," Lillian said before walking away.

Cal knew she was not talking about the card.

When he reached his car, his phone rang, and he checked caller ID before answering. Charity's friend, Susie. He should answer, at least to apologize for not responding to her last three voicemails. But what would he say? *Sorry, Susie. Starting a new relationship, and it's been a little rocky. Don't have the bandwidth to add your charming presence to the mix?* He'd think of something more proper later.

Right now, he wanted to bask in the warmth of Bryony's willingness to keep going, even when she was confused and unsure.

His own family dynamics notwithstanding, he had to admit his sister had been right when she said it would happen to him someday. And though he might not tell her any time soon, he had to acknowledge, at least to himself, he was smitten.

# BRYONY'S PAST IS NOT HER FUTURE

*E*nding a brief phone chat with Cal, Bryony smiled and went back to work cleaning the service counter.

She was in love like never before, and she knew it.

Since their mutual confessions about past failed relationships, Bryony now thought of her life in terms of BC and AC, Before Cal and After Cal. Before Cal, she had more time to herself. After Cal, she had more fun, even when she was alone. Before Cal, she had worried about Mitch's worries. After Cal, she rarely had time to worry.

Between dates, dog-walking, and phone calls three or four times a day, joy filled her life, maybe for the first time ever. He had asked if she would accompany him to Cleveland for a Halloween party with his family. She declined, of course. They had only been seeing each other officially for a few weeks. But she wondered if she should have accepted the invitation.

Having Cal in her life felt more natural than breathing. With one foot in reviewing their most recent interaction, the other in the BeanHereNow moment, any urge to wonder, *Is it real? Can it last?* fluttered away, no match for the swirling upward trend of energy Cal brought to her life.

Without telling anyone about Charity's offer, not even Lillian, Bryony had declined. That phone call had garnered more self empowerment than any of the self-help books or videos Bryony had devoured during the transition to her new, improved life.

Another customer approached the counter and said, in an artificially deep voice, "Bryony Green! I haven't seen you in years."

The woman's face appeared as if she had just come from makeup for the next scene in her starring role. Bryony looked beyond the age-defying foundation, concealer, blush, eye liner, mascara, and bold red lipstick. "Susie?" Surely there were some well-hidden scars. Nobody her age could look that young.

"You didn't recognize me right away, did you? I'm thrilled." Susie leaned forward and whispered behind her hand. "I put a lot of my ex's money into this face."

"Susie Quatman." Bryony breathed out slowly. "It's been a few years. What would you like?"

Lacquered fingernails tapping the counter, Susie deliberated while Charity Henderson stepped through the door and walked to the counter.

"Hi, Bryony. I'd like a chai tea."

Bryony nodded and moved to fill a mug.

Susie had been Charity's number one henchwoman in high school, putting into play any number of ploys designed to degrade the less popular students. Bryony had been on the receiving end more than once.

"Five dollars, please," Bryony said.

Charity started to open her purse, but Susie interrupted with a throaty command. "Let me pay!"

Mr. Parker looked up from his crossword puzzle, seemed to assess the situation, and returned his eyes to the paper beneath his pencil.

While Susie ordered her drink, Etta arrived for the day. She sat down at her usual table, pulled out her laptop, and opened it.

Having completed her order, Susie swung away from the counter and called over to Etta. "Excuse me. We were going to sit there."

Etta cocked her head to the side, the overhead lights glinting off her nose ring, her black hair moussed and standing on end.

"Yes, you." Susie pointed first at Etta, and then away from Etta's table. "Please move your computer elsewhere."

She turned back to the counter. "Will you please clean off that table, Bryony? Charity and I called that spot."

Astonished by Susie's use of a phrase which should have been held back in high school, Bryony found herself lost in the memory of how the popular kids had "called" the picnic table in the shade, the first row in the auditorium, the corner booth at the downtown diner.

Forcing herself back into the present, she managed to say, "There are plenty of open tables."

"But we want that one." Susie turned again to Etta. "Please move your stuff so Bryony can clean the table for us. We're ready to sit down."

"How can this be your table?" Etta asked, "When my butt's in the seat and yours is not?" Henry Winkler could not have done a better impression of Fonzie.

Mr. Parker and Abby looked up, silent witnesses. A flashback cry of *girl fight* rang out in Bryony's head.

Susie sneered and began to huff a reply, but Charity touched her arm. "Plenty of tables over there."

After Bryony served her coffee, Susie threw a toxic glance at Etta and followed Charity to another table as far from Etta as possible.

Some might have called Etta's behavior rude, but Bryony liked to think of it as evidence of a hidden superpower, one for which Bryony yearned.

In high school, nobody crossed Susie or Charity. Bryony's adolescent self fist-pumped power to the little people as she gathered a gift to pay homage. She carried it through the opening in the counter with both hands and placed it gently before her new hero.

Etta looked down at the plated bagel. "I didn't order anything."

"It's a gift," Bryony said.

"What for?"

"For being a valued customer," Bryony answered. "Cinnamon raisin."

"My favorite." Etta looked up and smiled.

The past scariness disappeared. Underneath the piercings and tattoos lived someone who could be counted on, the expression on her face pleasant, knowing, kind.

Bryony returned to her post.

All customers served and satisfied at present, Bryony moved to the back of the workspace and slipped on disposable plastic gloves to shift warm bagels to the baskets lining the wooden shelves. A wave of confidence started to take hold inside her, something akin to what she had read about in those self-help books. With this newfound sensation, images of what she wanted to do with the rest of her life burst forth, a full blown vision.

Lillian returned from an errand. "Did you see Charity and Susie out there?" she asked, and answered herself right away. "Of course you did. You waited on them." She washed her hands at the small white ceramic sink beside the door to her office.

Bryony had lost interest in Charity and Susie the second her future life materialized in her mind.

"I do want to make pies," she said.

"I love your pies. " Lillian rubbed her hands dry on a white towel. "Bring one in tomorrow."

"You don't understand. I want to make pies every day."

"Like a business?" Lillian asked.

"Yes, like a business." Like the business of how she would spend the rest of her life.

"All of a sudden you're sure?" Lillian asked. "Where did this decision come from?"

"Pies," Bryony repeated. They didn't always come out perfect —crust baked a little too long, or filling a tad too sweet—but one could always adjust the amount of sugar or the temperature of the oven for the next batch. Unlike most of life, pies were within her control. She could do this.

Lillian looked at Bryony, one eyebrow arched, and asked, "What happened?"

"I'm serious, Lil. I want to make pies. Let's talk." Bryony grabbed two mugs and headed for the coffee pot.

When presented with the steaming coffee, Lillian took the mug, and with a deadpan delivery said, "Okay, if any other customers come in, I'll have Mister Parker tell them to serve themselves and leave the money on the counter."

Bryony rolled her eyes. "The morning rush is over. Let's split a bagel. I'll bring a few chairs behind the counter." She was already moving toward an unoccupied table to collect the chairs.

"I'll butter the bagel," Lillian said, the concern on her face shifting to an expression of humoring one who may have gone bonkers.

Unconcerned about whether or not Lillian thought she was bananas, Bryony situated the chairs far enough away from the customers to allow for privacy, but close enough to tend to anyone who approached the counter. She settled onto one chair and patted the other. "C'mon, Lillian. Sit. Let's talk."

"What's gotten into you?"

"I want to start my own business." She remembered the strength behind Etta claiming her space. Bryony wanted her own space, too. She wanted to delight in the messy reality of what it would take to visualize and create a business doing what kept her centered in her own superpower. She wanted to bake pies.

Lillian sat against the chair back, her spine straight, hands clasped in her lap. "When did you decide this?"

"I have realized"—Bryony lowered her voice further—"that I am going to die an utter failure if I don't do something meaningful, memorable, fun, starting now."

"Excuse me." Susie leaned over the counter as if searching for someone back there to help, though Bryony and Lillian sat in plain sight. "I'd like a refill. Can I get service here?"

Lillian started to rise, but Bryony rose quicker. "You sit. I'll do it." She took Susie's cup, refilled it, and passed it back across the counter.

"Thank you, Bry," Susie said. "Love your outfit. You always did know how to make classic seem a little less dull."

All through high school, Susie had made fun of Bryony's clothing. Was she still mocking her? Without thinking, Bryony quoted Coco Chanel. "'Fashion has two purposes—comfort and love.'"

Susie looked up and paused, her fingers a few inches from the mug handle.

Bryony followed up with, "I go for both, and if it looks good, that's a bonus. Let me know if you need anything else."

"My, oh, my," Lillian said when Susie was out of earshot, and Bryony again sat opposite. "What's gotten into you? You're on fire."

"I'm tired of not being heard, of not making my mark in the world."

"I think you can do anything you want," Lillian said. "And if pie is your thing, then I'll back you up in any way I can. I've been running this shop for ten years, and no one thought I'd make it."

"No one?" Bryony asked. "Not even Rick?"

"He thought it would sink us both, but he loves me, so he took the risk."

Bryony thought of Cal. He'd been the first to articulate the idea of selling pies, but she realized now the notion had been brewing in her since she started making the pie list so many years ago. Would he be as encouraging if he would be impacted by the outcome?

"Excuse me." Susie leaned over the counter again. "Can I buy some bagels to go?"

Again Lillian started to rise, but Bryony moved faster.

"Sure, Susie. What kind would you like?" Bryony snapped open a paper bag and positioned herself in front of the bagel bins.

"Which are the freshest?" Susie asked.

"All made fresh today."

"You make them here?" Susie asked.

"We have them shipped raw from a shop in Columbus, and we bake them here."

Susie deliberated, one finger lodged in her right dimple.

Seconds passed. Bryony counted. By ten, her irritation decreased. By twenty-five, she wondered if Susie tested her. By forty, she knew Susie played some kind of game. By sixty, Bryony knew who was winning. She stopped counting and smiled. "Take your time, Susie. I've got all day."

Susie flipped her hand away from her face and said, "Oh, it doesn't matter. Put a variety in a bag. I'll take a dozen."

Bryony filled the bag and rolled the top to close it. Triumphant, she handed it to Susie and ran her card.

Before leaving the counter, Susie said, "I'm hosting a gathering at my parents' house this Saturday night. A few of the girls from high school will be there. Would you like to come?"

In any other circumstance, Bryony might have pointed out the "girls" were in their mid-to-late fifties, but she stood on the polite side of the counter. "What a nice invitation," she said. "I'm busy, but I appreciate your thoughtfulness."

"Come on over if you change your mind," Susie said. "You know the house, right? The party starts at eight." She started to leave, but stopped, throwing a final jab. "Oh, and leave your husband at home. You are married, aren't you?"

Bryony took a breath and held her ground. "No, not married. Hope you have a great time."

Susie smiled and walked to the door to join Charity, who waved at Bryony before departing. Bryony lifted her hand, then returned to her seat facing Lillian.

"Where do I start?" she asked. "With a business?"

# "CAL COME HOME"

*A*fter school, Cal stopped by BeanHereNow as he did every day. The pumpkin Bryony and he had carved sat among other Jack-o'-lanterns. Garlands of orange, red, and yellow leaves, gourds, black cats, and full moons decorated the front of the shop,

Unusually affectionate, Bryony's fingertips feathered across his hand before clasping his credit card. She told him she had big news. He invited her again to come to Cleveland for the party on Saturday. She declined again, saying it was too soon.

She asked if he needed any help while he was gone. Would she like her to bring in his mail?

He liked her asking, but said his Saturday mail would be there when he returned Sunday night. He did not need help with his dog. He would take Bailey with him.

They spoke on the phone later in the evening about highlights of the day, and Bryony's big news. She told him she was serious about starting a pie business, though she had no idea how her plan would evolve over time. Maybe she could start at home, make them in her kitchen, sell locally to people she knew.

He encouraged her, made her promise to let him taste test every experiment, and vowed to not blame her for extra pounds around his middle. She laughed.

They were doing okay, better than okay.

Right before turning off his bedside light, Cal's cell phone rang. The voice on the other end disappointed his hope of Bryony calling again, but his warmth was honest, real.

"Heidi!" he said. "Can't wait to see you this weekend. How are the munchkins?"

"They're fine," she said, her voice weary. "But Dad fell this morning."

"Oh, no!" Cal took off his reading glasses and laid them on the book he had been reading. "Is he okay?"

"We took him to the ER, and they checked him out and released him. I made him come to my house. You know how he is. He wants to be in his own house. Can you come sooner?"

Cal rubbed his cheek with his free hand. He had planned to drive up Saturday morning. "I've been subbing in a trivia championship on Friday nights, and we made it to the final rounds."

"Trivia?" Heidi asked with disdain. "Where are your priorities, Cal?"

"It's work related, Heidi." Bailey jumped on the bed and snuggled his head into Cal's armpit. "The principal is the other member of the team. And I'm, uh, kind of dating his sister."

Heidi huffed. "Another train wreck?"

"I don't date train wrecks," Cal said, distracted as his mind worked through the classic dilemma of can't-be-two-places-at-one-time. Mitch would understand, he thought. Family trumps bar games. He would tell Mitch to find someone else. "I'll leave right after class on Friday."

"You're not bringing the sister with you, are you?" Heidi asked.

"I invited her twice, but she declined."

"Good for her!" Heidi said. "Because you couldn't possibly know her well enough already to bring her home to meet the family."

"You'd like her, Heidi. She loves making pies." He changed his phone to his other hand so he could rub Bailey's belly.

"We need you here. Come home and find someone in Cleveland. Besides, you're too old to start over someplace else. You need to be around people who know and love you."

"I'm not too old!" Cal looked at Bailey. "She says I'm too old. What do you think?"

"Is she there now?" Heidi asked, mild panic in her voice.

"I was talking to the dog." Bailey rolled onto his back and wagged his tail. "Tell Dad I'll pick him up Friday night and take him home."

"Thanks, Cal."

"Sleep well, Heidi."

"You, too."

Cal tapped the screen to disconnect the call. He knew his father was in good hands, and trusted Heidi's judgment about the fall being no big deal. Still, he looked forward to being able to see for himself. He tapped the screen again and put the call on speaker.

"Hello?" Bryony's sleepy voice answered.

"I'm sorry, did I wake you?" Cal asked.

"I was watching a movie, must have dozed off."

"Sure you won't come with me to the party in Cleveland?"

"I'm sure." Her voice sounded alert now, but still soft and sleepy. "Sure you don't need help with anything while you're gone?"

"All covered," Cal answered. "But you can soothe my anxiety about your brother's competitive spirit. We have a championship round Friday night, and I have to leave town. Dad fell."

"Oh!" Sounding fully awake now, Bryony asked, "Is he okay?"

"Heidi had him checked out. He'll stay at her house until I get there. They'll do okay together until Friday, I think. I hope." Cal settled against the pillow. "Will Mitch excuse my absence or give me detention?"

"Mitch is serious about his trivia," Bryony said.

"To take trivia seriously is an oxymoron because trivia, by its very nature, should be seen as something trivial."

"One might think so," Bryony said. "Unless they had grown up in a town where the details obscure the overall reality."

He loved the way she responded to him. Her mind worked well. "Are you calling your fellow townspeople blind to the bigger picture? Narrow-minded?"

"When it comes to trivia," Bryony said. "Mitch and his friends have tunnel vision, and the tunnel is lined with graffiti of obscure facts and useless information."

"No information is useless," Cal said.

"And now you sound like my brother. I'm not kidding. Mitch can be petulant when someone disappoints him."

"A true weakness for someone in school administration." Cal switched off the bedside lamp and sank into the bed.

"This is a small town. We have learned to tolerate the less-than-stellar qualities in our leaders because we prefer people who think like us, talk like us, and act like us."

"And by 'us,' you mean 'them,' right? Surely you're not as parochial in your thoughts and desires?"

"If by parochial you mean wedded to traditional ideas, I have to remind you I am as American as apple—"

He interrupted to finish her thought with, "Of course, the pie thing. But you did tell me," he said. "You want to make and introduce pies from all over the world. Your goal speaks of someone whose mind moves beyond the cultural boundaries of a small midwestern town."

She yawned. "I would like to see the world someday."

"We both have to rise early," Cal said. "Get some sleep." He stopped himself from finishing with "darling." They ended the call. Bailey jerked his paws and whimpered in his sleep.

Right before he fell asleep, Cal remembered Mitch's words after they won the semi-finals. *Okay, Forster. I'm counting on you. On the night of the finals, be there or say a prayer.*

Punching his pillow, Cal laid on his side and found the right spot for his head. He would cancel with Mitch in the morning. The man would have four days to find a replacement.

What was the worst that could happen?

After all, it was only a trivia contest.

# BRYONY'S PEACE PIE

On Thursday morning, Bryony pulled into a parking spot where she could see both the main entrance to the high school and the staff lot. The morning sun glinted in her side mirror. Fog hung low on the athletic fields behind the school.

In spite of knowing she was about to intervene in matters that were not her business, and out of her control, she chided herself for not acting sooner. Making a move before Cal had a chance to tell Mitch about pulling out of the tournament would have been better.

Last night she and Cal had their first real disagreement. Mitch acted childish, according to Cal, when he heard Cal had to leave town. Bryony tried to explain her brother's need for competition, how winning seemed to be his main pleasure, but Cal argued. He asked why Bryony defended her brother. He said Mitch was inappropriate, which was "putting it mildly." He said if he were being completely honest, he thought Mitch had always been a bit of a bully to Bryony. Cal's last comment stuck in her mind.

"Bad behavior tolerated," he said, "is bad behavior validated."

Instead of arguing back, Bryony invited him for a walk and took him to a park he had never seen. They held hands for the first time. Before he left, Cal kissed her forehead and apologized for being hard on her earlier. She told him to not worry. He was right, and she appreciated his lack of pretense.

She knew Cal didn't mean to put her in the middle of his trouble with Mitch, but she was. Instead of being pulled in two directions, she decided to see herself as a bridge, someone who might connect her brother and Cal, two men who were important in her life. She didn't want to see them warring.

Mitch's car travelled down the driveway. Bryony slid her hand under the foil-covered tin pie pan, warmth spreading through her fingers and palm. Lifting the gift, she slid out into the morning air and waited for him to park.

"What are you doing here?" Mitch sounded annoyed as he stepped out of his car.

"Peace offering," she said.

"Who's fighting?" He stepped over the cement parking block and approached her, his gray blazer unbuttoned and flapping in the breeze. "It's cold out here!"

"I have something to warm you up." Bryony held out the quiche.

Mitch sniffed under the edge of the covered tin. "Onion, sausage, and dried tomato?" he asked.

"Your favorite." Bryony had discovered she had, in fact, baked more pies on her list than she remembered, not because they were on the list, but because she had continued baking off and on over the years. Onion, sausage, and dried tomato was number fifty-five. Only eighty-two more to go.

"I remember the first time you made this." Mitch took the pie from her. "I was in college." He smelled it again before lowering it to waist level. "But I think you should stop feeding people and get a real job to feed your IRA. Oh wait"—he held up his hand feigning a change of heart—"don't listen to me. I'm only your brother."

"I appreciate your concern, Mitch." Bryony stepped forward and kissed his cheek.

"What's the kiss for?"

"For caring about me, and for going easy on Cal."

Mitch threw his head back in disgust. "He asked you to do this? Coward."

"He didn't ask me to do anything." Aware of other staff arrivals, and the close proximity of teachers walking by, Bryony lowered her voice. "Don't be too hard on him. He's a good guy."

"What's really going on with you two?" Mitch asked.

"I manage his student, and we are sort of dating."

Mitch was quiet.

"He can't show up for trivia at the bar because he has to go home to help with his father," Bryony said. "You know how it was when Mom was sick." Maybe Mitch would remember, though she had done most of the work.

Mitch smelled the pie again.

"So, let him off the hook," she coaxed. "Go easy on him. Okay?"

"Is this a bribe?" Mitch held up the pie. "Is this supposed to make me a gracious loser? Because without Cal, I will lose. He seems to know something about everything." A ray of sun emerged from a cloud and struck his face.

"I know someone else who knows something about everything," Bryony said. "He reads the newspaper and completes crossword puzzles every morning."

"Who?" Mitch looked at her sideways.

"His name is Mister Parker. He's a voracious reader."

"Is he reliable?"

"Like a Rolex." Bryony knew all of her brother's deepest desires.

"Let me know if he's interested." Mitch walked toward the building, raising the pie. "Thanks for this, and Bryony?"

She waited.

"Don't get too attached. He's leaving at the end of the school year."

When would he stop treating her like she was fifteen?

Bryony made it to the corner at the end of the drive by the time Cal arrived. They passed as she pulled onto the street and he into the driveway. He waved with a puzzled look on his face as she continued without stopping and drove away. She had wanted to avoid seeing him because he would wonder why she was there, and she didn't want to lie to him, by omission or otherwise.

She hoped her gesture with Mitch might ease Cal's day. She would do anything she could to help him.

# CAL PUSHES PRINCIPLE

Cal watched Bryony's car exit the school drive and disappear from view. She must have known she would miss his morning coffee run. What was she doing at the school, and why had she left right when he arrived? Had he offended her? Or worse, had she reached the end of her ability to tolerate his mega ability to meta communicate? He should tone it down. Good thing he would be gone for the weekend. She probably needed the rest.

A minute before the start of first period, Mitch came to the door of Cal's classroom and asked him to step into the hall.

"Am I in trouble?" Cal asked as he quietly closed the door behind him.

"My sister brought a pie to me today to manipulate me into being nice to you. She confirmed with me that you two are officially dating now. What happens when you leave? You'll break her heart, and she'll quit the measly job she has and end up on the street."

"You're making me late for my class to talk about this?" They were in a sitcom, right? Cue the laugh track.

"What are your intentions, Forster?"

"My intentions?" They'd already been over this. "My intention is to spend some time with your sister to get to know her." He enunciated like he was talking to someone new to English. "She knows the score, Mitch. If I leave in June, no harm, no foul." The football metaphors were beginning to wear on him, but he used them anyway, so Bryony's brother might finally hear him.

Mitch seemed to deliberate, started to speak, stopped himself, appeared to think again, and finally said, "I want you to know I talked to Justin Hicks. He won't be bothering your student anymore."

"How do you know?" Cal asked, unfazed by Mitch's absurd cross-examination, his frenetic pace. He'd never met the person who could outstrip the speedy lane-change of his own thoughts.

"I told him I would talk to his father if I heard any additional complaints about his behavior. I used to coach his dad. Great football player with good values, but he can be a mean son of a gun. You don't want to cross him."

Cal winced. What was life like for young Justin at home?

Mitch started to leave, but turned back. "Another thing. Did you help your students register to vote?"

That again. "I did not," Cal answered.

"You didn't?" Mitch looked puzzled. "Are you telling me you didn't order your students to register to vote or risk having their grades lowered?"

"I can deny the allegation with a clear conscience," Cal said. "I would never lower my students' grades for any heartfelt desire on my part, no matter how civic-minded."

Footsteps ran around the corner behind Cal.

"Walk!" Mitch commanded.

The footsteps slowed, and a short kid with red hair fast-walked past them, his head down.

"I had two parents call and express concern," Mitch said.

"One of them sits on the school board. How is it they both called and told me basically the same story?"

Cal shifted back and forth on his feet, quelling his snarky side. "I did offer my eighteen-year-old students extra credit for presenting evidence they were registered. I offered the same extra credit for those under eighteen if they wrote an essay on voting rights."

Mitch scratched his arm. "Yeah, they did say something like that, but it seems these parents have a legitimate concern. A few years back, a school teacher ran into legal problems because she helped her students register to vote."

"I know about the case," Cal said. "The teacher ran afoul of a ludicrous regulation, in another state, enacted to suppress voters."

"There are no laws to suppress voters," Mitch said.

After thirty years of teaching, Cal had reached the point where the ignorance of administrators failed to hook him. He was not going to argue voter suppression with Mitch any more than he would argue whether the world was flat or round. "Reading about the earlier case inspired me to take action," Cal said. "I checked. I am not breaking any laws."

"But it wasn't in the syllabus," Mitch said. He leaned forward, a former bulky offensive lineman.

"I teach what's in the syllabus," Cal said, inching forward himself. "Including the parts I find lame or distracting. I teach it all, and I teach it well."

"Separation of politics from education is vital," Mitch said. "When levies come up, we need voters on both sides of the aisle."

Cal spoke with restrained passion. "Every one of my students over eighteen registered to vote, and those under eighteen wrote thoughtful essays about voting rights. I teach civic duty, not politics. I would expect you, of all people, to want our students to become responsible, engaged community members."

Mitch stepped back a hair. "Calm down. This isn't a debate. Frankly, I don't care what you do in the classroom, as long as you don't date the girls and drink with the boys. I'll go back to those with concerns and settle them down. We don't want any problems around here, Cal. Next time you want to get creative with the syllabus, run it by me first, okay?"

"I need to get to class." Cal started to turn toward his classroom door.

"I'm not done yet." Mitch waved him back.

Cal looked at him, waiting.

"I've spoken with the head of the school board and it looks like the budget for your program will likely be cut next year."

"Cut?" Cal shoved his hands into his pockets to keep them under control. "I was hoping we… Chuck… could expand."

"Expansion's never going to happen." Mitch laughed. "We can barely afford to pay teachers."

"How much of a cut are we talking about?" The program could work with less money, Cal supposed.

"All of it," Mitch said. "They're going to reallocate the money to the STEM program. Science, technology, engineering, and math are the future. We need to develop new programs in those areas."

"STEM's important," Cal said. "But what about the people who need an extra hand to get there?" Most of his students wanted to work for a variety of reasons. His program kept them in school and increased the likelihood of graduation. "I'm not knocking STEM, but people also need to develop work skills and the confidence to know they can go out in the world"—he rolled his hand forward, trying to make a visual for progress—"which may result in them eventually going to a trade school or college."

"Like I said," Mitch said. "It's likely to be cut. All the more reason to not spend too much time getting to know my sister. Because even if you wanted to stay, there will be nothing to stay for."

Cal crossed his arms over his chest, reigning himself in. "How much did you push for the program, Mitch?"

"Not at all, Cal. I agree with the school board."

"Is this about Bryony?" Cal dropped his shoulders, squaring off. "Or the trivia game?"

"What?" Mitch's surprise seemed authentic.

"Are you trying to sink the program because you don't see me as a dependable team player, because I don't always follow your lead?"

"What an absurd idea. I'm not that shallow." Mitch's cell phone buzzed. He flipped it open and brought it to his ear. "Let me call you back. No, I did not say I would dress up like a turkey for a pep rally in November. Tell Brian to do it. He's the biggest turkey around here." He closed the phone and looked back at Cal. "What was I saying?"

"Brian's a bigger turkey than you are," Cal said.

"No, I mean about the—oh, yeah, the trivia game. I wouldn't allow my personal feelings to sway my professional judgment. What difference does it make anyway? You're the one who made it clear right from the start you'd be gone at the end of the year."

"Whether or not I'm here is irrelevant," Cal said. "The program is important. I'd hate to see it cut because you didn't see the value in it, or the value in someone like me."

"This has nothing to do with you, Cal. The program's a lost cause. They've been trying to eliminate it for years. I'm not surprised it's on the chopping block, and I'm telling you, there's no going back. It's a done deal."

Cal waited until his head felt less explosive. "Are we done here?"

"Yeah." Mitch cuffed Cal's shoulder and smiled. "Get in there and mold those young minds."

Cal stood in front of the closed door and watched Bryony's brother leave. Mitch opened his cell phone, put it to his ear before rounding the corner ahead, and disappeared from view.

The program would be cut after this year. Why did he care so much? Because he might lose something more important than a temporary assignment? This thing with Bryony could upend all of his plans. In the back of his mind he'd been wondering if Chuck would consider team-teaching. Then Cal would have a reason beyond Bryony to stay because he knew she wasn't ready to be the one reason, and he needed more time with her. He was willing to give her all the time she needed.

The last time Charity called, she said Chuck was feeling better, ready for visitors. Cal would call him at lunch.

In the meantime, he had a class to teach. He took a breath, let it out, waltzed into his classroom, and asked, his voice ringing with as much zest as he could muster, "Who's up next for their three minute marketing pitch?"

# NO CHARITY FOR BRYONY:
## PART II

$\mathcal{T}$he idea to bribe Mitch had seemed perfectly rational at four in the morning, but now Bryony was under-slept and overwrought. Would her plan backfire? If so, what was the worst that could happen?

Todd was out sick, and Lillian had left to attend to a family obligation. The focus required to serve a steady stream of morning customers by herself failed to dilute Bryony's worries. There was nothing she could do except wait for Cal's possible irritation about her interference.

Maybe upsets were a sign their relationship was moving beyond the polite phase. Maybe it was time to get real.

The fixtures had been served and were settled in at their regular tables. The line of customers trickled down until nobody stood at the counter. Bryony left the work area to clean off a few tables and muster the courage to talk to Mr. Parker about the trivia contest. She chastised herself for offering him up without asking first. She should know better than to listen to ideas cooked up and acted on when she should be sleeping. She blamed her behavior on her budding relationship with Cal. Men brought out something akin to adolescence in her, hormones gone wild.

As she passed Abby's table, Bryony commented on the tiny animal forming on the end of a crochet hook. She could see it was a gray elephant with pink inside his ears.

"It's the first in a series," Abby said. "I plan to make an entire menagerie."

Etta tapped away on her laptop keyboard. Bryony stepped over to her table and picked up an empty plate, then wiped the unused side of the table with a damp cloth. Etta seemed oblivious.

Moving to the next table, Bryony spoke to the man behind the newspaper. "Hello, Mister Parker, anything worth reading today?"

"Only if you're interested in sports, politics, human interest, fashion, cooking, or world news," Mr. Parker said. He lowered the newspaper and peered over his glasses. "We live in a fascinating world."

Bryony pulled out the chair opposite him. "Mind if I sit for a minute?"

His right eyebrow arched. "Sure, have a seat."

"I have a request," Bryony said, lowering herself into the chair. "My brother, Mitch, needs someone to fill in on his trivia team for a tournament, and I hear you might be the man for the job."

"Where did you hear that?" Mr. Parker asked.

"Todd told me he's never met anybody who knows as much as you do. And I see you reading the newspaper every day. Your resume is your daily routine."

"Where and when does this tournament occur?" he asked.

"Tomorrow night. The sports bar on Taft Street. They start at eight o'clock." Bryony held her breath as he deliberated.

"That'll interrupt my usual bedtime, but I suppose I can help out."

"Thank you, Mister Parker," she said in a rush of exhalation. She asked him to write his phone number on a fresh napkin.

"It's the least I can do," he said. "That pie was just like my wife's." He returned her pen, raised the newspaper, and disappeared behind it.

Bryony stood and pushed the chair back in gently, guessing he had dismissed her, but as she started to walk away, he lowered the newspaper again. "Thank you for asking me to help out." His voice was softer, his eyes misty.

She smiled. He raised the newspaper once more, and she knew with certainty this time the conversation over. One hurdle cleared, her worries about Cal calmed.

IN THE AFTERNOON, Lillian returned from transporting her granddaughter "from point A to point B."

Bryony greeted her with a cheery, "Hello! What a beautiful day, huh?"

"Charity and Susie are here again." Lillian exchanged her jacket for her apron.

"Yes, they are." They were customers to Bryony, nothing more. Every new sighting lowered her visceral response, desensitization in action.

"They've been coming in often," Lillian said.

"I guess we're the new hot spot in town."

"I ran into Charity the other day." Lillian crossed her arms and smiled. "Chuck continues to improve."

"Happy news," Bryony said.

"I thought you might want to know."

Bryony tried to brush off the comment. Only Lillian knew the endurance of Bryony Green's special fondness for the cute—then handsome—boy she met the first day Chuck moved to town.

"Charity has no idea how instrumental you were in keeping them together," Lillian said.

Bryony shrugged her shoulders.

She and Chuck met the day he moved into a house down the block. He asked about the local library. She gave him a tour of the town.

They became inseparable, for a time. Chuck called her his "best bud," and Bryony dubbed him her favorite neighborhood nerd. They had fun together, and though Chuck never tried to kiss her, or even hold her hand, Bryon confided in Lillian that she was ready, waiting, and wanting him to make a move.

But then Charity moved to town, and Chuck's interest in his neighbor shrank to times of angsty romance trouble. On those days, Bryony would walk with him and listen, always asking, "What do you want, Chuck?"

Chuck would always answer, "I want Charity." After wise counsel from the girl who had been his "best bud," and would never be his girlfriend, Chuck would reconcile, every time, with the girl who would someday be his wife.

"Did you know Cal knows Chuck?" Lillian asked.

"What?" Bryony dropped a bagel.

Lillian offered an empathetic grimace. "Chuck's the reason Cal took the job at the high school," she said.

"What are you talking about?" Bryony bent down to pick up the warm ring of dough.

"They grew up together as boys in Cleveland, before Chuck moved here. I thought you might not know since you hadn't mentioned it."

Bryony's solar plexus issued a sick little pang. Cal and Charity had a connection through Chuck? She thought she had transcended those old less-than feelings conjured up by flawless, perfect Charity Henderson. And here they were, back to plague her with the same mood-killing, mind-numbing, body-shaming potency as before.

She tossed the fallen bagel into the wastebasket. Cal said he came to Fieldstone because of an old friend, but he hadn't mentioned Chuck. The information grew around her like a prickly raspberry patch. Would dating Cal put her in the vicinity of the two people she had spent the last thirty-plus years avoiding?

"I wanted you to hear it from me"—Lillian's expression changed from bearer-of-bad-news to eyes-on-the-prize— "because I knew you would do what you're doing right now."

"What am I doing?" Bryony asked.

"You're letting yourself lose again, and this isn't a contest. Cal seems partial to you. Charity is not a threat. What happened in high school is ancient history." Lillian swatted Bryony's hip as she walked to the office.

"Ancient history," Bryony said, glancing over at the table where Cleopatra and Salome rose to put on their coats. Neither of them looked back before leaving the coffee shop.

Bryony plodded through the rest of the day, dreading the hour when high school students would rush in. She knew Cal would show up, and he did, right on schedule.

"What can I get for you today?"

He leaned on the counter, closing the distance between them. "Will you have dinner with me tonight since we can't do the movie on Friday?"

So, no obvious blow back from her efforts on his behalf, which was a relief, but he seemed completely unaware of her mood, which made sense. How could he have known that she just found out he was tangled up with her worst memories? She wanted to be with Cal. She knew she did. With tough resolve, she decided she could not let Charity get in the way one more time.

Just as she started to accept his invitation, Cal said, "I've been invited for dinner at the Hendersons. Chuck and Charity. Do you know them?"

Bryony choked back the affirmative reply on her lips and stumbled over her words. "Casually, it's a small town."

"I'd like you to come," Cal said. "I got some bad news at school today."

Had Mitch given him a hard time about canceling on trivia? Cal spoke again before she could ask.

"Mitch told me the school board will probably cut funding for the work study program next year. Cut it completely!"

"That's terrible," she said, doing a miserable job of feigning surprise. Mitch had warned her, and she had failed to pass on the information to Cal. So much for being a bridge. Too much pressure, and she collapsed because there was no way to maintain integrity with both of them at the same time. "Todd's been great for us."

"Right?" Cal straightened his back, and Bryony could see the taut muscles in his neck. Trim, fit, attractive, intelligent, and right in front of her, asking her to be with him. "I need to meet with Chuck," he continued. "Will you join us? I'd like your support."

"Chuck and you need to discuss business," Bryony said. No way was she going to dinner at Charity Henderson's house. "You and I can get together when you return from Cleveland."

"I'd really like you to come," he repeated. "And you're still welcome to come with me to Cleveland."

Conflicting thoughts pushed hard against the deep confusion of not knowing what to do next. Bryony's feelings were all over the place, riding high from the past few weeks of being with Cal, lower than low from the news of Cal's connection to Charity through Chuck.

And Cal seemed oblivious. He just kept talking.

"Sorry. I know it's rude to continue asking after a woman says no, but about tonight, I asked Charity if I could bring a date, and she said she would love the company." He leaned forward again and stage-whispered, "Their house is enormous.

Pool table, ping pong, theater room with a huge TV, a sauna. I'm sure you two could find something to do while Chuck and I talk."

Spending an evening with Charity Henderson in her pretentious home topped Bryony's list of not-going-to-do-that-ever. "I've been feeling a bit off today," she said, her voice catching.

Still oblivious, Cal countered with, "Sure I can't change your mind?" He cocked his head, wrinkles bunching the skin on his forehead.

Warmth returned to her midsection. "Did Bailey teach you how to beg with your eyes?"

"I'm not good at it, am I?" Cal asked.

On the contrary, those lovely blue eyes almost convinced her, but she stood firm. "You and I can reschedule. Do you want to order something?"

Cal looked around at the three young people waiting for their turn to order. He again faced Bryony. "No, thanks. Bailey calls. I'll call you later tonight?"

"Please do." The warm feelings bubbled inside again. He waved and ran, technically jogged, to the door.

When the line of teenagers dwindled, Lillian laid her hand on Bryony's shoulder and smiled. "That's funny," she said.

"You heard?" Bryony asked.

"The universe conspires to help you release grudges."

"Would you stop?"

"I have always said you won't find your soul mate until you forgive Charity Beaman for stealing the love of your life right out from under you."

"Chuck Henderson was not the love of my life."

"Now you're talking sense," Lillian said. "Maybe the world is in order, and you weren't meant to meet your soulmate until now. Maybe Chuck and Charity were meant to be together all along. Maybe the love of your life is Cal."

"I hope not," Bryony said, the words reflexive, untrue.

"Will you listen to yourself?" Lillian flicked her fingertips across Bryony's upper arm. "If you let Cal Forster slip away, I will never forgive you."

No words came. As much as she would like to protest, Lillian was right.

"Look." Lillian patted the place on Bryony's arm still stinging from the flick of frustration. "I know Charity was mean to you from the beginning. Her first day in a new school, she saw you and Chuck sitting together at lunch, and she set her eyes on him. I've always told you, she saw you as a threat. But Charity seems different now. She's changed in the last few years. I see her as approachable now, less regal."

"If a snake sheds its skin, it's still a snake," Bryony said.

"That is harsh, my friend. I think you would be happier if you could let go of old grievances. People can change."

Again, Bryony had no words. Lillian made sense, and Bryony admitted, at least to herself, pining for Chuck Henderson had become so much a part of her life she didn't notice it, like she didn't notice her heartbeat, or her breathing.

She remembered how Nathan's defection hurt in large part because it reminded her of Chuck choosing Charity instead of her. Every man she ever dated had been compared to the man she lost before he was a man. Except for Cal.

Not once had she considered how Cal stacked up to Chuck.

"Do you still have time to meet with me tonight?" Bryony asked.

"Are you still not planning to call Cal back and accept his invitation for dinner at the Hendersons?" Lillian asked.

"I am not planning to accept that offer, but I will answer the phone tonight when he calls."

"Will you?" Lillian asked.

In some small ways, Lillian was like Mitch. She liked to be right, and she liked to win. The big difference between Bryony's best friend and her brother was the extent to which Lillian being right coincided with Bryony's best interests.

"Yes, I will. I promise."

Lillian hugged Bryony around the shoulders. "There's hope for you two! What time shall we meet?"

"If I can leave a little early, I'll bring supper to your house at six."

"Perfect!" Lillian said. "Rick will love that!"

Bryony would pick up a few things on the way home and make the next item on her list. Chicken Pot Pie. An appropriate choice since she was too chicken to face her feelings about Chuck and Charity. So chicken, she knew she might choose to waddle away from Cal and remain cooped up in her safe, singular life for the duration. That's how chicken she might be, too chicken to change.

# CAL TRIES TO HELP

"Sorry your date couldn't make it." Charity Henderson ushered Cal into the two story reception area of her home. "I took the liberty of inviting Susie to join us." She led him down the wide hall and into what appeared to be the family room. In addition to two couches, matching recliners, a wall of book shelves above closed cabinet doors, and a wide screen television installed on the far wall, there was a bar at one end of the room.

Susie, wine glass in hand, and Chuck, empty-handed, were seated together on one end of the nearest couch. Her head leaned toward her pale, thin companion, a look of deep concern etched across her face.

They both looked up when Charity and Cal entered the room.

"Good to see you," Chuck called out, his voice stronger than expected.

"Hey, buddy." Cal sat on the armrest closest to Chuck and offered his hand.

Susie turned to Cal, her expression a little too attentive. Was he auditioning for a role?

"You haven't called me back yet," she said.

"Sorry about that," he said. "I have been so busy."

"We still have time." Susie tipped her glass in his direction.

"So, how's old Fieldstone High treating you this week?" Chuck asked.

"Still a huge culture change," Cal answered, his tension easing.

"Another world?"

"Another era at least," Cal said. "I feel like I'm teaching in 1957."

Susie laughed. "You are, dear."

Both he and Chuck paused to acknowledge Susie's comment, but returned to their two-way conversation in short order.

"Big city problems exist here," Chuck said. "But they're tempered with a good deal of old fashioned tradition."

"And a huge measure of economic wealth," Cal said. "I know you've suffered in the downturn, but from all accounts, Fieldstone is still able to provide jobs or some kind of assistance to the majority number of people living here."

"Here, here!" Susie held up her wine glass. "Let's hear it for good old Fieldstone, Ohio!"

If he were a betting man, Cal would lay down ten on Susie having started with a glass of wine, or three, before the one she now held aloft.

Charity handed Cal a glass of wine and settled herself on the other side of Chuck, her hand resting on his knee.

"Spending time here has been a bit dull," Susie said. "But after thirty years in Cleveland, I needed a break from the traffic, the noise, the stress. Fieldstone's so much cozier, don't you agree, Cal?"

"Mmm," Cal hummed over the rim of his wine glass. He finished swallowing and put the glass on the table. "I'm pretty partial to Cleveland. My family lives there."

"So, you won't be staying in Fieldstone after the school year ends?" Charity asked. "I hoped you would. I'm trying to talk Chuck into retirement."

Cal looked at his old friend. Had he not told his wife about the budget cut?

Chuck smiled. "She knows."

"Knows what?" Susie asked.

"I know the school board is threatening to cut Chuck's program out of the budget," Charity said. "They threaten every year."

"Is that why you all invited me tonight?" Susie asked. "Do you need to talk about fundraising?"

"The idea hadn't crossed my mind," Charity said. "But since you mentioned it, let's chat."

&#123;&#129;&#129;

BETWEEN BITES AT DINNER, they brainstormed strategies to address the impending funding cut. Susie displayed a superficial understanding of how to explore the problem. Charity, however, presented a new, impressive side of herself. She talked strengths, weaknesses, opportunities, and threats as well as any strategic planner Cal had ever encountered.

After she had made one more astute statement about how to strategize around saving the work study program, Cal shifted the course of the conversation to ask, "Where did you learn how to lead?"

Before Charity had a chance to answer, Chuck said, "When the kids were still in grade school, Charity was the youngest school board president ever. I always said if I'd been able to have the babies, Charity would have been the better breadwinner."

Charity shook her head and grinned.

Initially, Cal had wondered what Chuck saw in his wife

besides her poise and beauty. Now Cal was seeing a whole other side of her. She possessed the mind of an organizer, a developer, a shaker and a mover, and she knew how to use it.

"If I had inherited a load from my parents, I would have had children and volunteered, too," Susie said. "I moved to Cleveland with my husband, God rest his soul, and took the first job offered because Tom couldn't make enough to keep me happy." She slugged down the last of her wine.

"Tom's not dead, Susie," Charity said. "And I think he's been very generous."

"Oh, that he were, on both counts," Susie said, her voice higher pitched than before.

"Susie knows business development," Charity said. Cal could see that she was trying to reign in Susie's drunkenness.

"Yes," Susie said, sober now, at least in tone. "I have been the force behind promoting many small businesses, and I have written a few grants on the side."

"Cal has ideas about expansion," Chuck said. "Maybe you two should get together and see what you can come up with."

"You don't have to ask twice." Susie laid her hand over Cal's.

Cal pulled his hand back to pick up his wine. How did school funding dovetail with small business funding? He didn't see the connection, but he didn't know everything. Maybe Susie could offer something useful.

After another round of discussing ways to address the school board, the four of them took their coffee into the family room.

Charity and Chuck sat together on the couch. Cal chose the seat edge of the nearest recliner. Susie milled about the room picking up objects for inspection and setting them down again.

"That dinner was lovely," Cal said.

"The chicken and green beans were easy," Charity said. "But I can't take credit for the dessert. I picked it up in Columbus yesterday when I was shopping. You can't get a good pastry in Fieldstone."

"Oh, really?" Cal said. "I have a friend who's thinking of starting a pie business."

"One of your students?" Susie asked. She wandered over and sat on the armrest next to Cal.

"A friend," Cal said.

"Who is it?" Susie asked, leaning forward, her elbow on her knee, chin in hand, and fingers playing across her lips.

Cal didn't know what kind of script she was writing in her head, but he knew whatever the plot, she would see herself in the starring role.

"I haven't been given permission to share much information," Cal answered. "But do you all think a pie shop could make it in a town this size?"

"A specialty food business sets a town apart," Chuck said. "Look what ice cream did for Jerseytown."

"And chocolate for Grant City," Charity said. "Those towns have festivals every summer centered on their specialty food shops."

"Can you imagine Fieldstone becoming the pie capital of Ohio?" Susie said, straightening up, raising her arms to jazz hand as she continued. "We could score a feature in Small Town Ohio magazine, or be part of the show on PBS, the one where the celebrity goes around and highlights unique food in unlikely spots. Fieldstone's about as unlikely as they come!"

Charity and Susie talked on and on about the ways pie could revitalize Fieldstone. Every so often, Chuck would offer a suggestion, his face showing heightened color, a brightness in his eyes which had been missing when Cal arrived.

He wished Bryony had come with him. Cal was sure she would be excited by their encouragement, their ideas.

# BRYONY'S COMPANION PLANTS

*A*pparently Cal's evening with the Hendersons was so titillating, he didn't even bother to call until long after Bryony had gone to bed. She said she needed to sleep, steeling herself against the corrosive damage done by so many years of being an afterthought.

After the brief call, she lay awake most of the night, wondering how she could continue to see him if this is how it would be. She tried to reason herself out of backing away from him—he'd known the Hendersons all along and not been irresponsible about arranged plans with Bryony before last night—but old habits take on a life of their own when challenged by forces beyond one's control.

She went to work the following morning with red eyes and dark circles.

Cal had shown up for his morning coffee. Again, he didn't apologize for not calling earlier the night before. She told him she was too busy to chat, and he left with a smile and a wave, heedless of the barrier she sensed between them now.

Lillian noticed Bryony's worn down appearance, but accepted the insomnia excuse, she too suffering from that at times, which allowed for escape from relationship scrutiny. That bit of respite was the highlight of Bryony's day thus far. She rinsed a fresh cloth in warm water, grabbed the bottle of spray sanitizer, and moved beyond the counter to wash tables.

At Abby's table, she stopped to admire the young woman's current project, a baby blanket crocheted on the diagonal. "Taking a break from the animals," Abby said. "Check out the yarn."

Fingers stroking the surface, Bryony said, "It's soft."

"Bamboo," Abby said.

"I love it."

"I'd trade you an afghan for six pies," Abby said. "I could give Grandma one pie a month for half the year."

Imagining an afghan draped over the back of her couch in shades of green, a hint of pink, maybe a subtle yellow, Bryony said, "It's a deal."

"I'll bring in yarn samples tomorrow," Abby said.

"What can I trade for a pie?" Mr. Parker asked.

"How about cash?" The question came from the short-haired woman whose face, for once, was not buried behind her computer screen.

"I'd be happy to pay for a pie." Mr. Parker looked back at Bryony. "You name the price."

Bryony continued to look at Etta.

Etta shrugged her shoulders. "I heard you say you want to start a pie business."

Bryony turned her attention back to Mr. Parker. "Showing up for trivia night will be worth a second pie."

"I said I'd be there." He looked back down at his puzzles.

Abby resumed hooking and pulling her yarn, but Etta continued to watch Bryony, her laptop abandoned for the time being. Bryony approached Etta's table.

"Sit down for a minute," Etta said.

Bryony sat, the damp cloth clutched in her right hand.

"I'm not a busybody," Etta said. "But I can't help but hear what goes on back there"—she pointed to the work area—"because I sit right here every day. I would sit farther from the counter, but the opening and closing of the door makes me cold!" She smiled, and little lines crinkled at the corners of her eyes. "I keep hearing tidbits of information about you wanting to start a pie business, and you don't know me, but I think I can help you."

"How?" Bryony asked.

"I help small, independent food producers," Etta said. "I'm not saying you need my services at this point, but if you want to pick my brain, I'd be happy to give you information about how to sell your pies online, how to price them, and how to advertise them."

"Sell pies online?" Bryony asked.

"You can sell almost anything online," Etta said. "Here. Take a look." She tapped her keyboard and turned her screen toward Bryony. "Look at this. These prices range from twenty-three to forty-five dollars a pie."

"So much?" Bryony's eyes widened.

"Lots of money out there," Etta said. "Don't sell yourself short. I don't have time to talk right now, but like I said, if you want to talk some afternoon, I'm happy to help."

"Yes! I need all the help I can get." Forty-five dollars a pie? Unbelievable.

Etta smiled. "Now if you'll excuse me, I have to get back to the office." She pointed to the computer screen.

Bryony eased out of the chair. "Thank you, Etta." A giddy giggle tickled Bryony's belly. She squelched it. Way too soon to start celebrating.

The rest of the day breezed by, all worries about Cal and the Hendersons submerged by the prospect of selling the one product Bryony loved producing.

At four o'clock Cal arrived and ordered a latte.

Still afloat from knowing pies could be marketable and profitable, Bryony greeted him with less concern about where they would end up. For Heaven's sake, they had only been seeing each other a brief time. And he had said from the beginning he would leave at the end of the school year. Silly to allow her feelings to become so dramatic.

"Did you have a nice dinner?" she asked as she assembled the latte.

"Stimulating," Cal answered. "I am more confident the funding for the program might come through. Charity's friend, Susie Quatman, was there. Do you know her?"

"From school. She moved away after graduation." Hearing that Susie had been there barely hurt. Knowing she had a future with or without him insulated Bryony from the harsh winds of days gone by. She had a life of her own. She glanced at Etta's usual seat. What a difference a day can make.

"I hope you don't mind," Cal said. "I ran the idea of a pie business past them last night. I think if you wanted to reach out, Charity and Susie might have ideas about how to promote your business."

Armor up, Bryony's jaw set. Her shoulders tensed. "I'd appreciate you not talking about my idea with anyone. It's too soon. I need time." She needed trustworthy allies.

"Sure," Cal said. "I didn't tell them you were the pie maker, but they were excited. Chuck, too. I think discussing the idea revived him a bit. He said he's a big pie lover."

Bryony bit her lip.

"Make my latte to go," Cal said. "Bailey's in the car. We're on our way to Cleveland."

Bryony poured the drink into an insulated paper cup and snapped on a lid.

Cal handed over a credit card. "I look forward to seeing you Sunday night."

Bryony slid his card through the reader.

"I'll call later tonight," he said.

"Okay." The reply sprang automatic, like, "please," and "thank you."

He offered his usual wave from the door, and Bryony moved on to the next customer in line. If Lillian hadn't been called away to provide care for a sick grandchild, Bryony would have taken a break. As it was, she would have to manage her feelings and the line of thirsty, hungry people all by herself.

Two lattes and two bagels followed by a dozen plain bagels and copious amounts of distraction wrapped up the next two customers. She accomplished far more excellence in service for customers three, four, and five. By the sixth customer after Cal's departure, Bryony was able to bring herself back to the moment, far removed from the not-so-buried memories of Susie and Charity when they were young.

The regular customers, seeing the enormous task of managing the afternoon rush alone, helped as much as they could. They brought their mugs and plates to the counter and threw away their trash. Their kindness reminded Bryony she had not merely survived her youth, she was in a better place, surrounded by people who didn't insult or taunt her.

Her calmer mood lasted into the evening, but when she pulled the peanut pie out of the oven, number seventy-five on the list, she thought about the comic strip and Charlie Brown's gullibility. She was done being the gullible one. The next time the Lucy factor in her life pulled the ball away, Bryony would not end up on her back.

When Cal called at eight o'clock, she didn't answer her phone.

# CAL'S CLASH

*R*aindrops left black dots on Cal's dark gray canvas sleeve. He jogged to the coffee shop door from his car. Once inside, he unbuttoned the front of his coat and wiped his shoes before stepping off the flowered welcome mat.

The coffee shop buzzed with activity. Todd, Lillian, and Bryony flew around each other, three birds angling and swooping, their wings flapping with precision. He'd hoped he might catch Bryony for a minute. Not much chance of that happening too soon in this much hubbub.

Between his father, the munchkins, the Halloween party, and several heart-to-heart discussions with Heidi about how to help their father, Cal had only been able to call Bryony at odd hours the entire weekend. He hadn't been surprised when she did not answer.

On the trip back to Fieldstone, he'd called from the road to cancel their Sunday night plans because he left Cleveland later than originally planned. That call, too, went to voicemail.

He only had a few minutes before he needed to leave for school.

Chuck, Charity, and Susie occupied a table halfway between

the service counter and the door. Susie saw him first and waved him over.

He walked to their table, his eyes on Bryony. Hers were on the people directly in front of her, on the opposite side of the counter.

"I'm so glad we didn't give up our extra chair," Charity said. She removed her leather bag and patted the chair seat. "Come and sit, Cal."

He sat on the brown chair, across from Chuck, without removing his coat. "You're out early this morning."

Chuck sported a fresh haircut. A navy blue sweater brought out the lighter blue of his eyes. "Doc gave me a good report yesterday," he said. "He says if I keep this up, I could maybe start working again in the spring." He did look better, but he still needed more bulk and tone in his muscles.

"Whoa there, champ," Cal said. "I'm not ready to give up my post."

"No worries. I'm taking the rest of the year off, as planned," Chuck said.

Cal smiled, his hands in his jacket pockets. He glanced at the service counter and could only see Lillian and Todd now.

"Cal," Susie said, louder than necessary.

He brought his attention back to the table but remained more interested in the person he could not see, hoping the flow of customers would ease so he could talk to Bryony. The weekend had been fun, but hard in some ways. He had seen the difference his absence made to his family, the need for him to be there.

"I heard the other day that you know our little Bryony," Susie said. "She's not the Shy Bry she used to be."

"I never thought of her as shy," Chuck said.

"Don't you remember that time she was called on in World History to answer a question, and her face turned so red we all thought she might burst into flames?" Susie asked. "We had a good laugh about that."

"I don't remember that," Chuck said.

"I do." Charity's voice was low, and her expression hard to read.

"Of course you do," Susie said. "Bryony was famous for being the sweetest of the least noticeable girls. I always thought she might be pretty if she put any effort in."

What was Susie up to?

Cal stood. "Sorry, I need to grab a latte and run. Chuck, Charity, have a great day. Susie, I'll see you at four?"

"Let's meet here?" Susie asked

"Sure," he answered. Perfect. Closing time would limit their meeting time. He didn't want to meet with her at all, but Susie had insisted she could help find additional funding for the work study program. Cal owed it to the young people to do all he could to help.

Three people stood in front of him when he joined the line. After they were served, he approached the counter while opening his wallet.

"Good morning, Mister Forster," Todd said. "What would you like this morning?" The young man who had hung his head for the first few weeks of class now stood tall. There was no reward greater than this.

"I'll have a latte and a turkey sandwich to go."

"Coming up!" Todd moved deftly to fill Cal's order.

Bryony was nowhere to be seen.

"Where's Ms. Green?" Cal asked when Todd delivered his order.

Todd looked around the coffee shop. "I don't know. She was here a minute ago. Do you need to talk to her?"

"No, I'm fine," Cal said. "I'll talk to her later."

He walked out into the morning air with less pep in his step. He did need to talk to her because he had a big decision to make. A lyric line by The Clash about choosing to stay or go played in his head. The minute he thought the line, his brain provided an instant replay that looped until past lunch.

§.

AT FOUR O'CLOCK in the afternoon, Cal returned to the coffee shop.

Lillian took his order and arched one eyebrow as she set his tea on the counter, her non-verbal communicating with such volume Cal felt clairvoyant. "Bryony was here a minute ago but had an emergency errand," she said. "An errand she remembered after Susie asked if we'd seen you."

"Is Susie here?" Cal asked, looking behind him, his curiosity aroused. Why would Bryony avoid Susie?

"I think she went to the restroom," Lillian answered.

"Susie and I planned to meet at four, a school thing," he said, returning his gaze to Lillian, his own eyebrows raised now, inquisitive.

Lillian slid the tea across the counter. Cal started to reach for his wallet.

"This one's on me," Lillian said. "I think we can start considering each other as more than customer and shop owner."

Cal wrapped his hand around the warm mug and studied Lillian's face. She continued to look directly at him without flinching, her expression relaxed but strong, telling.

"And does this more-than-customer status," he asked, "give me the right to probe into the peculiar looks and innuendos regarding relationships between people who have grown up in this town?"

"Yes, it does." Crescents formed on each side of Lillian's grin. "Now or later?"

"Quick as you can," Cal said under his breath. "One line."

"A tall order," Lillian said. She took a breath and began to speak.

"Cal!" Susie called from the far side of the seating area. Cal turned to nod at her. "Let's sit here." She pointed at a table. "And can you please bring me a cup of whatever you're having?"

Giving a thumbs up to Susie, he turned back to Lillian.

"Whatever Bryony has, Susie wants," Lillian said. She pulled a mug off the rack, filled it with hot water, placed it on a saucer with two tea bags, and slid it across the counter. "This one's on me, too. See you later, Cal."

He nodded in understanding and turned to carry the two cups to the table.

"Tea?" Susie looked at the mug with distaste. "I prefer something sweet and milky with loads of caffeine, but okay."

He put the tea in front of her. "So, tell me how you know Bryony."

"Bryony?" Susie said. "Bryony Green? Oh, we go way back. I think we met when we were in first grade." She put a tea bag in the water.

"Were you friends?" he asked.

"When we were young," Susie said. "But then she got kind of weird, and I stopped hanging out with her."

Gone was the smooth, sophisticated look she'd portrayed when they first met in Cleveland. He was finally meeting the real Susie, the one underneath the makeup, surgical lifts, and orchestrated vocal affect.

"Weird?" He dunked his tea bag.

"You know, she couldn't keep up. In fact, she hasn't changed at all since high school. She still looks the same, wears the same kind of clothes, and look where she ended up." She scoffed. "Working in a coffee shop."

"Anything else?" Cal asked.

Susie leaned in, conspiratorial, a devious grin on those

painted lips. "I was instrumental in steering Chuck toward Charity. I think Bryony saw him as hers."

"Chuck?" Bryony and Chuck knew each other? She hadn't said a word. In fact, he remembered her indicating familiarity with his old friend, but nothing more.

"Chuck spent a lot of time with Bryony after he moved here. But when Charity came along, she was so obviously the right match for him, right? I mean, they're the couple we all wish we were, or had been."

"Uh huh." Cal sipped his tea.

"To tell you the truth, I don't think Bryony ever got over losing Chuck. She dated this one guy for a while, but then he ended up dating me." Her face made an "oops" expression followed by a cutesy smile. "I mean she's never been married. As far as I know, she's single and obviously not trying to attract anyone. It's kind of tragic."

"Tragic," Cal said.

"So, enough about Bryony Green! If you want to expand the program you're teaching, I think I can help. I've written many grants over my career, and one thing I can tell you about money for kids, any way you can tie it to people with disabilities and minorities is a plus."

"Mm hmm," Cal sipped his tea.

"I'll need to use one of your students as the 'face' of the program." She made a frame with her hands and overacted looking out from it.

"Use?" Cal asked.

Her hands fell, and she assumed a more professional tone. "You know what I mean."

"I think I do," Cal said. He stood and put on his coat.

"Where are you going?" Susie asked.

"I think we're done here."

As he walked out the door, Susie called out, "Do you want to go out later, grab a drink?"

Cal didn't answer.

He was thinking about a surprise he'd been preparing for Bryony, and he had a lot of thinking to do about something else, too, something unexpected, potentially life changing.

Being home over the weekend, seeing the love between his sister and Mark, between his nieces and their spouses, confirmed what he had been coming to for weeks, and now he was torn between his family and the woman he loved.

Yes, he knew that now. He loved the woman with flaming cheeks and auburn hair.

They'd only been playing at dating up to this point. And she certainly seemed ambivalent about him at times. But when he thought about his overall experience with her, he realized that he wanted to give the idea of them being a couple a real shot. Because he'd never met anybody who made him happier, or more agitated, or more willing to forgive, or—most of all— more ready to settle down, wherever and however that might happen.

He simply wanted to be with Bryony Green.

No one outside of his family of origin had ever factored into his life plans, and now Cal couldn't think about next year without including *her* somewhere, somehow. Should he plan to stay and find another teaching position in or near Fieldstone, or go back to Cleveland, where he belonged in every way possible with the exception of Bryony?

He needed to talk to her, to know where she stood, what she wanted.

Should he stay, or should he go?

# BRY BACKS OFF TO BAKE

*B*y Tuesday morning, Bryony was convinced. Falling in love with Cal had been a mistake. Chances were Cal was already having second thoughts about her anyway. He hadn't tried to call again over the weekend until Sunday night. When she had listened to his voicemail, she wasn't surprised he canceled their date.

And so she had made up her mind. As in the past, Bryony needed to pull up her big girl pants and move forward on her own.

Avoiding him at the coffee shop would be a breeze, as she had demonstrated to herself on Monday. She could soldier on through the rest of the school year until he was gone. Supervision for Todd could be accomplished on the phone or on paper.

But she knew Cal was not the kind of man to quietly disappear. He would want to establish something he might refer to as *closure*. He would think he owed her that. She owed him that, too, she supposed, sooner or later, her preference being later. But later came sooner than expected because Bryony could not refuse his late Tuesday afternoon invitation for a walk after Lillian had ordered her to, "Take off for an hour and talk to the man."

Cal helped her into her coat and asked, "Ready?"

She faced him. "Where are we going?"

"Not far."

He held the door, and Bryony stepped out into the quiet downtown.

She needed to tell him, tell him now, in a way he would understand, a practical way. She had too much on her plate. She needed time, space, distance.

"Cal, I've been thinking," she started.

He shushed her. "I do want to hear what you've been thinking, but first I want to show something to you."

Bryony put her hands in her pockets and looked at him. "Okay."

"First stop, the coffee shop," he said.

"We just walked out of the coffee shop."

"Yes, but I want you to see what's on the outside." He walked to the edge of the building and began to speak like a tour guide. "This building was erected in 1890, making it the second oldest building downtown, the oldest being the courthouse. A man named Robert Fieldstone designed this building to house his dry goods store. Robert was the great grandson of the town's founder."

Stepping to the side, he pointed to the metal plaque and asked her to read it.

Screwing up her face into a silent request for knowing what the heck was going on, Bryony read the plaque. "Where's Robert's name? It says the building was built for Charles A. Smith & Co."

"Robert's name isn't there," Cal answered, "because after he bought the land and designed the building, he lost a load of money in the financial panic of 1884. Due to those losses, he lacked the capital to build, so he sold the land and design to Smith."

"How do you know all this?" Bryony asked.

"One of my students researched the town's financial history," Cal said. "I learn far more from my students than they learn from me. If I want to learn about something, I make up an assignment. My students come through every time."

"If you say so," Bryony said, smiling. She couldn't help herself. Cal reminded her of every PBS show she had ever seen, including those with Barney and Elmo.

"Robert went on to open a small hotel catering to business people," Cal said. "His customers turned his business into a sought-after location because of his wife's cooking. Her specialty? Pie."

"You're making this up," Bryony said, amused, which was dangerous. Amusement weakened the thicket she'd grown around her heart in the past few days.

"In fact," Cal said, "his restaurant and hotel were so prosperous he was able to eventually buy this building back from Charles Smith. He opened his dry goods store, which serviced the town through the Great Depression."

Skepticism seeped into her amusement. "Is all of this true?"

He nodded with vigor, saying, "I fact-checked," and led her to the next building.

"This building has housed seven different businesses since it was built in 1923." Cal again assumed the tone of a tour guide. "The most interesting was a yarn shop which opened in 1965."

"I remember that yarn shop," Bryony said.

"Did you ever go in?" Cal asked, dropping the theatrics, sounding like himself again.

"No. I wasn't interested in learning how to knit or crochet."

"You should try it sometime. I hear it's good for the brain. Anyway," Cal again assumed the announcer's tone again, "the woman who owned the business tried four different times to open a yarn business, and she failed every time, until she located here. Maybe it was timing, or maybe the location, but she was able to keep the business open in this building until her health failed in the year 2000."

"I wondered what happened to her," Bryony said.

"Her name is Cassandra, and she lives in a nursing home," Cal said. "She said her investment resulted in a profit consisting of 'lifelong friends and memories to carry me through the hardest of times.' My student included the quote in the paper."

"Okay, I see what you're doing," Bryony said.

"And the storefront over there"—Cal pointed to a vacant building—"used to be an ice cream place. It moved on to a larger location on the edge of town."

"Parmiters," Bryony said. "Their ice cream is fabulous."

"The people who started that business failed three times before they hit the right recipe."

"Okay," Bryony said. "Message received."

"Most of us fail over and over. Be brave, Bryony. It's never too late to make your dream come true."

Nobody except her mother and Lillian had ever demonstrated such clear, unwavering support. "Thanks for being so nice to me," she said.

"Lecture over," Cal said. "You have something to say to me, and I have something to talk about, too. Where do you want to go?"

She suggested the diner down the street and led the way. Neither initiated small talk. Whether she matched Cal's pace or he hers was open for debate, but neither of them seemed to be in a hurry.

Once inside, Bryony sat down at the nearest table. Cal sat in the chair opposite her. Three dead flies lay belly up on the window sill.

A familiar face walked over with her paper pad. "Hey, Bryony. What's new?"

Gloria's white polyester button-up top stretched across her pot belly and her short, brown, rolled hairstyle hadn't changed since high school. Bryony introduced her to Cal, saying they weren't there to eat.

"So, coffee for two?" Gloria asked.

"Sure," Bryony answered.

As Gloria walked away, Cal asked, "Another friend of yours?"

"She graduated with Mitch."

"And she owns the place?"

"Her brother does. Their grandparents opened it."

Cal wrinkled up his nose and whispered, "I'm open to liking it, but it makes me want to break out the cleaning supplies."

Bryony smiled and shrugged. "I know. I've learned to ignore it. The food is fresh and good." As was the impact of Cal. Cutting off her feelings for him had required numbing her entire body. She tried to shut down again, but pleasant little tingles and bursts of wellbeing plagued her.

"Seems like you know almost everyone in town," Cal said.

"I never met Todd before he started working at the shop." Talking about Todd was safe. It pulled her attention away from feeling back to thinking. "I can't thank you enough for bringing him to us."

Cal tilted his head. "So formal. This isn't a business meeting."

Her stomach tightened. Being with Cal confused her.

Gloria arrived with the coffee, said, "Let me know if you need anything else," and left the table.

"I understand you know my friends, Chuck and Charity, and their friend, Susie," Cal said.

Bryony took a deep breath and noticed she could still breathe, a good sign. "Yes, I know them."

"That Susie's a piece of work," Cal said.

"What do you mean?" What did he mean? He sounded displeased with the wealthy woman who seemed to acquire everything she wanted, never mind the expense.

"I mean she's kind of a cougar. Whenever I'm with her, I feel like I'm bait." He shook his shoulders and shuddered. "Wouldn't want to be caught up in anything with her. Forget what I said about her helping with the pie business. I don't trust her."

Warmth flooded through every cell of Bryony's body. Her face flushed with pleasure. Someone else finally saw the world the way she did. "Sorry about disappearing for a few days," she said.

"You're here now." Cal started to reach across the table, but Bryony withdrew her hands and put them in her lap. He looked puzzled as he asked, "So, what's been happening in your world, Bryony Green?"

They talked for over an hour. When he asked if her phone had been out of service, she chose honesty. She had needed time to think. And her thinking was she needed to not be dating anyone. She hoped he would understand. She would like to be friends only, not his temporary date while he lived in Fieldstone.

She saw more regret in his face than she had anticipated, but he said he did understand and would be whatever she needed him to be. She didn't know what he meant by that, and he seemed quieter through a second cup of coffee, but he still showed interest in hearing about her life, like a friend, which is what she had wanted, she guessed.

When she asked about his family, he said she had missed a good party, but didn't elaborate.

After paying, Bryony walked Cal to his car. He slid in behind the steering wheel, and she saw sadness in his smile, which surprised her, but he sounded upbeat when he said, "Gotta run. Bailey awaits. Have a good rest of the day, Bryony."

"I will," she said.

She walked back to the coffee shop and started taking her coat off as the door closed behind her.

Chuck and Charity Henderson sat with Susie Quatman, all

three settled in close to the door. Bryony walked over to the table, greeted each one by name, and asked, "Do you need anything?"

"We're good," Chuck said. "Nice seeing you, Bryony. Great place!"

Hearing his words and taking in the warmth generated by his smile reminded her of when they had been close. "I heard you had surgery," Bryony said. "I'm happy to see you're doing well."

"Thanks," Chuck said.

"We were hoping we'd run into our friend, Cal Forster," Susie said. "He seems to spend a lot of time in here."

"I just left him," Bryony said. "He ran home for his dog."

Susie's countenance fell.

"I'm glad he's found a friend in you," Chuck said. "We practically begged him to sub for me for the year, and then abandoned him when he arrived. I had no idea I'd be down for so long."

"You're doing great now." Charity patted Chuck's knee.

When Chuck looked at his wife, Bryony saw love passing between them. They were not merely aged versions of iconic high school sweethearts. They were a mature, married couple surviving a crisis together.

"I hope to see you in here more often," she said.

Chuck smiled at her. "I hope we see more of you, too."

Bryony carried her coat to the rack in the back of the store, lifted it to the hook, let it drop, and sighed.

Chuck and Charity Henderson were not the people she had known in high school. She was not the person they had known then either. Everybody grew up—everybody except maybe Susie—and moved past divisions related to the competitive nature of high school. They could all be friends—except maybe Susie—including Cal.

That night she made a tomato pie. Bryony had read that

dreaming of tomatoes was a sign of moving in a new work direction, one that would go well. Maybe daydreaming while working with tomatoes would have a similar effect.

Over the weekend, catalyzed by Etta's encouragement, Bryony had mapped out a vision for her pie business, a bold plan starting with a state-of-the-art kitchen sufficient to produce enough pies for both local and online sales.

After the tomato pie cooled, she removed a piece to taste test. The savory tang of new adventure hit her tongue like the spicy scene in a novel or movie. She would be fine without Cal, and he without her. They would be friends doing their own things, as it should be for two independent adults, neither of whom had ever been married, neither of whom expressed a strong desire to head toward matrimony. Why muck up two perfectly refined single lifestyles?

She took another bite, and then another.

The taste lost its tang after the fourth bite, but she kept eating, for comfort and joy, neither of which she achieved as she swallowed forkful after forkful until the entire piece was gone, leaving only crumbs on her plate.

She started to press her finger into the crumbs to eat those, too, but stopped. After a deep breath and a chance to allow for introspection, she took her plate to the sink and rinsed it.

Crumbs were not her future.

# CAL CALLS FOR HELP

The time between the end of dinner and lights out constituted the hardest part of Cal's day.

Over the past several weeks, he had settled into an evening routine of reading his way through a new detective series recommended by Chuck, who said the stories helped during his recovery.

The main character—a middle-aged man tracking crooked colleagues and various kinds of trafficking rings from which imperiled people required rescuing—mourned his wife and daughter after the author killed them off in the first chapter of the first book in the series. Cal could relate to the loss of loved ones. The drama in the stories distracted him from missing Bryony.

Though they had run into each other a few times and been cordial, he had not called her, as she had not called him. They were both wise enough, he guessed, to know when to cut their losses. But tonight the loss of her loomed larger than usual. He needed to talk to somebody.

Chuck and he had not spoken in a few weeks, so Cal picked up his phone and pulled up his contact list. He wanted to check in. He hoped to hear good news.

After observing a few social amenities related to family, sports, the national news, and which volume of the series he was reading, Cal asked, "Any word yet from the school board?"

"Nothing," Chuck said. "Charity's pulled out all the stops with every contact she has. Seems like someone's feeding the board information which makes our program seem redundant, unnecessary. Charity keeps hearing the word, 'useless,' passed around, and the phrase, 'no evidence basis.'"

"Didn't they read the report you sent in?" Cal asked. "We documented the rise in student attendance and the reduction in detention over the last five years for seniors entering the program." Did the school board know anything about the young people served by the program?

"I don't know, Cal," Chuck answered. His voice sounded tired, though stronger than a few months ago. "I only know it's not looking good at the moment, which can change. They won't vote on next year's budget until after the new year. I'm not sure what I'll do next year if the program ends."

Whether or not the program continued would have little impact on Cal. He would leave after the end of the school year. The idea of staying had been short-lived and exclusively tied to his feelings about Bryony. Feeling foolish now, he was surprised he could be taken in by his need for someone to call his own. Rock ballads came to mind. To yearn for one's own great love story may be entertaining, but not pragmatic.

"You can always move back to Cleveland," Cal said.

Chuck laughed. "If there's no place for me next year in this school system, I'll retire and do something else. Maybe I'll be a greeter at Walmart."

"Their loss, Walmart's gain," Cal said.

Chuck laughed again, paused, and said, "Listen. If the weather gets bad and you can't drive to Cleveland on

Wednesday, you're welcome to come to our house for Thanksgiving."

Cal appreciated the invite, though short of a blizzard, he knew he would be going home.

They ended the phone call. Cal spent the rest of the evening grading papers. Right before bed, he walked Bailey again and locked up for the night. In the morning he would finish the last few papers at school before the students arrived. Not stopping at the coffee shop gave him another thirty to forty minutes every morning. He missed the lattes, but he didn't need all those extra calories anyway.

The scent of fresh sheets welcomed him to bed. Seeking the right neck support, Cal stuffed the pillow under his head. Bailey jumped on the bed and settled in beside him. "No snoring, buddy," Cal said, and closed his eyes.

He woke to the sound of his ringtone. The clock registered twelve thirty. The caller ID on his cell read "Heidi."

Cal sat up and switched on the light.

"Hey, Heidi," he said. "What's up?"

"Don't panic, but I need you," his sister said.

"Not a good way to start a call. Are the kids okay?"

"They are, but Dad fell again." Her voice was rushed, and he heard sounds in the background—a car starting, an electronic voice reminding the driver to fasten their seatbelt. "We think he was rolling his garbage can back up to the house," she said. "The neighbor found him in the driveway and called the squad. They took him to the ER. I'm on my way there now, but it doesn't sound good."

"What was he doing outside this late?" Cal threw off the covers and swung his feet over the edge of the bed.

"I don't know. The nurse who called said Dad was confused. He might have bumped his head, or he fell because he was dizzy or disoriented."

"I'll be there as soon as I can." The blankets on the other side of the bed erupted into a plume of shaking dog fur. "Sorry, buddy. Didn't mean to bury you." He pulled back the covers, and Bailey jumped to the floor.

"Are you talking to your dog again?" Heidi asked.

"Yes," Cal answered.

"Can you leave him home?" Heidi asked. "One less thing to worry about. We might all be pretty busy."

"I'll figure something out. Call if anything changes." Cal made a mental list as he strode to the closet—dress, pack, call Mitch to arrange for a sub, establish pet care. Tomorrow he would call to have his mail held. He had filled the gas tank yesterday.

"Drive safely," Heidi said.

"Always."

After slipping on the jeans and T-shirt he had worn earlier in the evening, Cal opened his closet and pulled out his duffle bag. Bailey sat beside the bed scratching his ear. "What am I going to do with you?" Cal asked.

Heidi was right. He couldn't take Bailey with him. If Cal needed to be at the hospital round-the-clock, he didn't want to leave Bailey alone at his father's house. Heidi and her kids would step up if needed, but Cal didn't want to impose. They all had busy lives.

After stuffing jeans, khakis, underwear, socks, and T-shirts into the duffle bag, he went to his closet and pulled out three button down shirts. He would hang them in his car. Mission accomplished, he sat down on the bed and hit a contact number. Mitch answered the phone, his voice sleepy but surprisingly gracious about being awakened.

"No problem, Cal. Good thing Parker's on board for trivia. Take all the time you need."

Cal thanked him and ended the call, noting the cynical thought that Mitch would probably be happy if he didn't return at all. And then, without thinking twice, he pressed the very number associated with Mitch's assumed preference that Cal would return never.

"Cal?" Bryony asked.

"Sorry to call late," he said.

"I was awake," she said.

"I have to go to Cleveland. My dad fell tonight."

"I'm sorry," she said. "Is he okay?"

The concern in her voice caused a hitch in his throat. She was someone with whom he could have shared his fears about someday losing his father. He ignored the surge of feeling and pressed on. "I don't know. I'm leaving in a few minutes. Would you mind taking care of Bailey while I'm gone? He's very little work. A walk in the morning. A walk at night. Food in his bowl. Water. He won't drag you through the mud again. I'll make him promise. I'm so sorry to ask last minute, but I think Bailey and I would both be happier if he stayed home."

"I guess so," Bryony said. "I've never taken care of a dog before."

"He's not much trouble. I have a cat now, too. You aren't allergic, are you?"

"You have a cat?"

"Buggy showed up a few weeks ago." Cal didn't say, *about the time you and I ended.* "She's a stray, and for some reason Bailey loves her, even though she bugs the heck out of him, hence the name."

In addition to the addictive detective series, caring for the cat had kept him interested in something other than making a nuisance of himself with Bryony.

"Wow," Bryony said. "I'm amazed. I don't see you as a cat person."

She was right, and Cal wanted to tell her the whole story, but that would never happen. He needed distance from her. A clean break. Because even though he'd declared himself understanding of her need to back off, nothing he thought or felt agreed with that plan. He'd only called Bryony for help because he couldn't think of anyone else to ask on such short notice, in the middle of the night. "The cat requires minor oversight. I'll leave a note and put everything you'll need on the kitchen counter."

"What if I mix them up, give the dog the cat's food and vice versa?" Bryony asked.

Cal laughed. "They'll be waiting at the door with sharp knives when you return."

"I'm overthinking," Bryony said. "Leave a note. I'm sure we'll be fine."

"I have a note ready to go." He'd prepared it for his Cleveland dog-sitters. He would print it and make a few edits with a pen. "Thanks, Bryony," Cal said. "I've missed seeing you." His whole face immediately tensed, wishing he could take back the words. They matched his feeling, but not his better judgement.

Bryony's silence said it all. She hadn't noticed his absence. Better that way, cleaner, no drama.

"I'll leave a key under the front mat," he said. "Thanks, again. You're a good friend."

"Not a problem," she said. "Drive safely. I hope your father's okay."

They ended the call, and Cal finished the tasks on his mental to-do list.

The temperature outside had dropped. His car was cold. Cal threw his bag in the back seat, hung the shirts, and started the engine. It had been less than twenty minutes since Heidi's call. Remembering one more detail, he turned off the ignition and exited the car to slip the house key under the porch mat. Prior to starting the car again, he took a breath and went over the list once again, ticking off each item in his mind until he reached the end.

List double-checked, he was good to go.

Backing out of the driveway, he reviewed his phone call with

Bryony. Had he missed telling her anything vital? He didn't think so. She had his number and could call if she had questions. He could count on her. And she could count on him to be a friend. An appropriate, distant friend with no other expectations. Cal turned on the radio.

Hard rock would keep him awake and drive away the worry and regret thrumming through his mind and body.

# BRY FALLS FOR CAL'S KITCHEN

*S*treetlights still on, Bryony climbed the three steps to Cal's front door. The key lay under the front mat as promised. Apprehensive, she unlocked and pushed open the door to enter.

In the brief time they had toyed around with dating, they spent all of their time together away from their homes because they always had somewhere else to be. She felt odd walking into his house now, too curious, like a trespasser, like an intruder.

"Bailey?" she called. Cal's dog bounded down the last few steps of a staircase, fur flopping and tail wagging. He stopped at her feet, sat, and looked up panting, his tongue hanging out one side of his mouth.

"Aren't you the well-behaved one today?" Bryony asked. She patted his head. Bailey slurped her hand. Maybe this wasn't going to be so hard after all.

"Show me around the place," she said as she started wandering down the wide hallway.

Bailey wagged his tail and followed.

Cal lived in a neighborhood a notch up from hers. Bryony assumed homes like these were always owner-occupied. Maybe

Charity knew the owners. Maybe she had suggested the arrangement.

The first door on the left opened into a massive living room, the second into a dining room.

At the end of the hall, she pushed open a swinging door, located the light switch, and gushed, "Wow!"

The house may have been built fifty to seventy-five years ago, but the update on the kitchen was recent, no more than five to ten years.

Floor-to-ceiling oak cabinets surrounded a granite counter reflecting under-counter lighting on its polished surface. A double sink with a gooseneck faucet sparkled. The six-burner gas stove sat atop a double-oven. Overhead lights bounced off the built-in microwave and a stainless steel side-by-side Sub-Zero refrigerator freezer.

Bryony sank onto a chair. Cal had been holding out on her. Had she known about the kitchen, she would have suggested a dinner date at his place. She sat for a full five minutes, reverence and peace descending over her. She belonged in a place like this, a shrine to that which made her spirit puff up like a perfect pastry.

Bailey sat in front of the kitchen sink, watching her. Bryony noticed cans and boxes on the counter. She pushed herself out of the chair to investigate. A page-long list of dog care tips quelled any leftover fear about not knowing what to do. And now she knew they had surpassed the proper time for a walk per the line, *Bailey will expect you take him out the minute you walk in the door. All will go better for both of you if you follow his guidance.*

A dog leash lay beside the boxes and cans. Bryony hooked it to Bailey's collar. Two colorful plastic bags were tied to the grip end.

"Okay, boy," she said. "No chasing cats, no digging in flower beds, and no knocking me down."

He led her out the front door and peed on the first tree they came to.

"I guess we left at the right time," Bryony said.

She had never lived with a dog. When she was five, she begged for a pooch, but her father nixed the idea, saying he had a dog when he was kid and he *was not going through that again.* Later, she learned her father had witnessed the dog's death under the tires of a speeding car. As an adult, she could understand why he chose to not risk a repeat of such loss. But the five-year-old in her still yearned for a living being like Bailey, someone, or something, who would greet her with unrestrained welcome every time she returned .

Bailey walked her around a five block tour of his territory. He seemed to need to acquaint himself with every hydrant, bush, tree, and post they encountered. Instructions in the note were to let Bailey sniff until he was done, so Bryony did, impatient until she started to enjoy the morning air, hints of pink in the eastern sky, and architecture revealed by porch lights and lamp posts.

A few friends in elementary school had lived in these houses. She remembered a summer day with pony rides for a birthday party at a house around the block. Those were the years when everybody in the class had been invited.

Bailey made one long last sniff at the tree in the neighbor's front yard, then trotted up to his front door and wagged his tail. Bryony dug the key out of her pocket and unlocked the door. She might as well put it on the metal ring with her key fob and house key.

The door latched behind her. Bryony went back to the kitchen counter to read the note again. There were handwritten additions. The one at the top read, *I attached the business card for my local vet.* She glanced at the card for Benson's Veterinary Services. Across the left margin of the page, Cal had scrawled,

*Call me on my cell, day or night, if you have any questions. Thanks for being a good friend. Cal.*

Maybe they could be friends. He had invited her into his home without him being there, and trusted her enough to place his animals in her care. But her version of friendship implied effort to spend time together. Once the "dating" thing fizzled, Cal seemed too busy to come around. But Bryony supposed she had done the same, making little effort toward him.

A note was scribbled in the right margin of the paper. *Leave a can of fresh cat food in Buggy's bowl in the morning and evening. Fill her water bowl. Put her food and water on the middle shelf in the pantry and leave the door open. Otherwise, Bailey consumes it. If you want to see her, you'll have to search. She hides under the bed or in the den.*

Bryony opened a can of cat food and dropped it into one of the bowls stacked on the counter. The food smelled fishy, like being at the ocean, but a tad more nauseating.

She carried the cat bowl over to a door and opened it. Stairs led down. She shut the door and opened the one beside it. Light from the kitchen revealed a large walk-in pantry with mostly empty wire shelving on both sides.

An empty bowl like the one in her hand sat in the middle of a shelf halfway up to the ceiling. Bryony picked up the empty cat bowl, replaced it with the full one, and picked up the empty dog bowls from the floor.

After refilling Bailey's food and water bowls and placing them back on the floor, curiosity about the rest of the house convinced Bryony she wanted to meet Cal's cat. She left the kitchen to explore.

Book shelves rose to meet crown molding in what appeared to be a formal office. Cal had said his rental came partially furnished. Surely he had not contributed much to this monumental decor.

Heavy maroon curtains covered a window behind a large,

shiny desk. A brown, leather, wingback chair sat in one corner, a floor lamp beside it. A small round oriental rug lay in front of the chair. Dog hair along one area of the rug's border provoked an image of Cal sitting in the chair at night, his glasses on the end of his nose, a book in his lap, Bailey at his feet. Bryony opened a door in that room to reveal a closet. It held a vacuum cleaner and a few empty hangers, but no cat.

She moved on to the living room and flipped on the overhead lights. Wall-to-wall off-white berber carpet spread beneath a black three-piece set of couch, loveseat, and chair. They were arranged in a circular pattern with plenty of floor space around them to spare. Each piece of the set had end tables with blue ceramic lamps that plugged into outlets in the floor.

The lamps matched a blue ceramic hearth, and the fireplace had a substantial mantel.

Simple off-white window curtains hung from black iron rods. Large abstract paintings covered the walls around the fireplace and the wall opposite. Smaller framed art—landscapes, barns—hung on the third wall. A grouping of even smaller canvases with whimsical black stick figures dancing in and around colorful backgrounds hung on the fourth wall. Bryony looked closer at the stick figure art and read, *To Cal, my favorite among favorites. Peace out, SH*, scrawled above the signature.

Cal had interesting friends.

Still no cat in sight, Bryony opened the front closet. Coats she recognized as Cal's hung neatly in the middle. A pair of cross country skis leaned in one corner. Bryony smiled. Fieldstone rarely had enough snow for skiing.

She opened another door to a half bath off the hallway, and then wandered through the arched doorway to the formal dining room where she circumnavigated a massive table with twelve chairs. She found a few stains on the carpet, but no cat.

Having explored the rest of the downstairs with diligence, duty called to check the upstairs as well. Being in Cal's home, seeing how he lived, gave rise to the regret she'd been hiding from herself. The house bespoke a man who could take of himself without requiring too much upkeep on her part.

But she had yet to check the refrigerator, or his bedroom. She needed to find something fresh to validate her decision to back off from him. Otherwise, she would spend a long holiday weekend walking his dog, stalking his cat, and kicking herself for kicking him out of her life.

Ascending the carpeted treads to the second floor one at a time, Bryony called out, "Kitty, kitty. Here kitty."

The first and second doors off the upstairs hall led to empty bedrooms with open closets and no signs of a cat. The third door opened to a master bedroom, which also had no furniture. The en suite bathroom and walk-in closet were open with no cat in sight.

Another hall door opened to a full bath, a fifth to a linen closet, a sixth to a stairwell leading up. She was not going up there. Bryony shivered and shut the door.

When she reached the seventh and last door, she hesitated. Should she open it? This room had to be Cal's bedroom. She wanted to see it, but now she knew she was stalking Cal, not the cat. If he wanted her to see his room, he would have left the door open. Maybe this was where he hid those bachelor tendencies, left his bed unmade, threw his underwear on the floor.

A loud meow issued from the other side of the door, a plea for release. Without thinking, Bryony turned the knob and pushed it open. A huge yellow tabby padded forward and wrapped itself in and around her legs, purring. Bryony bent down and picked it up. "My word!" she said. "You must weigh twenty pounds at least! Cal should worry about you eating the dog food, not the other way around."

She carried the cat downstairs, her purring a constant

vibration, and placed her in the pantry. Buggy leapt to the shelf with the cat bowls and chowed down.

Bryony looked around one more time. Satisfied she had covered all required bases, she locked the house and returned to her car.

Backing out of Cal's driveway, she remembered being so overwhelmed by the size and sound of Cal's cat, she forgot to look at his bedroom. She would check it out tonight, to make sure all was well, because Cal had entrusted her to keep his pets and his home safe. Yes, she convinced herself, she wanted to inspect his bedroom for purely reasonable reasons.

# A NURSE FOR CAL

The manager on his father's hospital unit had supplied a blanket and pillow for a chair which opened into a cot. Cal slept on and off for a few hours with monitors beeping, the light from the hall shining in his eyes, and wake-ups by the phlebotomist, the patient technician, and the night nurse. Every time they asked, his father could recite his name and birthdate, and they seemed satisfied.

At eight in the morning, Cal Sr. rustled his sheets.

"What is it, Dad?" Cal moved off his cot and picked up his father's hand.

"Doodads fiddling the thing around, and nobody remembered to catch the fish when it fell off the bridge."

"What?"

"Is that you, Cal?" his father asked, awakening now.

"Yeah, Dad, it's me. What's that you're saying?"

"I don't know. I think I was dreaming." His father looked around the room. "What am I doing in here again?"

"You fell, and they worried you'd bumped your head."

His father pushed back the sheets. "What did they do with my clothes?" He started to move his feet to the edge of the bed.

"I swear those doctors need new motor homes. Why else would they make people spend the night for no reason at all?"

"Hang on, Dad." Cal moved to the edge of the bed, blocking his father's escape.

"Move, Cal!" his father ordered. "Have you seen the bills they send? Astronomical. Take me home."

"Let's wait and see what the doctor says this morning."

His father gave up and lay back on his pillow. "They'll take one look at me and say, 'There's another semester of tuition for my kids, a new set of tires, and a month in the Adirondacks.'"

Cal covered his father with the sheet and blanket. "Your sense of humor is intact."

His father lifted his head off the pillow. "Why are you here? Don't you have to work today?"

"And you're aware of the day. Is there anything you can't remember?"

"I don't know," his father said. "Let's find out if I can remember how to live my own damned life." He again threw off the blanket and sheet. "If you don't move, I will report you for unlawful entrapment." He pushed against Cal's hip, shoving him a few inches from the bed.

If his father was that strong, and he could make sense, maybe he was right. Maybe he could go home. Cal watched as his father pushed himself to a sitting position, dangled his legs off the edge of the bed, and used his arms to leverage himself upright.

"You're all hooked up to tubes on this pole here," Cal said. "Let's get a nurse to help."

"Rubbish. You can help. The pole will roll with me. Watch." Cal caught his father's arm as he stood, and provided support while he steadied himself. White hair stuck out in all directions from his head, and his legs were splotchy with purple spots around the ankles.

"Are you sure this is okay, Dad?"

"I'm sure they'd prefer I make it to the bathroom. Shake a leg, son, and hold the back together, will you? I know how distracted these nurses can be when they see a set of well-seasoned buns."

Cal laughed and moved with his father, dragging the IV pole into the bathroom and waiting until his father was situated, at which point the patient ordered his son out, saying he could be left on his own for a few minutes. Cal stepped outside the bathroom to give his father privacy.

The nurse's head popped around the door to the hallway. "Is he all right?" she asked.

"He's in there," Cal said.

"Let's have a look." She opened the room door wider and came around to the bathroom door.

"How are you doing in there, Mister Forster?" she asked, and disappeared into the bathroom.

Cal could hear her talking and his father's muffled replies.

Within minutes, the nurse opened the door and walked with her patient out of the bathroom. She held the gown together in the back until his father sat on the edge of the bed, then helped him swivel himself onto the pillow and lift his feet back onto the mattress.

"Golly, Rachel," Cal Sr. said. "I'm weaker than I thought. What have you all been doing to me?"

She laughed. "I don't think we did the doing. Need anything else right now?"

"No, dear. Thank you for everything." She tucked the sheet around him. He grasped her arm and asked, "Are you married?"

Nurse Rachel laughed again. "I am not. Are you looking for a date?"

"Lord, no, honey. But my son over there is a good catch. He's single, too. Best fellow you could ever want. Maybe I'm only here for the meeting of you two."

She gently tucked his arm under the cover. "Call if you need anything."

Before exiting the door, she looked at Cal and said, "He's doing much better."

With deep brown eyes, unblemished smooth skin, and sleek black hair cut even with the bottom of her ears, Nurse Rachel stood a few inches shorter than Cal.

"I was on duty yesterday when they brought him up," she said. "He was confused, and slightly dehydrated."

"Can he go home today?" Cal asked.

"I doubt they'll let him out today, but it's the doctor's call."

"He hears you talking about him," his father said. "He's not deaf."

Nurse Rachel smiled. "He's feisty," she said, and left the room.

"Everybody treats me like I'm a kid," Cal's father said. "Get me out of here, son."

"Okay, Dad. I'll see what I can do."

They spent the rest of the day together. Heidi visited in the afternoon, visibly relieved both by her father's improvement and her brother's presence. Before she left, she told Cal she would cook the turkey this year. He should focus on their father.

Cal agreed, saying he would do whatever she wanted, and they shared a warm hug. Grateful to be able to help both of them, Cal settled into the chair once more to watch his father snore.

He wondered how Bryony was doing with Bailey and Buggy. Pleased to have a reason to call her later, he let himself drift into a nap, and dreamed of a nurse with auburn hair who wanted to play doctor.

# BRYONY'S MILLIONAIRE PIE

$\mathcal{J}$n the evening, Bryony returned to Cal's house. This time she leashed Bailey first thing, and he took her for a long walk. When they returned, Buggy waited at the door. She curled her plump feline body around Bryony's lower legs, leaving a layer of long cat hairs on black tights.

After feeding both of them and washing their dirty food bowls, Bryony explored Cal's fully equipped kitchen cabinets—surely the owners had supplied the pots, pans, mixing bowls, baking dishes, and cooking utensils—and, inspired by what she found there, set up a few needed items on the counter beside the sink.

Then she made a quick trip to the store for ingredients.

When she returned, she pulled her hair into a ponytail and commenced with pie making in the most luxurious kitchen she had ever seen in real life, similar sightings limited to high end makeovers in glossy magazines.

First, she made two graham cracker crusts. Next, she blended cream cheese, condensed milk, and whipped topping. To the dairy base, she added a can of drained crushed pineapple and chopped pecans. All of that she poured into the graham cracker crusts and put them into the refrigerator to chill for the evening.

Millionaire pie.

Because being in Cal's house and preparing food in his fabulous kitchen made her feel like a million bucks.

After cleaning up the pie-making mess, Bryony curled up in the wingback chair to read a book. Animals need companionship, she reasoned. Feeding them was not enough. She needed to stay with them, to remind them they were not forgotten.

Thirty minutes into her book, Bailey came to lie on the rug, and the cat jumped to the back of the chair, her tail swishing over Bryony's ear. The tickling sensation made her smile. She could get used to this.

When her phone rang, Bryony picked it up, checked the number, and put it to her ear. "Hi, Mitch. What's up?"

"Dad said you're thinking about starting a pie business." No greeting, not a question, his announcement brusque.

"Yes, I am." She'd mentioned the idea to her father a few days ago, and might now regret having done so.

"These days you need about a million in assets to retire comfortably," Mitch said. "Remember the old lady who used to babysit for you? She smelled like popcorn and always had her hair pinned down with those thingies."

"Bobby pins," Bryony said. "She curled her hair with bobby pins."

"Whatever," Mitch said. "My point is, she had to work because she was poor. Nobody wants to be poor when they're old, Bryony. Dad pays over four thousand dollars a month to live at RestHaven. As his needs increase, so will the fees. Think about how much the cost will add up to over time if he lives to be a hundred."

"Do you want him to die to save money?" Bryony asked.

"You're not listening." The volume of his voice rose with

irritation. "What happens if you lose your shirt starting a business? I'll have to support you. I don't want to work for the rest of my life, Bry. Do us both a favor and take an accounting job for another sixteen years. You'll have maxed out on social security, and if you invest up to the limit on IRAs every year, you'll be swimming in dough."

"Not the kind of dough I want to make, Mitch." She probably knew more about personal financial management than her brother. "I don't expect you to support me when I'm older, okay?"

Bailey looked up at her and wagged his tail. "Thank you," she mouthed to him.

"That's not the point," Mitch said.

"What is the point, Mitch?"

Bailey put his head between his paws and continued to make eye contact.

"What if I want to stop working and do something different? I don't have that freedom, and it irks me to hear you think you do."

How dare he try to manipulate her. "I don't think I have that freedom, Mitch. I know I have it. I won't starve. I want to be happy. Can you understand that?"

Bailey stood up and barked.

"Nothing you say makes sense to me. Where are you?" Mitch asked. "Did you get a dog?"

She wasn't going to tell him she was at Cal's house. "Can we agree to disagree?" she asked.

"Not an option," Mitch said. "Worrying about you keeps me awake at night."

He would say or do anything to control her, and his final attempt unleashed her anger. "Think of me as one of your students," she said. "You're good at compartmentalizing when it comes to them."

"What does that mean?" Mitch asked.

She had nothing else to say to her brother. "I think we're at an impasse. Let's not make it worse. I'll see you on Thursday."

"Don't forget the pies," Mitch said.

She couldn't think of a snappy comeback, so she said, "I won't. Goodbye," and hung up the phone.

Bailey barked again.

"Do you need to go out?" Bryony asked

Cal's dog lay down and put his head between his paws, watching her.

"Bark if you want to go for another walk."

He rolled to his side and closed his eyes.

Buggy started to purr.

Sandwiched between the dog and the cat, Bryony opened the book again and noticed how punching back a little invigorated her. Tomorrow night she would make and deliver a bean pie to Mitch because beans, beans were good for the heart, and he was full of hot air.

# CAL MAKES A CALL

O n the Wednesday before Thanksgiving, Cal pulled into the driveway of his father's house.

"The doctor sure was angry with you," his father said.

"He wasn't mad at me." Cal turned off the car. "He was frustrated with you."

The doctor had tried to educate Cal Sr. with facts and figures about the risk of falls to older adults. His patient replied with taunting suppositions about the doctor's motive, asking if he owned stock in companies providing care for the aged.

"It's my choice," his father said as he unfastened his seatbelt. "I'd rather die miserable at home than live in one of those places they stick you in to suck as much money out of you as they can while you slowly waste away."

"We're all trying to keep you as healthy as you can be," Cal said. "Nobody wants to see you in a situation where you're miserable, barely clinging to life."

His father flipped open the handle on the passenger side door. "I'll never cling to life, Cal. Miserable or not, life clings to me."

Once inside the house, Cal helped his father to the living

room. Earlier in the day, Heidi's husband and son-in-law had moved in an adjustable twin bed and potty chair, just in case.

After settling his father into the recliner beside the bed, Cal asked, "Do you need anything else?"

"You look worse than I do," his father said. "Go to bed."

"Heidi's bringing over dinner soon."

"I'll be fine." His father waved him out of the room. "See you in the morning."

"Okay." Cal backed out the door. "Call me if you need anything." He held up his cell phone.

His father touched the cell phone on the table beside his recliner. "I'm fine, Cal. Go to bed."

Trudging up the stairs, Cal pulled a slip of paper out of his pants pocket. Nurse Rachel had slipped her phone number to him after she wheeled his father out to the car. Cal keyed it into his cell phone with her name, laid the phone on the table beside his bed, and undressed.

He slid between the sheets, hoping for a quick nod off, but his mind raced. He picked up the phone and made a call, which was answered right away.

"Hi," he said.

"I'm glad you called," Bryony said.

Her voice was sweeter than anticipated, almost seductive.

"You are?" Cal's mind calmed as he focused on her voice. He thought about the kindness in her eyes, how it soothed him.

"How's your father doing?" she asked.

Cal sighed. "We made it home. He's comfortable. My sister's bringing dinner for him. I'm exhausted. I wanted to thank you for helping. You've made this all so much easier for me."

"Not a problem. How long do you think you'll be staying with your father?"

"I have no idea." Cal yawned. "We'll follow through with the discharge plan. Hire somebody to stay with him until we're sure he's stable, or longer. I think I'll be up here more often."

"Let's get together when you get back," Bryony said.

Cal's heart swelled. He needed this, something to look forward to. "I'd like that." He was so exhausted, so appreciative of her presence on the phone, he teared up.

"Sleep well, Cal."

"You too, Bryony."

Cal put his cell on the bedside table.

"Who was that on the phone?" Heidi leaned against the inside of the open door, her arms crossed.

"A friend."

"A friend who makes you happy."

Cal punched a cradle in the pillow for his head and said, "Yeah, she does."

"Someone local?" Heidi asked.

"She lives in Ohio."

Heidi waited a moment before saying, "Nurse Rachel was nice."

"Yeah, she was."

"She said she'd help us find help for Dad."

"Yeah, she told me that, too," Cal said. "She has a little home health gig on the side." Nurse Rachel was nice, maybe a little nicer than she needed to be. Yeah, she had gone out of her way to be nice. "Did you pick up the turkey?"

"I did."

"I'm so tired I can barely think." A vice of muscle tension pressed on both sides of his forehead. He hoped he hadn't picked up a virus in the hospital.

"I'm sorry," Heidi said. "You rest. I'll make sure Dad's comfortable before I leave. We'll eat at two tomorrow."

"Will you call Rudy and invite him?" Cal asked. "He ate alone last year."

"I can do that. Thanks for coming home, Cal."

"See you tomorrow, Heidi." He tugged the blanket around his shoulders as he turned to the wall.

"Goodnight, Cal," Heidi said. "Sounds like Rachel will be able to help us out with Dad." The door shut softly.

He and Rachel had a chance to talk while his father slept. Turned out she and Cal were the same age. She said she had worked at the hospital for over thirty years. She had grown children. Her husband had died of a heart attack a few years ago.

She seemed solid and kind. If he were looking to date someone in Cleveland, he might choose her.

# A MOUTHFUL OF PIE CHART

On Thanksgiving Day, Bryony delivered her father and five pies to Mitch's house. Knowing her family would prefer an assortment of traditional favorites, she chose sweet potato, pumpkin, walnut, and pecan, but added a savory surprise for the main meal.

Carol welcomed them into the house and took their coats while fawning over "Papa Green." He grunted appreciation, his head down, not looking at his daughter-in-law as she led him into the living room to seat him on the couch. As his grandchildren, their spouses, and his great grandchildren arrived, Bryony's father barely acknowledged them. Mitch's arrival elicited only a slightly warmer greeting.

The younger generation filled the room with overlapping conversations and human heat. Bryony tried to keep up, and when she couldn't, sat back and listened. Mitch asked his children, their spouses, and his grandchildren questions and used all of their short replies to reflect on his own experiences. Nobody tried to include Bryony or her father in the back and forth.

Finally, Carol called them to the table.

Making it all the way through the main meal without saying more than, "Yes, please," and "No, thank you," Bryony's father managed to keep his delivery civil until Mitch commented on how nice it was to have the family together again.

At that point, her father looked up from his dessert plate and said, "I don't see why Alma couldn't come. There's always enough food for a battalion, and an army could fit in your house."

"We wanted it to be just family," Mitch said.

"She's family to me," her father said and stuffed another bite of pie into his mouth.

"We'll invite her next time, Papa Green," Carol said. She turned to Bryony, speaking louder than necessary. "Mitch tells me you're thinking of starting a pie business, Bryony."

Bryony's fork halted an inch from her mouth, and she laid the bite back down on her plate. Her sister-in-law's record for perfect timing remained unbeatable. "I'm in the dreaming stage at this point."

"You always were a dreamer." Her father wiped his mouth on a cloth napkin. "Always with your head in the clouds. That's why you'll always be an old maid. No man wants a woman who doesn't put dinner on the table every night."

*In 1955, in your dreams*, Bryony thought. She and her father had been getting along so well, but back in the dynamic of their family of origin, he reverted to his old surly self.

"He's only telling it like it is," Mitch said. "Starting a business at this stage of the game is beyond ridiculous. Do you know how many fail in the first year? Twenty percent. Those are not good odds, Bry. You'd do better to go back to working full time until you can't anymore. I do not want to rescue you from financial collapse. I am not made of money."

The other adults around the table had gone silent.

Unwilling to further ruin their holiday meal, Bryony thanked her brother for his concern and said she would take his advice into consideration. The tactic seemed to work as he turned his focus to asking for another piece of pie, "with more whipped cream this time," and then lamented about how much he had already eaten and how horrible he would feel in the morning.

Enduring until the end of the meal, Bryony offered to help clear the table, but the younger adults insisted on cleaning up. Carol escorted her father-in-law into the family room. Mitch announced his plan to retire to his recliner in front of the football game, but before he left the table, Bryony asked if he could give their father a ride back to the Assisted Living. When Mitch started to complain, his daughter stepped up and offered a ride for her grandfather. Relieved of duty, Mitch started to head for the recliner. Bryony cut him off at the doorway to the family room.

"Mitch, can I talk to you for a minute?"

He sighed deeply before escorting her to his home office—a small room off the front hallway—and, once inside, stood with his arms folded across his chest. "What is it, Bryony?"

"I want you to look at something." She pulled an envelope out of her purse. "Not that it's any of your business, but it seems like you need to have this information."

"What's this?" He extracted the documents and unfolded them. "Is Dad getting kicked out of that place? All the more reason for you to move in with him...." His voice trailed off as he scanned the first sheet of paper. "What is this?"

"That's a spreadsheet of my assets and liabilities." She hadn't intended to show her spreadsheet to Mitch, but she had it in her purse because she met with her financial advisor a few weeks ago and had yet to refile it. Given her brother's incessant insistence that she would end up poor, or that he would end up having to support her, showing him evidence to the contrary just made sense. "If you want, you can turn to the next-to-the-last page to review the totals of all of my accounts.

The last page is just a colored pie chart of where my assets are located."

Her brother did as she instructed and—following a word that might have resulted in a high school expulsion—blurted out, "Is this for real? How did this happen?"

"I've been investing money since I was eighteen," she answered. "I own my house and car, and have budgeted for needed repairs. Even if the stock market plummets, I'll be in good shape because my financial holdings are dispersed over a wide range of risk tolerance."

"You have more money than I do!" Mitch exclaimed.

"You had more people to spend your money on," Bryony said to soften the blow.

She took the papers from his hands and slid them back into the envelope.

"You could lose all of what it would take to start a business and still have enough money to fund a long, comfortable retirement," Mitch said, still sounding incredulous. He sank into his desk chair. "You really don't need me to take care of you."

"That's what I've been telling you, Mitch. I haven't needed anybody to take care of me for a very long time."

Her brother looked dazed.

"Are you okay?" Bryony asked.

"This changes everything," he said, shaking his head. "I just can't believe it."

Bryony shrugged her shoulders. "I wasn't trying to hide it." Maybe she and her brother should have had this conversation years ago.

Mitch sighed deeply, pushed himself out of his chair, placed his forearms on Bryony's shoulders, and looked her square in the face. She wasn't quite holding him up, but she could feel his weight pressing down.

"Little sister," he said. "I apologize for all of the times I have doubted you. Clearly, you have much to teach me."

Tears sprang to Bryony's eyes. "That's that nicest thing you've ever said to me."

Before she could offer a hug, Mitch removed his arms and stepped back. "Now go on home before Dad figures out you left without him. I have a game to watch."

Halfway to her car, Bryony heard Carol call from the porch, "Thanks for the pies. They were delicious."

Bryony walked back, gave her sister-in-law a warm embrace, and said, "Dinner was wonderful. Thanks for having me."

At home, she took out the yellow legal pad provided by Etta when they met to discuss a business plan. Together they had worked on a pitch. Bryony crossed out everything she had written and flipped to a fresh sheet.

*Nobody can sell love*, she wrote. *You can't buy peace. You have peace and feel love when you savor the moment. All over the world, families share a pie when they gather for holidays, for funerals, for a special meal together. Take the time to notice those around you. They are the foundation of your purpose, your passion. Savor those moments. Share a peace today.*

Satisfied, she put the pad face down on her desk and gathered her overnight bag.

Tonight she would sleep in Cal's bed.

Because being in his house made her feel more comfortable than she had ever felt anywhere.

Bailey met her at the door. After walking him, and feeding both him and Buggy, Bryony settled into the reading chair. Soon Buggy came in and assumed her place on the back of the chair, smelling of the sea, brushing Bryony's cheek with her tail and licking her paws right behind the top of Bryony's head. Bailey positioned himself at her feet.

All was well with her world.

Cal called at nine o'clock. "Do you need to roll around on the floor to distribute the extra calories?" he asked.

"No." Bryony laughed "I paced myself."

"Smart," he said. "How are the kids?"

"They miss you. Buggy threw up a hairball." Bailey thumped his tail. "Do you think Bailey understands English?"

"I do!" Cal said. "Thank you for noticing. Everybody thinks I'm crazy when I say he knows the difference between Vivaldi and Mozart. He always chooses The Four Seasons."

"If you're crazy, I'm crazy, too," Bryony said.

"Nice to know I'm not alone."

This was how they used to talk, before Bryony withdrew from him, which seemed ridiculous now. She slid into the familiar back-and-forth as she moved to the floor to rub Bailey's back and belly. She talked until she was hoarse. Cal listened, but never remained silent for long. He asked for details about where she was on her pie list and lamented not having sampled all of them, making her promise to repeat the performance when he could taste test. As before, she found their conversation intoxicating.

After a few hours, Cal yawned.

"Go to bed," Bryony said. "You have to be ready for your father tomorrow."

"And you have to be ready to cheerfully greet each customer on the biggest shopping day of the year."

They talked a few minutes longer until she insisted she had to go to bed because Cal sounded like he was falling asleep.

After they both hung up, she carried her small suitcase up the stairs and opened the door to Cal's room.

Bailey brushed past her and climbed onto the bottom of the bed. Bryony laid her clothes on the chair and put on her nightgown. She went to the bathroom to brush her teeth, came back to turn off the overhead light, and crawled in between the sheets.

The pillow smelled woodsy, like Cal's aftershave.

Inhaling deeply, Bryony started listing gratitudes. Cal topped the list, and he came at the end, too.

Life was good when it began and ended with Cal.

# CAL CHOOSES

$\mathcal{T}$he Sunday evening after Thanksgiving, Cal pulled into the driveway of his rented house in Fieldstone. Front and back porch lights cast yellowish glows in the freezing drizzle. Lamps left on in the living room and hallway sparked a tiny hope Bryony's car might be hidden away in the garage, but Bailey alone greeted him at the front door.

Dropping everything he carried onto the floor in the hall, he leashed up his dog and took him for a walk. When he returned, he wiped Bailey down with a towel, then carried his laundry to the washer and his bag up the stairs.

The house felt different. A whiff of Bryony's perfume hung in the air. He found small yellow notes stuck in various locations.

On the bed, the note read, *I washed your sheets so you wouldn't have to bother with them when you returned.* Not likely he would have given clean sheets a second thought, but he liked the gesture.

When he returned to the first floor, he found a note on the kitchen counter. *Bailey and I made a pie last night. Most of it is in the fridge. I did some shopping. I hope I picked out what appeals to you.* Cal opened the refrigerator and found oranges, boxed salad, a quart of milk, eggs, sliced turkey, cheese, cottage cheese, celery, carrots, green and red peppers, and a pumpkin pie with a tiny sliver missing. He pulled out the pie, cut his own tiny sliver, and ate it in three bites.

"Oh, my, Bailey. Did you try this? It's delicious!"

Bailey sat on the mat in front of the sink and cocked his head to the right.

In the pantry, Cal found bananas, apples, sweet potatoes, Idaho potatoes, onions, granola, tuna, a fresh jar of mayonnaise, and a loaf of whole grain bread. He stepped out of the pantry to find Bailey still sitting on the mat. "Did you see all that food in there? I'm counting on your help, buddy." Bailey cocked his head to the left.

A hand-crafted ceramic mug, one Cal rarely used, sat upside down in the dish drainer. He habitually chose the stained giveaways from The Ohio Teachers Association, The Red Cross, and The Good Shepherd Funeral Home. Bryony's taste in drinking vessels exceeded his. He should follow her lead in that area.

He opened the cabinet to take out a small plate and pulled the pie from the refrigerator. Cutting off a sizable piece, he placed it on the plate, collected a fork from the drawer, and sat down.

Two bites in, he pulled his phone out of his pocket and selected Heidi's number.

She answered after one ring.

"I made it home, Heidi."

"Home is here, Cal. We need you."

"I have to finish out the school year," Cal said.

"I'm not ready to handle this on my own," she said. "I don't think I have another six months of emergency calls, trips to the hospital, meal preparation, and running over there two or three times a day."

Cal brought his hand to his neck and massaged. "Let's hire someone to live in."

"And where are we going to find someone we trust?" she asked.

"Rachel, you know, Dad's nurse at the hospital. She said she would help."

"It'll be expensive," Heidi said.

"He has the money." Cal didn't know his father's total worth, but he knew there was plenty. Cal Sr. would never go broke.

"He won't want to pay," Heidi said.

"You're his POA for finance. Talk him into it. Remember when you wanted the hundred and eighty dollar prom dress?"

"You remember that?" Heidi asked.

"I cowered in my bedroom. You two had a heck of a fight."

"I got the dress," Heidi said.

"You can talk him into anything."

She was silent for a few moments, then asked, "When are you coming back?"

"I'll drive up Friday night," Cal said. "And I'll come home every weekend until we have someone living in."

"Don't get too close to your new friend," Heidi said.

"She's not interested that way."

In spite of their extended phone conversations the last few nights, and his helpless hoping for more, Bryony had expressed no interest other than friendship. She would stay in Fieldstone and bake pies. He would return to Cleveland and help his sister help their father.

"Will you call Rachel and arrange to have an aide?" Heidi asked.

"Sure." Until he could be there in person, he would do what he could to help from a distance.

"When you call her, why don't you set up a date for next weekend? Dad liked her."

Cal chuckled. His sister was so predictable. "You want Dad to date Nurse Rachel?"

"That's not funny," Heidi said. "Ask her out."

"I should ask her out because Dad likes her?"

"She's nice, Cal."

"I'll think about it," Cal said.

They ended the call, and he polished off the pie before opening his phone again and deliberating.

Rachel's last name was Gebhart, and her contact information sat right on top of Bryony's on his "G" list. He should call Bryony first, to thank her for helping out with Bailey and Buggy. He thought about their wonderful conversations, about his desire to have them become a nightly habit. But, he reminded himself, she had been firm in her decision to be his friend, nothing more. To try to convince her otherwise would be rude.

Sooner or later he had to call Rachel. Heidi was moving toward burnout, and his father's care needs would only increase, but the call would signal something more than just a business transaction. Rachel had gone out of her way to show interest in him. She was attractive, intelligent, actually quite appealing.

The ear worm started up again. Should he stay, or should he go?

He looked one more time at Bryony's number and selected the contact above it.

# CHARITY FOR BRYONY

*B*eanHereNow welcomed customers to the holiday season with a nativity scene for those celebrating Christmas, a Kinara with red, black, and green candles for those celebrating Kwanzaa, and a menorah with white candles for those celebrating Chanukah.

When a young man sporting a T-shirt reading *God is Dead* asked, "What do you have for the atheists?" Lillian replied, "All the love in my heart and everywhere that is not decorated." The young man's countenance softened, and he paid it forward for the customer behind him.

Bryony loved working in the coffee shop.

Even the sight of Cal standing in front of the counter failed to dull her mood.

"Christmas will be here soon," he said. "Do you have all your presents wrapped?"

Bryony pushed his latte across the counter and smiled. "I haven't finished buying them."

She had hoped to have a reason to buy something for him, but when he returned after Thanksgiving, he seemed distant. The short set of daily phone calls while he was in Cleveland had ended with no explanation. He had sent a sweet note with a gift card in the mail to thank her for helping out with Bailey and Buggy.

Barely recovered from the embarrassment of sleeping in his bed, imagining a future with him, Bryony marveled at her ability to face him without blushing. "I have good news," she said.

His eyes lit up and, for a moment, the old Cal was back. "What is it?"

"Lillian and I plan to merge my pie business with the coffee shop. We're going to expand into the next building." She filled him in briefly. A friend's mother-in-law owned the building next door and had offered it for a hard-to-beat price. Mr. Parker's brother, an architect, had drawn up a preliminary plan. A regular customer helped price equipment and other start-up costs.

"I'm so happy you're going after what you want." Cal sounded supportive, like a teacher, like any caring person, but not like someone who would be around to celebrate when the shop opened.

She wanted to go after him, too, but, "I'm thrilled," was all she could get out before Charity Henderson walked in the door and headed straight for the counter.

"Hey, Cal. How's commuting back to Cleveland every weekend? How's your father doing?"

"Cranky," Cal said. "We're shoring up his care so he can stay home as long as possible."

"Good luck with that!" Charity said. "We struggled to find the right person when I needed help with Chuck."

"We're ahead of the game," Cal said. "Dad met a nurse when he was in the hospital right before Thanksgiving, and she's taken a special interest in him."

"We all need someone with a special interest." Charity turned to include Bryony in the conversation. "I want to apologize to both of you for suggesting Susie Q could help either of you in any way. She's more bluster than business. Always has been. Anyway, she's gone off to California now, so good luck to her there." She pulled off her gloves and laid them on the counter.

Cal chuckled. "Susie Q—that's funny." He picked up his cup. "Gotta run. You two have a good day." He held his coffee aloft with a "thanks for this" to Bryony and headed to the door.

Bryony looked at Charity and smiled.

Charity placed her fingertips on the counter. "Bryony, I also want to apologize for something else."

The shop door closed behind Cal. Bryony brought her full attention back to Charity. "What for?"

"For being such a jerk to you all through school." Charity steadied herself on the counter, her symmetrical, perfect face sober. "You were always nice to me, and I acted terribly after Susie convinced me that you had a thing for Chuck. I have a grandchild who was recently cyber-bullied." She lowered her head and shook it slowly back and forth. "Some of those text messages she received were pretty reminiscent of how we treated you. I now realize how awful that can be for the person on the receiving end." She raised her head, and Bryony could see the contrition on that beautiful perfect face. "I am asking for your forgiveness."

"In Susie's defense," Bryony said. "I did kind of have a thing for Chuck in high school."

Charity's countenance softened, and she chuckled. "Of course you did! Every girl had a thing for Chuck back then."

When Bryony smiled this time, a flood of warmth filled her chest. "True."

Placing her hand over Bryony's, Charity asked, "Will you come to our holiday gathering this Sunday? We'd love to include you in celebrating our good fortune."

Without hesitation, Bryony said, "I'd love to come."

"Thank you." Charity removed her hand and picked up her gloves. She started to leave, but turned back. "I almost forgot the reason I came in. I heard you're opening a pie business. Do you have time to bake some for the party? We'll need about a dozen."

"I'd love to," Bryony answered, amazed she had spoken that phrase twice within two minutes to Charity Henderson and actually meant it.

"Great! You pick what kind to make. Bring them with you. The party starts at four."

"Okay," Bryony said. "I'll be there."

Charity left, and the next customer came through the door behind her.

The natural light in the shop suddenly brightened, as if a cloud had passed and the sun could shine unfiltered again. Forgiveness was a wonderful thing. If only one could bake it into a pie and feed it to the world.

# CAL CHOOSES, AGAIN

*C*al sat down at the kitchen table for his morning call with Rachel. He put her on speaker and laid the phone beside his cereal bowl.

Their mix of professional and personal had seemed like a good idea in late November. Now he wasn't sure. The phone time felt like a chore, one more task to complete in a day filled with a never-ending list of tasks.

"Your father's doing great!" Rachel said. "The girls love him. He walked around the block with Ellie last night."

"Whose idea was that?" Cal asked. His father had given up evening walks when he retired.

"He insisted," Rachel answered. "Said he's ready to resume his *daily constitutional* to inspect the neighborhood."

"Great to hear, Rachel." Cal would be forever grateful to the nurse who had organized an entire posse of young women to look after his father. They cooked, cleaned, ran errands, took him to appointments, and learned his favorite games. In short, they were a new kind of family for Cal Sr., a family based on providing every need possible until his life ended, as it should be for everyone.

"What time do you arrive tonight?" she asked.

"I'm not coming this weekend," Cal answered.

"Why not?"

Cal sighed. He liked Rachel. He appreciated her help, her wit, her zip, but the disappointment in her voice concerned him. She seemed wounded by his decision to do something other than what she expected. "Papers to grade. And a friend's having a holiday party on Sunday."

"Do you have a date for the party?" she asked, coyly.

"No," Cal answered, not too bothered by the need to play along with her teasing way to ask for reassurance. "I told you. I'm a one-woman-at-a-time kind of guy."

"I could be your date for the party," Rachel said.

"What?" The implication jarred him. Rachel in Fieldstone?

"I don't have any shifts at the hospital," she said. "I could drive down."

"Umm, wow." He rubbed his head. "Let me think for a minute, okay? Talk about it tonight?"

"Sure!" Her upbeat tone sounded forced. "Call me tonight."

"Will do!"

He ended the call, finished his breakfast, and rinsed his bowl. Why not ask Rachel to come with him to the party on Sunday? She would like Chuck and Charity. They would like her. Win-win all around. But then there would be the issue of her spending the night. He stepped around Bailey as he walked away from the sink.

"What do you think, buddy? Are we ready for a sleepover? It's been a long time." Bailey yawned.

All the way to school, Cal thought about whether or not he should invite Rachel to the party on Saturday. By the time he parked his car, he was still undecided. He walked into the school continuing to deliberate.

Before he could make it past the door to the administration

suite, Mitch stepped out into the hall and called to him. "I have news. Come on in."

Cal switched direction with his legs while his heart continued down the hall. Listening to Mitch was not how he wanted to start the day, but he followed him into the suite and through the door to his office.

"Close the door behind you and have a seat!" Mitch's smile gleamed bright, and he exceeded his usual level of polished appearance.

"Fresh haircut?" Cal sat on the edge of chair facing Mitch's desk.

Mitch smoothed his hair back, though it lay sculpted against his scalp. "Important meeting tonight. Gotta last through the day." He sat back in his chair and put his feet on the desk. "Listen, Cal. I have the final word from the board. They refused to consider an extension of the work study program. They are pouring every resource into STEM. They're removing funds from the music and art programs, too."

Cal stood, disgusted when he found himself mimicking Mitch's behavior, his hand stroking back his own hair, but not for the sake of grooming. Cal was trying to keep his head from exploding. Cutting the work study program was bad enough. Killing music and art bordered on educational collapse. He could not keep the vitriol out of his voice.

"STEM has given way to STEAM, inclusive of arts programs," he said. "And now there's even STREAM, which incorporates reading into a truly collaborative curriculum. The arts keep our spirits alive, and reading is essential for everything."

"We have limited funds," Mitch said.

"You have limited imaginations." Cal knew he was over the line.

"You have no idea how our budget works."

"If you'd read my resume, you would know that I finished a

principal licensure program ten years ago, and I have an associates degree in accounting." He cut loose the anger he'd been sitting on since meeting the man. "You appear to have no idea how people work."

Rather than yell back, or get red in the face, Mitch folded his hands against his stomach and smiled. "I like you, Cal."

"What?" What in the world was Bryony's brother talking about? Whether or not he liked Cal had nothing to do with supporting the young people of Fieldstone. Mitch Green must be insane.

"I like you, and I'm going to let you in on a big secret."

Cal waited, his temper cooling as he seriously wondered if Mitch was losing his mind.

"In the past month, I have learned something about myself. You're right. I don't understand how people work. How they think, how they feel, who they really are. And pretending I do understand them exhausts me."

For the first time since meeting him, Cal wanted to listen to the man. He sat in the chair opposite the desk and waited.

"That is why"—Mitch lowered his feet to the floor and leaned forward in his chair—"I am tendering my resignation tonight, effective the end of the school year. And you know who I'm recommending to fill my spot?"

"Who?"

Finger pointed, Mitch announced the candidate. "You."

Cal cocked his head to the side. "Me?" Rarely would he have been able to label his reaction as flummoxed. This was one of those times.

"You're qualified and know people, Cal. That's what this job demands. Are you up to it?"

As much as he tried to maintain composure, Cal could not keep the corners of his mouth from turning upward. "I'm flattered."

"Think about it. Who knows? Maybe you'll be able to turn

them around about the work study program, hang on to art and music, weave in that reading thing you were talking about."

"Is that a dare?" Cal asked.

"It's whatever it will take to push you to say yes."

"I'll think about it." Cal stood, realizing he would think about it, which might be dangerous. He walked to the door and pushed it open.

"And Cal?" Mitch said.

Cal turned to face him again.

"I gave Bryony a hard time for going out with you because, well, I had a hard time seeing her go out with anybody. I watched our father mistreat her practically every day of her young life, and I am ashamed to admit that I was a silent witness. As an adult, I have tried to protect her like I should have protected her back then, when we were young."

Cal took a step back in to the room and started to say, "That's actually quite insight—" but Mitch cut him off.

"Let me finish, Cal. I have recently discovered that not only can my sister care for herself better than I can, but I now see that she deserves someone like you. Treat her right."

Cal deliberated. Should he tell Mitch his sister had shut down any possibility of a future together? Should he stay and offer Mitch perspective on why that might be? Because he might be wrong, but Cal was fairly certain the guy who had just admitted he knew jack about how to treat people, the same one who had silently witnessed his father mistreat his sister, that guy had probably also played a more direct role in his sister being too frightened to take a chance on love. He'd seen how Mitch addressed bullying, how he disciplined students. He terrified them.

Nah. He wouldn't say any of that. Nothing to gain by going there.

He left the office, closed the door behind him, and made a fresh decision. He would not think about Mitch's offer. As planned from the beginning, Cal would leave Fieldstone at the end of school year.

Why wait until tonight to call Rachel back? He pulled out his phone to send a text. Having her visit would be a good thing. Mitch recommending Cal as the next principal was a great ego boost, but he would be moving back to Cleveland at the end of the school year. Rachel would tie him to the place he belonged.

Besides, he reasoned as he hit the icon to send the text, having Rachel visit would also help him properly bury his feelings for Mitch's sister because Bryony had been very clear.

She only wanted friendship, and he didn't think he could live with that if he had to continue to run into her on a regular basis.

# BRYONY'S DEVASTATING MISTAKE

**B**ryony drove to work on Monday, reliving the Henderson party for the umpteenth time. On the plus side, Charity and she had spent a long time sitting at the kitchen table chatting about a host of topics, and Chuck had a smile on his face every time she looked at him. Also, Lillian and Rick were there. And everybody raved about her pies.

The plus side was no match, however, for the devastating impact of seeing Cal with a date, a nurse he had met in Cleveland. Her name was Rachel. She seemed to be a good fit for him. Warm and friendly, athletic-looking, she might have been a stand in for Meghan Markle.

During the party, Lillian pulled Bryony to the side to apologize profusely for pushing her to date him. *I'm so sorry, honey. I won't stick my nose into your love life ever again. I promise.*

Unable to speak the truth, Bryony said, *My heart is not broken*. What was that thing Cal found unforgivable, lying by omission? Guilty. She had omitted everything she truly felt and thought when she rejected him. She had been lying to him and to herself since. No point in changing that now. He'd moved on.

After parking in her usual spot, she headed for the door of

BeanHereNow. Lillian had decorated the front of the shop with deep green garland, red bulbs, faux snow on the windows, and a huge wreath on the front door, which was unlocked.

The lights were on inside the shop, but when Bryony entered and called out, "Hello," nobody answered. She took a breath to still her thoughts. Lillian had talked about letting Todd close by himself. Had she entrusted Bryony's charge with the ultimate responsibility, and had he utterly failed?

Yesterday morning a shipment of specialty cups and thermos mugs sat in the corner waiting to be unpacked. Now all four boxes were gone, but they weren't on display in the customer area. She made a quick check of the stockroom and office. No boxes, also no Todd, or Lillian.

Panicked, Bryony checked the hiding place for the cash box. Lillian insisted on keeping several hundred dollars on hand, in case they ever ran out of change. The small green lock box was gone.

Bryony went into Lillian's office, which was also unlocked, and dropped into the desk chair. She had shown the location of the cash to Todd last week.

There were only two explanations for the missing money and merchandise.

Either Todd had left the door unlocked and someone robbed them, or Todd stole those items from the shop. The second explanation made the most sense. Who else would think to look for the lock box behind the paper products on top of the supply shelves?

Profound disappointment flooded her heart and mind. She had not only come to rely on Todd as a co-worker, she liked him.

The front door opened. She had left it unlocked when she arrived. Now what?

Bryony peaked out of the office to see Todd locking the front door from the inside. She set her posture, moved forward while readying herself for one of the toughest conversations of her life, and planted her feet behind the counter.

He turned and smiled. "Hey, Bryony. You should keep this locked when you're alone in here. No telling who might come in.

Walking toward her with a little swagger in his step, he wore his skinny black jeans, leather jacket, and boots. Bryony maintained eye contact, her lips pressed together.

By the time he reached the counter, his smile had faded. He stopped a few feet away from her and arched one eyebrow. "What's up?"

She could smell his soap, something herbal and so clean it heightened her sense of betrayal. How could he? She had been congratulating herself, at least in part, for his transformation. Maybe he would have been better off without it, without her, without responsibility. Turned out he couldn't handle it, any of it.

Todd reached out and put his hand on her arm. "You look terrible. What happened? Did something happen to Lillian?"

Bryony moved away from him. "Did you close up last night?"

He drew his hand back and clasped it with his other hand. "Yeah, why?"

"The door was unlocked when I arrived. Stock is missing. The cash box is gone."

"What?" Was that guilt or panic on his face? "I locked the door, Bryony. I remember locking the door."

"Then how did somebody get in here?" Bryony hated how her voice sounded, hard, dead.

"How should I know?" His eyebrows knit together now, and his face reddened.

She had to cut to the chase before Lillian arrived. Bryony would do everything she could to help Todd, but he had to acknowledge either being irresponsible or committing theft. "Whatever happened, I will help you work it out," she said, her voice softening a fraction of a decibel. "Tell me, Todd. Did you leave the door unlocked, or did you take the money and the new merchandise?"

"You think I stole that stuff?"

She forced herself to be calm. He would either admit to leaving the door unlocked or confess to stealing, show contrition, and return the goods and money. "You say you remember locking up, but when I arrived, the shop was unlocked, and we had been robbed."

"So, you think I did it."

"I think somebody did. Or you left the door unlocked. Which was it?" Focused on the only two possibilities that made sense, she needed to understand what he had done in order to help him.

He threw his hands up in the air. "That's just great!"

Bryony froze. Something wasn't right. He appeared anything but contrite.

"Screw you, Bryony. Screw you, and screw this place. I'm done." Todd turned and stormed to the door. He struggled for a second to unlock the deadbolt before pulling the door open and walking out into the early morning darkness.

Lillian walked in behind him, her head turned, her arms full. "What's wrong with Todd?" she asked as she unloaded bags onto the nearest table.

Bryony walked toward her. "Brace yourself. I have bad news."

"What happened?" Lillian pulled off her gloves.

Bryony sighed hard. "When I arrived this morning, the door was unlocked. The cash box, holiday mugs, and thermoses were missing. When I asked Todd about it, he quit. Should we call the police?"

"I don't think the police will be necessary, Bryony."

"Good." Bryony took a deep breath. "I'd much rather deal with this directly with Todd."

"First, you'll have to deal with me," Lillian said. "I left the door unlocked this morning when I took the merchandise over to Berry's Gifts. They'd had so many requests, I agreed to sell them over there, too."

Bryony's stomach clenched.

"And I moved the cash box to the bottom desk drawer after I replaced some petty cash I took out last week. I was in a hurry and didn't want to get back up on the ladder. I planned to put the box back up on the shelf first thing this morning."

"You did?" Bryony slumped into a chair.

"I did."

Bryony blew out a long breath. "I really screwed up."

"I take it Todd won't be working today," Lillian said.

"I think not." Chances were, he wouldn't be working today or any day after today. She didn't blame him.

"You put on the coffee," Lillian said, more Mom-voiced than ever before in their entire relationship. "I'll start the bagels."

"I have to call Todd first." Bryony pulled out her cell phone. She had to at least try.

"He won't answer," Lillian said. "Teenagers don't seem to know how to talk on the phone anymore. Text him. And don't write a whole explanation. Just text, 'So S-R-Y. I was W-R-N-G.'"

"S-R-Y? W-R-N-G?" Bryony asked.

"When I text the grandkids' babysitters, I take out the vowels and double letters. 'I apologize' should be conveyed in the first language of the one receiving the apology."

"I should have started studying this when we hired him."

"You should have investigated before jumping to conclusions."

"Don't rub it in." What a royal mess she had managed to make.

"Go make it right," Lillian said. "And don't forget to start the coffee when you're done texting him."

Bryony texted Todd immediately. She thought about texting Cal, but she didn't want to wreck the beginning of his Christmas vacation. Besides, Rachel might still be with him. If so, he would confide in her his great luck in dodging the small town bullet know as Bryony. The idea of them being together, talking about her, celebrating his escape, crushed her.

She flipped the coffee maker button to on.

Cal had said more than once he couldn't forgive people who hurt his students. Bryony had never dreamed she would be one of the people on his list. Todd had been their initial reason for coming together. And now Todd would be the final blow to anything beyond a passing friendship. Cal would move back to Cleveland in June to be with Rachel. Bryony would open a pie shop, maybe, if Lillian would forgive her.

She checked her phone. Nothing back from Todd yet.

Maybe she should talk to Charity about her old job. People were not her strength. She would prefer to face down a long line of million dollar mistakes than to ever again be the reason for the look on Todd's face when she had all but flat out accused him of theft or dereliction of duty.

For a brief moment, Bryony Green had found her place in the sun, but now she needed to retreat back to fluorescent lights and safe little spreadsheets. She'd never met a row of numbers she couldn't whip into shape, and miscalculations were easily repaired because math errors weren't devastated by her fallibility.

# CAL CHOOSES WISELY THIS TIME

"*D*id you sleep okay?" Cal asked.

Rachel stood at the sink filling the electric tea pot. "I can sleep anywhere."

"Thanks for last night."

She turned around to offer a slightly sarcastic smile. "You're welcome."

"No, really," Cal said as he stepped farther into the kitchen. "I am forever grateful for everything you've offered. Your understanding, your insight, not to mention how much you've helped my father."

Turning away from him to shut off the faucet, Rachel shrugged her shoulders and said, "I knew you were too good to be true."

"Now you're making me feel really guilty." Enervated by the previous night's insomnia, Cal sat at the table and ran his fingers through his hair. He guessed she had not slept much either.

After the Henderson's party, they had driven back to his house, both of them straining to have a congenial conversation. Finally, Rachel had broken through the pretense with a direct question about his interest in Bryony. She had seen the look on his face when he introduced them. A few well-worded questions had him confessing all. He had never wanted anyone as much as he wanted Bryony Green.

Rachel had listened with compassion and understanding. She said she was happy to find out now, before something more serious started between Cal and herself. She said she didn't want to be anybody's second choice, and he shouldn't settle for less than what he really wanted. Cal had expressed deep appreciation for her understanding. When she said she wanted to turn in for the night, he had offered her the bed, saying he could sleep on the couch, but she had insisted that the couch would be fine for her. She was used to napping on one at work during her breaks.

"You know," Rachel said as she brought two mugs to the table. "I sensed you were backing off, and I should have been more thoughtful, but you're such a keeper, Cal Forster." A bit of vitality crept back into her voice.

He reached out and took her hand. "Thank you, Rachel. So are you."

They worked together to prepare breakfast, and by the time they returned to the table, Rachel had completely recovered her usual joie de vivre. As they ate, they talked like old friends, compared notes about favorite sites in and around Cleveland, and discussed Cal's father.

Cal Sr. had come around to resembling the man he had been after he stopped drinking and before he retired. He lived every day as if the world mattered to him and he to the world. Cal realized his father did not need his son to ease the disappointment in his life. Rachel and her gang of aides and nurses had done that. The relationships these women provided had saved him.

"Enough about him," Rachel said as she sopped up the last of her egg with a bit of English muffin. "Let's talk about you."

"What about me?" Cal asked.

"What are you going to do about Bryony?"

"I'm not sure," Cal answered. "She said she needed to focus on her own life. Basically, she indicated that I was a bit too much for her."

Rachel laughed. "You're too much for anybody, Cal, but worth the effort." She stood and gathered their plates. "Besides, I saw the way Bryony looked at you." She carried the dishes to the sink, calling over her shoulder, "Try again."

"What about you?" Cal asked. Given the rapid shift in her mood and the content of her shared thoughts, he assumed he was safe in asking. "Any prospects out there?"

"Not really," she answered.

"Have you tried a dating app? 'Awesome widow seeks equally awesome life partner with whom to share life's adventures.'"

"I don't need awesome," Rachel said. "I'd settle for a reliable boyfriend. Preferably someone under the age of seventy who does not currently require my professional services."

Of course! Cal should have seen this all along. Rachel had never been meant for him. "Mind if I set you up with my friend, Rudy?" he asked.

Snorting a laugh, Rachel answered, "What have I got to lose?"

Thirty minutes later, they hugged in the driveway. Cal handed over a thermos of hot coffee, and Rachel left with a wave and no ill wishes. He felt nothing but relief that there was no mess to clean up there, not with Rachel, not in his own heart.

He only had the time it took to walk into the house, though, to be summoned to assist with someone else's mess.

Todd called, his voice frantic.

They agreed to meet in the parking lot of a cafe on the edge of town.

Once there, Todd laid out the story of what had happened

when he showed up for work, on time, at the coffee shop that morning. It didn't take a shrink to help him reflect on how Bryony questioning him had reminded him of what had happened to his brother. He felt guilty, even though he was innocent. The young man had remarkable insight.

"I did not take the money or the merchandise," he said. "And I locked the door when I left last night."

Cal continued to ask questions to help him focus.

"If only I'd been less volatile," Todd said. "Do employees ever recover from saying, 'Screw you,' to their bosses?"

"No worries, pal," Cal said, and recited the many times he had been almost as blunt.

After another round of processing fear that his reaction had cost him his job, Todd decided on his own to return to BeanHereNow at closing time and discuss the situation with both Bryony and Lillian.

Before they parted, Todd turned his phone on, checked his texts, and found an apology from Bryony. She had sent it before Cal and Todd had started talking.

All shadows of remaining hopelessness disappeared from Todd's face.

Cal offered to go to the coffee shop right away and smooth any remaining ruffled feathers related to Todd's reactive behavior. Then, he sent him off with a hearty clap on the back. Todd grinned and loped off to his car.

Having given Todd a helping hand, Cal needed to do the same for himself.

THE WINDOWS AT BeanHereNow were steamed on the inside, and the tables half full of customers. Most were hunched over their phones or computers.

The interaction Cal was about to have with Bryony scared

him. He stood on a precipice, ready to fall, hoping there would be no hard landing.

Bryony met him halfway into the customer seating area.

"Have you talked to Todd?" she asked, her voice low, urgent.

Cal took her elbow and led her to a little table off to the side, one they had used in the past.

"He's fine. He's embarrassed about his reaction," Cal said.

"He has every right to be angry. I was wrong." Bryony blushed but maintained eye contact. "I am so sorry, Cal. I let you both down."

"I appreciate you acknowledging the importance of your position." Cal put his hand over hers, and she didn't pull away. "In the long run, this will be a great lesson for him."

Bryony lowered her eyes. "I can't believe you're being so understanding about this. I was horrible to him."

"You've been great for Todd, and he appreciates you. He wants to know if he still has a job."

"Yes!" Her head flew up, and she locked eyes. "He wants to come back?"

"I told him to drive a hard bargain, to make you work hard for forgiveness. A raise might be in order." None of that was true. He was trying to make her laugh.

Tears filled her eyes, and she looked down. "I'm sure we can arrange something."

"Now." Cal gave her hand a little squeeze. "Can we talk about us for a minute?

"Us?" Bryony looked up again.

"Bryony," Cal began. "Todd didn't steal anything, but you have."

"I have?"

"You've stolen my heart, Bryony. I know you said you needed time to focus on yourself, but do you think you could let me do that with you?" He took his hand away from hers to search his pocket and pulled out the object that had been digging into his thigh for the past hour. He had found it in a dresser drawer at his father's house last weekend. He held it out now, his high school class ring. "Will you go steady with me?"

She looked surprised, then perplexed. "What about Rachel?" she asked.

"I'm not in love with Rachel." He could see she knew what he was saying.

Bryony took the ring and examined it. Tears ran down her cheeks, and she didn't wipe them away. "It's a little worn down," she said.

"Like the man before you. Worn with history, worthy of a future, hoping you'll let me wear on you a little longer."

She slipped it on a finger many sizes too small. "I'll have to get a chain for my neck."

Cal smiled. "I'm so happy to know I'll have a date for the prom."

Her eyes opened wide. "Can we really go to the prom together?"

He hadn't expected that. For a moment he saw the seventeen-year-old in her, and regret washed over him. What might have happened if they had met decades ago?

He embraced both of her hands and leaned forward. "We'll make it the experience of a lifetime."

# SIX MONTHS LATER

$\mathcal{T}$hree scents would forever stay fixed in Bryony's mind. The first, rain on warm cement. It swirled up from the sidewalk as she left her house at five-thirty a.m. on the third Saturday in June.

The second, buttery crust filled with cinnamon-spiced apples. The minute she stepped through the door of A L'il Coffee & Pie with Bry, the scent of tarts engulfed her. Todd met her at the door, his arms filled with roses.

"Aww," Bryony said. "You didn't have to bring flowers."

"Sure I did," Todd said. "Mom said roses are mandatory for every significant event."

"Then split those up and put them into three vases because today is significant for you, too, young man. You're a manager now!"

"The tarts come out in five!" Todd called over his shoulder as he carried the flowers to a table.

Lillian arrived five minutes later, and the three of them put the finishing touches on the expanded business. Family and a few others were invited to arrive an hour before the official grand opening. Bryony wanted everything to be perfect.

The contractors had done a tremendous job opening the common wall between the former BeanHereNow and the adjoining building. The order counter remained in its original location, and the combined business shared one expanded seating area that covered the fronts of both buildings. A commercial kitchen graced the area in back of the newer half.

Todd trimmed the roses and placed them in three vases. Lillian arranged and rearranged the Spring/Summer collection of gift mugs and coffee-making paraphernalia. Bryony put on her new apron, made from black lightweight canvas, embroidered with shades of green ivy. She pulled the tarts out of the oven, made coffee, heated tea water, and checked three times on the trays laden with mini pies and cut pieces of quiche.

Six friends had baked all day yesterday while she supervised. Leftovers would go to the residents at RestHaven. She had made sure there would be leftovers.

Lillian's family arrived first. As soon as they settled in, the fixtures arrived.

Mr. Parker hugged Bryony around the shoulders before seating himself at his usual table and pulling out his newspaper.

Abby Dunaway carried two bags through the door, one large and one small. After depositing her jacket and her larger work-in-progress bag at her usual table, she extracted a small crocheted animal from the smaller bag and held it out for Bryony's inspection. "I made these for the children who show up," she said. "There's a variety of different animals."

Bryony turned over the three-inch-tall stuffed bear in her hands. "I love these, Abby! Would you like to sell them here?"

"I might." Abby smiled. "Keep that one."

Bryony hugged Abby before slipping the animal into her apron pocket.

A new pair of flowered leather boots carried in the woman who had held Bryony's hand throughout the initial marketing campaign, and at many other steps along the way. "Are you ready to knock the socks off the world of the pie-loving public?" Etta Corning asked.

"We are," Bryony said, and gave Etta a big hug. "I couldn't have done it without you."

Etta brushed off the appreciation and the hug, but smiled as she said, "I'm here for the free food." She placed her backpack on one chair and sat on another.

Small hands banged on the front door. "Let me in, Bryony!" Cal's great niece pressed her face against the glass.

"Hell-Oh!" Bryony said. She opened the door. Small arms encircled her legs.

"Helen Marie, let go of her." Heidi kissed Bryony on the cheek as she entered the shop. "She almost tripped me the other day."

The four-year-old released Bryony's legs. Heidi's arms wrapped around Bryony's shoulders as she surveyed the interior. "How did you do all of this and still manage to visit us in Cleveland twice a month?"

"I had help," Bryony said.

The rest of Cal's family poured in through the door and moved toward the counter, where Todd poured cups of coffee and hot chocolate. Abby stationed herself nearby to distribute the animals. A few great nieces took up residence in a corner to play Southern Ohio Safari. Lillian's grandchildren joined them. Soon their animal imitations rose in pitch and volume.

"Can my zebra have hot chocolate?" Hell-Oh called out, holding up her stuffed animal.

"You can have as much as you want," Bryony said.

"You can have two," Hell-Oh's mother said. "None for the zebra. They're allergic to chocolate." She turned to Bryony. "My daughter knows no limits when it comes to chocolate."

"We have quiche," Bryony said. "I made some plain for those who think vegetables and breakfast aren't compatible."

Cal's niece hugged her. "Thanks for inviting us!"

Cal's father arrived, escorted by Rachel, his private nurse. She and Rudy were dating now.

"I hope there's a bathroom here," Cal's father said.

"There are three," Bryony said. "Two gender neutral, and one family friendly."

"I only need one, and I don't need it yet, but I will." He embraced Bryony. "Nice to see you, dear. The drive down was hellish on my sacroiliac, but you're worth it."

"Thanks for coming." Bryony kissed his cheek.

Rudy breezed through the door, hugged Bryony, and joined Rachel as she helped Mr. Forster, Sr. to a chair at Mr. Parker's table. Mr. Parker put down his newspaper and introduced himself to his new table companions.

Three of Heidi's grandchildren stationed themselves in front of Bryony. "There's a pool in the hotel, Bryony. Will you come swim with us?" Cody asked.

"We want to see your house," Melissa said.

"Can we come and stay with you this summer?" Chase asked.

Cal stepped into the shop and put his arm around Bryony's shoulders. "Back off, dudes and dudettes. Give her a chance to get through today before making plans for the summer."

One by one the children hugged her around the waist and ran back to the counter for drinks.

"Everything's free all day?" Cal asked.

"Payback for all the help," Bryony answered.

Everybody had helped. Rick's construction crew did the heavy lifting but, with Cal's help, he hired high school students willing to work weekends in exchange for a decent wage and training in basic carpentry and finishing skills. Rudy used his vacation time to help paint walls and stain woodwork. Gloria, from the diner down the street, organized a crew of friends to help make the curtains and tablecloths with matching aprons. Dewey's supplied the workers with meals and snacks to keep them moving.

The bell above the door rang again. Chuck and Charity Henderson walked in. Charity held out a ceramic pot with three kinds of plants. "The place looks wonderful, Bryony."

After Bryony found a place to set the pot, the two women exchanged hugs. When they parted, Bryony turned to Chuck. "You feeling okay?"

"Never better."

She and Chuck hugged. He looked strong, healthy. When Mitch announced his retirement, he recommended Cal fill his position, but Cal declined, supporting a more deserving educator, and the board voted unanimously to offer the promotion to Chuck.

Chuck pumped Cal's hand. "The board approved the funding at last night's meeting."

"They did?" Cal said. "That's great!"

Charity had worked with local businesses to tie the work study program to STEAM grants, and a committee of board members, administrators, and teachers were working on a strategic plan to shift to STREAM as soon as they could get buy-in from the teachers.

"Your job's secure as long as I'm around," Chuck said. "Will you stay?"

"Did you decide?" Bryony asked Cal. "Did you decide to buy the house?" When the owner decided to sell, he offered Cal first option. Was she ready to hear his answer? She wanted him to stay, but she knew now the depth of his commitment to his family. Whatever he chose, she wanted him to be happy. She steeled herself for disappointment.

"I made my decision a long time ago," Cal said.

She held her breath.

He looked around, took a breath, said, "Well I was going to do this later, but—" and dropped to one knee.

Todd's hand flew to his mouth. "Oh my gosh!"

Lillian beamed.

"What's Uncle Cal doing on the floor?" Hell-Oh asked from the far corner of the shop. "Did he get an animal, too?"

"Hush, Helen," Heidi said.

"Bryony, I'll stay on whatever terms you'll have me, but I think I'm ready to move beyond going steady." Cal put his hand in his jacket pocket and pulled out a ring.

Bryony's eyes darted to Heidi. "But that's your mother's ring."

"She would have loved you," Heidi said. Her eyes glistened.

Cal looked up, head cocked sideways, waiting for an answer.

Bryony put her finger on her lower lip and hummed deliberation. "Are you buying the house?"

"I know you have your eye on that kitchen," Cal said. "But I have a different idea. What if we bump out the back of your house, redo the kitchen, and add a sun room with lots of plants? We could finish the upstairs so the kids would have a place to stay when they visit."

She hadn't been expecting the ring, but more than that, she had not been expecting this, his plan to make her home their home. She had never shared with him her abandoned idea about finishing the upstairs in the hope that there would be children someday. Now there were children, more children than she could have hoped for. She looked over at them, all playing together. A big extended family.

The bell above the door rang.

Mitch crossed the threshold. "Is all the free food gone?" he asked. Carol slipped in and stepped up to stand beside him.

"Hey, there's my trivia partner!" Mitch said and started to move toward Mr. Parker, but Carol grabbed his arm and held him back.

The door opened one more time.

"We're here!" Bryony's father called out as he entered. "Better not be any pigeon in those little pies!" Bryony could see the teasing in his eyes. He would never know he'd eaten pigeon already, last Thanksgiving, the savory pie served with the main meal. He held open the door for Alma.

Her father's eyes dropped to Cal, and a wry smile uplifted the curve of his lips.

"Mommy, I need to go to the bathroom," Hell-oh called out, her strident voice followed by twittering laughter.

"What's happening?" Mitch asked.

"I think that's a little obvious," Bryony's father said.

Silence fell over the room.

Bryony looked down at Cal.

"Bryony," he said. "Will you marry us?"

"Do I have to give up the class ring?" Bryony asked, her hand rising to the polished ring hanging on the chain around her neck.

Cal held up the ring clasped between his thumb and index finger. "You can have both."

Bryony lowered her hand and spread her fingers.

Cal slipped the ring on her finger and stood to embrace her.

Everybody cheered. She looked around the room. Lillian and Rick leaned against the counter, their arms around each other's waists. Abby and Mr. Parker sat in their usual spots, their smiles fixed on Bryony, their hands idle. For once, Etta's computer was closed, and her eyes open to those around her. Heidi's grandchildren had abandoned their game for a moment, their smiles expectant, exuberant. Her father, Alma, Mitch, Carol, Charity, Chuck, Cal Sr., Rachel, Rudy—nearly everyone had tears in their eyes.

Bryony pulled away from the hug and looked up at the man she would someday wed. "Yes, I will marry you, Cal Forster."

The third scent Bryony would always remember was the fragrance of forever in Cal's kiss.

A lifelong resident of Ohio, Lee Barber walked a long and winding road to fulfill her dream of being a writer. Along the way, she learned about the goodness, resilience, and creativity of all people. When she is not writing, Lee collaborates with others to tell life stories, end oppressive practices and policies, and generate beauty and order in the world. For her, romance is finding that place of hope, and falling in love is for people of all ages.